After a monster attack to the capital city, Citadel, Sir Liam Bord seeks the witch responsible to bring him to the king for his trial and his punishment. Liam succeeds in capturing the witch, Reynald, a former royal mage whom Liam knew as a squire. Despite his attempts at treating Reynald as a prisoner, as Liam begins to understand Reynald's motives, he can't help but question the very system he's always supported. The way his heart races every time they're near each other only further complicates his mission...

AN IVORY FOX MASK

SITA BETHEL

A NineStar Press Publication
www.ninestarpress.com

An Ivory Fox Mask

CONTENT WARNING:

This book contains sexually explicit content, which may only be suitable for mature readers. Depictions of graphic violence/gore, past trauma, and war.

To John. You're pure magic.

Chapter One

Creed's hooves struck the cobblestone streets as Liam galloped toward the main square of Citadel's market sector. The horse's tail and mane were braided with bright blue ribbons. Gold and sapphire beads shimmered as Creed's tail whipped behind him.

The fountain of Saint Margaret gurgled. The dying sunlight dipping below the castle's parapets stained the water a vivid, fiery orange. All around the sculpture, people fled from the inns, taverns, and companion houses. Their screams circled the square. In the stories, Darius, the demon of vengeance and hunting, attacked Citadel as a great dragon, and Saint Margaret defeated him after being devoured and slicing through his stomach to escape. Liam pulled on Creed's reins. Dismounting, he dashed down the alley between the Naughty Mare and Candlewick Inn.

Liam's breath echoed along the narrow pathway. He skidded to a halt when he saw three crimson gashes of light burning in the shadows. The darkness moved and shifted, taking shape as the stryx crawled forth, as if from old wet-nurse tales, on four taloned feet. Liam unsheathed his sword, his shield raised to intercept any magical attacks, but the creature only screeched before spreading her wings and charging. The black feathers fluttered around the creature like smoke, her entire body semi-ethereal, a shadow bleeding onto an artist's canvas. Only the three needle-thin eyes were solid…vulnerable to attacks.

She snapped with her dark beak. Angling his sword, Liam thrust the blade toward the creature's third eye. The tip plunged forward, hilt-deep. Her body collapsed into a shower of black feathers. Though they tickled as they brushed Liam's sweat-drenched face, the feathers dissolved into wisps of smoke after settling on the ground.

Liam exhaled and smeared the sweat from his forehead with the back of his sword hand. Another scream—a human scream—pulled his attention away from the small victory. He glanced to his right and noticed one of the third-floor windows was open. A woman struggled to get away from the birdlike creature. She leaned half out the window and screamed again. Without hesitating, Liam grabbed the rusted iron ladder fastened to the side of the building as a fire escape and hoisted himself upward. Only a slender catwalk connected the ladder to the other rooms, so Liam hugged the inn's outer wall as he inched closer.

"Come out! There's a ledge!" He called to the woman perched on the windowsill.

She jerked her head in his direction. Her thick, brown curls danced around her head like streamers as a breeze blew past them. She saw the crest on his blue surcoat—a black stallion and golden scale—and relief washed over her expression.

"Sir Bord!"

"Come now." Liam beckoned her out of the hotel room. "I'll fight the creature, but I need you out here where it's safer."

The woman scurried onto the ledge. Her dress snagged on a stray nail, and she teetered, hands flailing. Liam hooked his arm around her waist and pulled her close. She gripped his shoulders. A blush dusted her cheeks.

"Sir Bord, you saved me."

His stomach twisted in an uncomfortable knot. As a knight, he was familiar with the expression on the damsel's face and knew he'd need to hurry before she tried to "reward" him with a kiss. Despite the danger in letting go, he released his grip on the wall in order to remove her hands from his shoulders.

"Hold tightly to the wall. Stay here until I clear your room and call you inside."

She nodded as a twitch of disappointment from his subtle rejection contorted the smile on her face. Liam grabbed his sword and dipped into the window. His shield caught the stryx's claws as she swiped at Liam's face. Liam sidestepped and parried, dancing around the torn sheets and broken chair as he fought. The stryx opened her mouth and shrieked, lunging for him. Liam saw an opening and pushed his sword into one of the beast's eyes, twisting like a key clicking home in a lock. Another burst of feathers showered him. He plucked one from his long, coiled hair and dropped it to the floor where it wisped into nothing. Liam stuck his head out the window.

"It's safe now."

The woman scrambled into the room, bowing in appreciation. Liam nodded and then raced out the door and back to the street where more creatures hunted for anyone who hadn't fled to the church. The blazing sunset burnishing the city a quarter hour ago was now bruising into a wounded red violet. The shadows stretched from each building. As Liam crossed the square, he could hardly tell Creed's outline from the stryx charging toward his horse. Creed reared, pawing at the stryx with his hooves. The creature paused for a moment, but realizing Creed couldn't hurt her, she darted forward. Her beak snapped, aiming for Creed's neck, but Liam managed to wedge himself between them with his shield raised. He pushed the stryx backward and slipped his sword into her right eye slit.

Liam's heavy breathing made his chest rise and fall. His armor was finely crafted mesh, one-third the weight of traditional plate, but he'd been riding and racing all over the city while hunting the stryx, and he felt like hot coals were packed between his shoulders and traps. He wasn't sure he could fight anymore, but a child's wail reverberated into the square.

Liam pivoted, searching. Around the corner, in front of a bakery, curled a dirty, bruised lad, perhaps eight or nine years old. The shadow creature stalking him wasn't like the others. She was larger, with four wings and a broader crest. A Matriarch, according to Liam's studies. A spark of hope flashed in his chest. She shared a bond with the witch who called her flock. If she died, the summoning spell would unravel and all the lesser stryx would vanish. Exhausted as he was, Liam wasn't sure he'd survive another encounter, but he didn't have to survive, he only needed to take her with him. Liam sheathed his sword. Stooping low, he snatched a stray stone from a flower bed in front of one of the shop windows and hurled the rock at the back of the creature's head.

"Hey!" he shouted.

She spun, screeching.

"That's right! That child's hardly a snack! Come get a proper meal!" Liam splayed his arms wide, inviting the creature to attack him.

He didn't bother drawing his sword again. His arms trembled from exertion. He no longer had enough strength to wield his blade with the finesse needed to hit the hair-thin mark of her eyes. Her talons clanked against the cobblestone as she trotted toward him, gaining speed when he didn't try to attack. He waited until the gap between her and the child was sufficient before pulling a small throwing dagger from inside his glove and flinging it into her eye.

Miss.

She turned her head half an inch, and it was enough for the blade to zip past her and bounce off the brick bakery.

"Shit." Liam leapt to the side.

His dragon-skin cloak flashed flame blue in dying dusk-light as he dove and rolled away. Jumping to his feet, Liam pulled the second of his three throwing knives. He aimed and released the blade, watching it cartwheel through the air, but the creature saw it whizzing toward her and ducked her head. She leapt; Liam feinted a final throw. As she turned to dodge the attack, he flung his real blade into her center eye. The small knife disappeared into the red crack and a flurry of feathers rained to the cobblestone.

Liam dropped to his hands and knees. The iridescent blue cloak pooled around him, and his locs hung like rope ends around his face as he caught his breath. After a few deep inhales, he stumbled toward the little boy still coiled near the bakery entrance. He ruffled the child's dish-water-blond hair, scanning him for injuries.

"You okay?"

Tears continued to flood from his eyes, but he nodded.

"Do you know where your mother is?" Liam asked.

The boy shook his head no, and Liam scooped the child into his arms. His steps were stiff and clumsy as he meandered along the road back to the square where Creed cropped the grass sprouting from a crack at the base of the fountain. Now the moonlight gave Saint Margaret's holy water a silvery shimmer. Liam set the boy at the base of the fountain and cupped his own hands into the water to ladle the chilled liquid high enough for the child to drink. After taking a sip himself, he sat the boy onto Creed's back. Limping, he held the reins as he led the horse through the town.

"What's your name?" Liam asked the child.

"Duncan," the child murmured.

"What's your mother's name?"

"Mama."

"Ah. Of course." Liam scratched the sweat from his scalp.

The square was deserted, so Liam headed toward the church where most of the townsfolk would have fled for shelter. He made it a block when a woman with the same fair hair as Duncan ran toward them. Tears poured across her cheeks, and she ran with her arms outstretched.

"Duncan!"

"Mama!" Duncan screamed, mimicking her gesture.

Liam grabbed him before he could fall from the saddle and tucked him safely into the woman's arms. She smothered the child with kisses. Stray hairs scattered around her cheeks and neck from a deflated bun, and her skirt was in tatters.

"Are you all right?" Liam asked.

"I killed one. I shoved a shard of my grandmother's broken plate into its devil's eye, but Duncan was gone." She continued to kiss him, despite his squirming. She paused, glancing up and truly noticing Liam. "Thank you, Sir Bord. You saved my son."

"It's my duty to protect Citadel with my life." Liam pressed his hand on his heart, over the golden scale emblem on his surcoat, and bowed.

From the direction of the church, the sound of a bell spread across the entire city. Liam allowed his shoulders to relax. It was the solemn, deep-toned all-clear bell, not the one that warned people of an attack. He and the other knights had managed to purge the city of the monsters before nightfall settled in and made them stronger. He never had a chance to learn Duncan's mother's name. The moment the bell rang, she cried out in her own relief and hurried out of sight. At least she didn't try to kiss Liam in gratitude. He hoisted his tired body onto Creed and guided the horse toward the castle, where the king would want to debrief the knights before dismissing them.

As the streets all converged near the inner wall protecting the castle, the city became a maze. Older sections had been built and rebuilt a dozen times. Fires destroyed old buildings; old houses had been re-bricked and worked into shops. The locals knew their way well enough—the children were masters of the smaller, half-closed alleys and hideaways—but Liam had to follow the same familiar streets to reach the castle without losing himself: Old Way to Huckleberry, left on Seller's Way, then follow the King's Path to the castle gates and courtyard.

The castle was a crowning fortress at the peak of a hill. Even in the deepening night, dozens of torches and braziers kept the palace sparkling like light-struck snow. Three defense walls separated the castle from the rest of the city. When Liam finally reached the courtyard, a stable boy took Creed to brush, water, and feed him. Despite his exhaustion, Liam wound his way into the castle to the war room. Inside, Sirs Tobyn Stelis, Lennard Hall, Kent Oldsworth, Abacus Finnegan, and Harold Pines gathered around the table. Bandages wrapped around Kent's head, Harold's foot was propped up on a stool, and a nurse was layering strips of cloth and ointment over Tobyn's burned forearm. Even young Lennard boasted a split lip and scrapes anywhere his armor and leathers hadn't covered.

"Look at our stallion with hardly a scratch on him." Harold snorted. He kept his hands tucked at his sides, but he was shaking from the battle.

The war had frayed all the knights, at least those left. Many, like Liam's and Lennard's fathers, had died during the Battle of Bridgewater. The three pine trees forming Harold's family crest were filled out by his growing postwar ale gut. His dark hair was still thick upon his head, but salt scattered through the strands. Liam couldn't remember exactly when this change happened. Only yesterday, Liam was the budding knight trying to prove himself, oblivious to just how corrosive the war would be on them by the end. And, while Liam could repeat the propaganda on the necessity of expanding the kingdom and gathering valuable resources for the benefit of the people, everything he'd heard off-the-record suggested the war was more a retaliation to the tariffs and trade embargoes Valen established after Seigfried's ascension to the throne.

Now? Lennard, the first to be knighted after the war, had the same gleam in his eyes with the recent city attacks. They were stories for him to act out his hero fantasies, while age snuck up on the rest of them. The others all had sons serving as squires, getting ready to be knighted as soon as they had the blessing of all their trainers and tutors, who would be as excited as Lennard to serve. Until then, those left would simply have to hold out. As much as they needed the help, Liam was holding his breath for the day the nobility would start commenting on how Liam had no sons, or even a daughter, to take up his shield when he finally fell. He dreaded those conversations more than he dreaded the shadow devils they'd fought all evening.

"I feel like I was wheeled over by a carriage." Liam dropped into the first available chair.

"Here. This will dull the aches." Lennard handed him a silvered stein filled with currant-infused lambic.

His grin was broad and honest. With his helmet removed, the flaxen curls fell into his eyes. He needed to shear them so they didn't blind him in battle, but everyone was too tired to lecture the rookie. Instead, Liam accepted the drink and nodded.

"Thank you."

Liam chugged the beer and wiped his mouth after draining half the mug. His hands were also shaking, more from fatigue than nerves, but he set his cup to the side so no one else noticed.

"Nothing like a drink after a battle." Abacus held his mug in his lap. His head drooped, and the wrinkles around his eyes seemed deeper, but who was to say if it was weariness or the shadows cast by the fire in the hearth.

"I don't even feel sore after two of these." Lennard raised his mug in a toast.

"That's because you're twenty." Harold sniffed. "We used to go to the Dirty Mare after missions and see who could outdrink each other. Remember?"

"Except for Liam, who's too chaste for our rowdy postfight rituals." Tobyn grinned, his broad nose wrinkling a touch with the expression.

Unlike the other knights who held large fiefdoms spreading out around Citadel, the Stelis family had always served as mayors of the city. The orchids on their purple surcoats were a clear sign that they were the guardians of the oracle, one of the only witches in Prophis legally allowed to practice her craft—under strict restrictions however.

"I'm not against a little drinking, but there was always something else to be done, and I never seemed to have the time," Liam defended himself. It wasn't the *drinking* he'd been avoiding; it was the women who'd keep them company afterward.

"Maybe you were the wisest among us." Abacus groaned as he shifted in his seat. "Now, after a fight, I just want to take a bath and lay in bed with my wife."

"A hot bath. Now, there is something we can all agree on." Liam nodded.

"There have been too many attacks. Three this month? What the hell is happening?" Kent touched the bandages around his head, checking his fingertips for blood, but though the linen was tinged pink near his temple, his fingers came back dry.

"The previous battles were all creatures from the Balbraid Thicket," Liam said. Balbraid was practically his home, his territory and the forest's borders twined together like two mating snakes. "But tonight? Tonight was different."

"Monsters, yeah? I think my wet nurse used to tell me stories of those beasties. I thought they had several hands, though, no wings."

"You're thinking about ponoi. Those are from a different fable. What we fought tonight are called stryx and act as the hunting dogs for the demon, Darius." Liam frowned. "I never really believed they were real. It's…unsettling to fight bedtime stories."

"You memorized a lot about them for someone who didn't believe they were real." Tobyn scoffed, but the sound was soft, good-natured, and not a proper criticism.

Liam shrugged. He loved bestiaries, and books describing ogres and musseri often included creatures from the hellish dimensions. Stryx were female pack hunters led by a Matriarch. They herded prey and carried their victims away. Surely the others had heard some of the same stories from the days of Saint Margaret, but before he could further explain, the door opened and Chancellor Cole stepped into the room.

"Chancellor." Kent was first to bow, his red surcoat more blood-colored than his actual blood-stained bandages.

"Sir Oldsworth." Cole nodded.

The chancellor walked through the room with a stiff, intentional gait. He always moved slowly, as if he had to think about each step. He had never mentioned an injury and never used a cane, but pride often prevented men from utilizing such aids even when they were needed, so Liam accepted his pace and held his tongue.

"Do we have any information on what happened tonight?" Abacus asked. "Liam's over here telling us bedtime stories about stryx."

Instead of beer, the chancellor poured a glass of brandy from a table near the fireplace. The firelight slipped through the liquor, giving it a bright amber glow. Cole eased into the chair closest to the head of the table, asserting his place as the king's right-hand man.

"We suspect a witch."

Liam remained stoic but wanted to roll his eyes. Cole always suspected a witch, always. Blight in the corn? Witches. Influenza sweeping through the city? Witches. Can't find your left stocking? Witches. Although, since there'd been a Matriarch guiding the other stryx, this might be one of the few times Cole was right.

"Have you consulted the oracle?" Tobyn asked.

"Her answer was…cryptic." Chancellor Cole sipped from his glass. "The king should be returning from her shrine shortly."

They sipped their drinks around the table and nursed their wounds. Liam closed his eyes and allowed the heat of the fire to wash over his face. The weariness nestled deep in the center of every bone in his body; however, when the king entered the room, all the knights, even the injured ones, dropped to their knees. King Siegfried wasn't much older than Liam, in his early thirties. He was tall, lean, handsome, and his hair always had a sun-kissed shine because of the lemons he imported from across the sea and used as a hair tonic. The long strands were plaited and adorned with opals. Liam was careful to focus on the king's feet to avoid staring at his pale lips.

"Sit," the king said. "How much damage did the city endure?"

Chancellor Cole pulled a booklet from his robes. "To the buildings? Minor damage only. We lost three lives, Your Majesty. Several injured, but most of the wounds were less severe."

"I see. And who killed the Matriarch?"

"The what?" Harold asked.

"The alpha of the pack," Liam explained in a way he thought Harold would understand. "The link between Darius and whoever summoned the stryx."

"Ah, it *would* have been you. I should have expected as much." Siegfried stepped closer to Liam. "Edeline mentioned I would send a stallion to hunt the one causing our troubles."

"Then it is a witch, my lord? Sending these monsters to attack?" Liam risked a quick glance upward before lowering his gaze again.

Liam's instincts nagged at him, telling him this wasn't fully correct. The way the stryx dissolved into smoke after Liam killed each beast was proof of them being a summon spell, yes, but the first two attacks, though magical creatures, weren't *magic*. They were strays from the Balbraid Thicket. Stopping a witch would be important, but if they didn't fix *both* underlying causes, the attacks would continue.

"Tonight's attack? Yes." Siegfried shrugged. "The oracle insisted the witch would attack the palace twice in the span of a week, so we should prepare for another battle within the next few days."

"Perhaps the oracle should recount?" Cole scowled. "We've already had three attacks."

"That doesn't mean all three were related." Liam spoke with a calm, deescalating voice, but Cole clenched his teeth and turned to Liam in his slow, unsettling way.

"How are these attacks not related? Witches can enchant beasts as easily as summon them." He turned back toward the king. "Don't put too much of our trust in the oracle, even if your father and grandfather used them before you, Seigfried. She's trouble. I feel it."

"You feel it?" Tobyn raised an eyebrow. "Sounds like magic. Are you a wizard as well?"

"Do not throw accusations at me, Sir Stelis. If any house should be investigated, it should be yours. Those orchids on your crest are a disgrace to this kingdom."

"Calm down, Chancellor. There's no need to rile the knights. Edeline's a tool. Useful. And mine to use." The king spoke in a bored tone, as if attacks were an inconvenience instead of a threat. "For tonight, you should all go home and recover from this battle, but we'll need to increase the number of soldiers patrolling the city and give them better training. The knights fought well, but our guards were all but useless. It's unacceptable. I shouldn't have to hire witch hunters from the east as mercenaries to protect a kingdom full of able-bodied men." The king dismissed them with a flick of his ringed fingers.

"I'll have a training program prepared by dawn." Abacus gave a final bow before being the first knight to exit.

The other knights were quick to bow and rush out as well. They wanted to go home and see their wives or mistresses, draft training regimens for their men, or drink themselves to sleep to forget another monster attack. Liam, however, lingered. He'd increased training drills after the ogre attack two weeks ago and hired both a counter-magic expert from Mascaria and beast specialist from the north. Like the city guards, Liam's men were well-disciplined against human armies but fell apart trying to deal with the colossal, chaotic fighting style of the ogres. Many of them had broken ribs or dislocated shoulders from attacks to Liam's own demesne caused by the expanding mills shrinking the forest.

"Is there something else, Sir Bord?" King Sigfried poured himself a glass of brandy, only giving Liam the slightest glance over his shoulder.

"Your Majesty, the first attack was dire wolves." Liam kept one knee planted onto the thick rug below him.

"Yes. I recall."

"And the second one was ogres."

"Correct again."

"Those are creatures who reside in the Balbraid Thicket, and earlier this year you ordered men to clear the Balbraid Thicket for mills and lumber."

"The oak and walnut in that forest are valuable exports to the arid lands of Suzdal," Cole said. "It is the king's right to use the resources of Phrophis to better our kingdom."

"Of course. I do not question the king's economics." Liam gave a slight bow, understanding the tension behind Chancellor Cole's words.

There'd been great unrest throughout the kingdom over whether the forest should be cleared or not. Universities from Phrophis and neighboring kingdoms had written letters beseeching the king to only harvest the wood in sections, giving areas to rest and recover while others were cleared, but the king was ambitious and wanted a swell of income in order to expand Phrophis and further industrialize it. Liam didn't have an opinion. He wasn't a scholar—he was a knight, and his job was to protect his liege and the people.

"However," Liam continued," it makes sense, with such large sections of Balbraid being cleared so quickly, that some of the creatures from the woods would get displaced."

"So the scholars keep telling me." Siegfried snorted. "But this is why I have armies to fight the low cunning beasts from the woods. Are your men not prepared to do their duties?"

"My men have been training beneath a Master Valinsir from Mascaria to better deal with whatever may escape from the forest." Liam lifted his gaze as high as the king's knees. "But, perhaps if we slowed the clear-cutting. At least until this new threat is dealt with—"

"Absolutely not." Siegfried chuckled. "Get up off the floor, Liam. Sit. Talk to me face-to-face."

"My lord." Liam took the nearest chair but did not have the nerve to face the king.

The chancellor crossed his arms over his chest, nakedly glaring at Liam, but Liam wasn't fazed by Cole's cantankerous scowl. He couldn't remember a time that the chancellor didn't follow behind the king and scowl at anyone who came within attacking distance—Seigfried now, but his father before him, and according to the stories, Seigfried's grandfather before even him. What unnerved Liam was the easy, lidded glance the king gave him, because it made his heart race and his palms sweat. The gratitude of a lovely woman held no power over Liam, but the slightest curl of Seigfried's lips ruined him completely.

"You understand, don't you?" Seigfried pouted. "I have already made contracts with the parliament of Suzdal. We can't show weakness to other nations. If we do, we might find ourselves with yet a third enemy on top of our current woes. The country hasn't recovered from our war with Valen, and the sanctions have stretched our coffers thinly. We need to rebuild."

"I see the wisdom in what you say." Liam nodded.

Seigfried was horribly oversimplifying, but Liam understood tight budgets made kings nervous, and at the end of the day, it didn't matter what Liam thought. His job was to serve and obey.

"At least allow me to assign some of my best men to protect you and train the city guard. The counter-magic techniques they've learned should be beneficial whether the next attack comes from Balbraid or our mysterious witch."

"Very well." Seigfried agreed without hesitation. "Send me a squad of men you think are best suited for the task."

"They'll arrive tomorrow morning."

"Your family has always been most loyal to mine. It does not go unnoticed, Stallion of Citadel."

Reaching out, the king rested his hand on Liam's shoulder. Liam's chest swelled with the casual contact, and Liam was grateful that his complexion would hide his blush.

"Thank you, my lord," Liam did his best not to stutter.

"If we're done here? We have other matters to attend to," Cole interrupted.

"You see what I have to put up with?" Seigfried winked at Liam as if they shared a private joke at Cole's expense. "Go home, Sir Bord. Rest. I'll have need of you soon, and we can't afford you exhausting yourself before then."

"Of course." Liam bowed and marched out of the study before he embarrassed himself.

Nonetheless, Liam was giddy as he navigated the maze of the castle and returned to the stables where Creed waited. He couldn't stop replaying the moment, the weight of the king's hand snug against Liam's frame. Liam wished he could accept the kisses and longing stares of the women he rescued, but even when he was a boy, serving as his father's squire, Liam always longed for the boys he'd see working the fields or strolling through the palace hallways—especially the royal magicians the king kept in the castle, always dressing in form-clinging damask robes and smelling of imported oils from faraway kingdoms. Liam sighed as he rode out into the countryside. One memory in particular haunted him—a game of hide-and-seek he'd played during a ball. While the rest of the castle spun and danced in the light of the ballroom, he and a boy his age with one brown and one blue eye chased each other all night. In his dreams, they kissed, but in reality, Liam had barely had enough courage to touch his shoulder when he'd tag him as "it."

Liam's manor was tucked in a crescent curving into the northern edge of the Balbraid Thicket. He'd spent most of his childhood hunting, fishing, and exploring the woods. He'd seen a dryad once and politely refused a kiss from her. He'd seen a satyr another time and accepted a kiss from him. His first kiss, sweet as summer blackberries, and one of the few kisses he'd managed to claim in his life. He still remembered the thick fur as he clung to the satyr's hips and how he had to stand on his toes to reach the satyr's mouth. Liam ignored the shiver tingling up and down his spine, and instead walked into his home and instructed his steward to have the servants prepare a bath.

He didn't need assistance removing his mail. The chained mesh was light enough for him to manage by himself. Stripping, he checked his body for scrapes and bruises. A small, purple welt marred his sternum, right over his heart, but he couldn't remember what he'd done to earn the mark. He prodded the bruise and winced. Not seeing any other damage, Liam slipped into the hot water and closed his eyes. He had no wife or mistress to greet him or help him wash, so Liam gave himself a few minutes as the heat soaked into his sore body. Then he scrubbed himself before wrapping into nightclothes and lying in his wide, four-poster bed with only the blankets and pillows to keep him company.

Chapter Two

In the morning, Liam instructed Valinsir—the retired Mascarian witch hunter now under his employ—to choose a squad of those best suited to protect the king and aid with further training. Liam sent them to the castle with letters of introduction, so Cole wouldn't harass them when they arrived, and he included a relocation stipend for their wallets.

After writing the letters and arranging the funds with his steward, Sam, he spent the remainder of the day training with the rest of his forces. Valinsir specialized in nonlethal capture methods, which was one of the reasons Liam chose him over several other recommendations. Most of the training involved how to bind a sorcerer to keep him from casting spells and how to unsummon various minor devils or monsters. He already knew stryx needed to be pierced in their eyes. Goetias were shapeshifters who served the demon Malphas. One had to trick them to reveal their horns and break them to banish them. The ipos could blur time around them, moving fast or slowing their prey. They hunted for the demon Focalor and only returned to their realm if their duck-like heads were severed. The ponoi were shadows with many hands bound to Erinyis and could be destroyed rather easily—if one could land an attack on them without getting overpowered, since they liked to swarm prey.

"But these creatures are all nursery tales and campfire stories." Liam glanced up from his notes.

"Sir Bord, you said Citadel was attacked by stryx yesterday." Valinsir raised a silvery eyebrow. He had the intense, yellow-green eyes commonly found in Mascaria.

"Honestly, I'm hoping what we saw yesterday were illusions meant to drive us to fear." Liam paused, glancing at the other soldiers, who were pretending to read but eavesdropping on their conversation. "The oracle said there'd be one more attack yet."

"It is likely to be more stryx," Valinsir explained. "It's…highly unlikely a witch would bind their soul to more than one demon. Contracts are complicated, more dangerous for the wizard than the demon, and have high prices."

"Then I'll recommend accuracy drills to Eli." Liam rubbed his neck. "At least the creatures from the Thicket are from *this* realm."

Liam pretended he couldn't hear the mutters. Demons and their pet devils were vague threats, but the ogre attacks had everyone in the Bord territories on edge. Liam waited for Valinsir to dismiss the others for fighting drills before continuing their conversation.

"Are witches in Mascaria…dangerous?" Liam asked in a low

voice, checking to make sure no one else was in the room with them.

"Some of them, but I don't believe every magic user is dangerous." Valinsir was careful with his words in a way Liam was accustomed to. Witch sympathizers were not often burned, but the stocks or long imprisonments weren't uncommon.

"Of course. The stories of localized stewards guarding towns and forests are far more common than tales of demons, so they can't all be horrible. Did you ever hunt someone dangerous though?"

"If you're asking me if I've ever faced someone who's made a contract with a demon?" Valinsir rolled up his sleeve, revealing scarred and mangled flesh from his wrist to above the elbow. "Once. It was harrowing. I almost didn't survive."

"If it comes to fighting whoever attacked Citadel, how will my soldiers fare in battle?"

"Optimistically?"

"Objectively."

"They'll die."

Liam winced but couldn't expect a better outcome only a few weeks into their training.

"Don't misunderstand. I don't think the knights will do any better."

"What about dire wolves attacking farmers? Will they be able to protect the local area?"

"They're getting there. Another few weeks, and I could arrange for patrols."

"Please do." Liam nodded. "I asked the king to slow the cutting while we deal with…whoever sent those things yesterday, but that's not an option, so I'm going to need our guards to be as well prepared as possible."

"Not an option." Valinsir gave him a dry, humorless laugh.

"Knights are for security, not counsel." Liam shrugged, ignoring the frustration building inside him. His duty was to the king. He didn't need to understand Seigfried's logic, only to follow his orders.

"Yes, our emperor is much like your young king." Valinsir dug through a pile of papers on his desk. "I'll see if there's any information that might help you in your witch hunt."

"Your services are invaluable." Liam bowed. "Excuse me, I better check on Eli and discuss next week's training plans."

That night, Liam studied his collection of bestiaries as he ate a simple dinner of pottage and bread with the rest of his men. He enjoyed his studies, finding griffins and dragons fascinating. If Liam could spend his days locked in his study reading, he probably would, but there were always drills, and tours of the demesne, and sitting in his hall to listen to civil cases from the people in his fiefdom. His reading was usually during meals, or a few coveted minutes before he fell asleep on top of the pages.

Another week sped by in a blur, the tedium melting time more effectively than an ipos could manage. Then, one afternoon, as Liam polished his shield and treated the scales with gold dust to keep them strong and flexible, a pigeon with a summons tied to his leg flew into his window and perched. Liam glanced at the message: the chancellor wanted to see him.

Liam finished treating the dragon hide and prepared to travel to the castle. Being the closest demesne to the capitol, it was a three hour plus ride to Citadel. Despite being a touch cool, the weather was pleasant, and Liam's thoughts wandered as the miles passed. When they neared the city, Creed flicked his ears and snorted, wanting to canter and play, but Liam kept him in check.

As he trod along Main Street, several shop owners bowed or waved. The children stopped their play and clustered on the edge of the cobblestone street to stare at the knight as he rode by. Liam was a sight with his blue dragon-scale cloak trailing behind him like a wave of peacock feathers and his twisted, loced hair flowing behind him like an actual stallion's mane. He waved in return and smiled and nodded his head. In an emergency, he needed the people of Citadel to trust him so they didn't panic during an attack, so he was always as friendly as possible when he was in the city. In other circumstances, he would stop by a few local taverns to gossip with the patrons, but Cole had no patience, so Liam hurried to the castle.

In the back of the courtyard, there was a stage where both jesters and magicians performed. The king sat swaddled in fleece, watching as two robed royal mages created colored lights that morphed into fantastical shapes. Seigfried's legs were crossed, and he toyed with the jewels in his hair as he often did when he wasn't actively presenting as a monarch. There was always a sense of wonder and glee when he watched the magicians perform. Liam indulged in a longing glance at Seigfried, distracted, before finding someone to stable Creed and rushing into the castle to avoid Cole reprimanding him for being late. He was not late, but the chancellor still glared at Liam. His once black hair had long since faded to iron gray, and he kept it cropped close to his head in the military style, although as far as Liam knew, he'd never fought in battle or for sport during festivals. Liam knelt in front of him.

"You called for me."

"We've had a poacher in the royal woods." Cole handed Liam a report. "Normally this would be a task for the hunt master, but as you can see in those documents, the poacher is killing unicorns."

"Hunting in the Royal Woods is unforgivable." Liam stood, flipping through the accounts of bodies found near watering holes. "But to hunt a sacred creature is blasphemy as well."

Liam's fists clenched around the papers. He could at least pity a poor villager poaching to feed his family. With the Balbraid Thicket shrinking, many hunters were struggling to find game. But the reports indicated that the unicorns were being slaughtered for their ivory, nothing else. This wasn't some desperate man feeding his family. The hair, hooves, and even eyes and teeth of unicorns could be sold in the black market for a noble's ransom worth of gold. Liam caught Cole's gaze.

"A witch? Gathering ivory for a spell?"

"A haughty witch." Cole agreed with a solemn nod. "Someone who doesn't care about squandering the rest of the magical components they're leaving behind. The king personally asked you to investigate. He's convinced this is connected to the ridiculous prophecy the oracle gave him."

"I'll leave immediately." Liam turned to go.

"The king wants the witch alive," Chancellor Cole said. "This is a serious crime, and the guilty party needs to be made an example. The king demands a public execution."

"I understand."

It was a pity Liam couldn't end the witch's suffering with a quick cut to the neck. He'd never personally watched the burnings, but he remembered the screams and the greasy smell the last time he'd brought a witch to the king to be tried and punished. His stomach twisted with the memories, bile rising hot against the back of his throat. Instead of dwelling on the criminal's fate, Liam gave the report another glance, deciding to travel south, sup and rest at the last village before the woods, and begin his investigation in the morning.

The Royal Woods lay southwest of Citadel. It was close enough for the king to entertain himself with personal huts, but because only nobility with royal permits could enter the borders, only a single hamlet stood between the city and forest. There was no traveler's lodge, but the singular inn doubled as a tavern. The cramped dining hall held a chill and reeked of smoke. The burning peat choked Liam and made his eyes water. He paid for a room and supper and didn't bother changing out of his riding leathers before sitting as far from the dimly lit hearth as he could. His cloak kept him warm. Whenever the air was cold around him, the dragon scales would radiate heat as if still connected to a living, breathing body.

Kulvacc the Greedy, a notorious dragon nesting in a volcano at the edge of Phrophis, lived 100 years ago. Liam's grandfather, Linnel, rescued Siegfried's mother as a girl after Kulvacc stole her for ransom. The battle had cost Linnel an eye and a section of the skin from his jaw. Afterward, Linnel spoke with a drawl from the twisted scar tissue beneath his lip and wore a patch with the golden scale symbol. To honor Sir

Linnel for his bravery, he was given a boon, which he used to request he marry a girl he fancied from the city, Liam's Grandma Lottie. Siegfried's grandfather also had seven magi craftsmen create a cloak and shield which had been passed down through three generations. An only son, Liam was not sure who he'd pass the relics on to after he died. He hoped to find an exceptional squire he could adopt so his family's legacy didn't end up in the royal treasury—beautiful but unused. The secret treasury full of magical contraband was supposed to be an exaggerated rumor, but Liam suspected it was real. Too many times he'd seen Sigfried with some oddity or another that was never sent to the church to be dealt with properly.

After dinner, Liam went to sleep. His room had a coal-burning stove. The smoke was less thick than the peat moss in the dining hall, but Liam woke up with his sinuses throbbing. He rubbed the crust from his eyes, washed in the basin near his bed, and limbered himself before re-swaddling his body in riding leathers, mail, surcoat, and cloak. He settled for some dried meat and apples for breakfast and ate on the road, heading for the forest as the sky brightened to his back.

Where the Balbraid Thicket was dense and wild and full of dangerous creatures, the Royal Woods had been cultivated by generations of botanists to be beautiful, more a garden than a proper woods. Regular controlled burnings kept the forest floor free of undergrowth, wild flowers had been imported from all over Phrophis, so goldenrod, arrow heads, and lobelia flourished around the sycamore and oak trees. A large moth, the color of polished jade, fluttered past Liam. He pulled his report from a leather satchel and found the area of the first victim. The glen was an ideal spot for unicorns, full of thistle, thyme, and clover for them to eat. A small waterfall poured into a pool, keeping it clear and free of algae. Liam thought he caught a silver-white flash through a copse of ash trees as he dismounted but saw only a cluster of wild bergamots when he turned to search the area.

The only tracks he found were deer, elk, and badger, nothing to indicate a human. Liam checked each area in the report, searching for a boot print dried in the mud, or a scrap of cloth snagged on a branch, or even a matchbook. Anything that could give Liam a clue about who was responsible for slaughtering unicorns in the Royal Woods, but he found nothing.

On his way to the final spot, he saw another flash of silver in the distance. Liam altered his course to follow the glint, and when he saw the white lump crumbled beneath the blackberry bramble, his gut twisted. Liam held his stomach but forced himself to march to the corpse. The glimmer had been sunlight striking her silver mane. The hair sprayed outward, one thousand filaments of spider silk scattering in each direction and glittering like starlight. Her tail curled in a loop the loop, the fringe at the end the same quicksilver as her mane. Her white coat had occasional flashes of pink or periwinkle, similar to the way greens and violets sometimes flashed within the blues of Liam's dragon scale cloak. Liam knelt, cupping the unicorn's cheek. The horn had been sheared at the base over the skull. Not a splinter of ivory remained, and no sword, no matter how well-forged, could manage a cut so perfect. It was undeniably magic.

"I'm sorry," Liam whispered. "I should have been here sooner and stopped this from happening."

He could have carried travel rations, rode directly to the woods, and camped in the forest overnight. He'd underestimated the poacher, moved slowly, and now a life was gone—an immortal life who should have never had to bear the tragedy of death that men like him accepted as part of their existence. Death wasn't meant to be part of her, shouldn't have been, but she was already stiffening as she lay in the clover. Faint purples and blues pooled around her bottom shoulder in deep bruises where her blood, no longer being pumped by her heart, settled and congealed beneath her coat.

And for what? What could possibly justify murdering something so pure? The wizard hadn't even taken all the useful spell components. Her heart, her tail, everything remained intact except the long, spiraled horn on top of her head. Not that he would have relished the site of a parted and desecrated unicorn, but there was an added layer of tragedy in the excessive waste. A starving man could have fed his family for the rest of their lives on the money an entire unicorn would bring. Liam simply couldn't fathom why anyone would take the horn and leave everything else. Desperate for any sign of the poacher, Liam scanned the scenery. The only tracks he found were the mare's and a stray fox who'd drunk from the pool before running off into the thick of the woods.

"Dammit." Liam pounded his fist against an oak trunk.

He marked his map, wrote his own record of the latest victim, and decided to check the last area. If he couldn't find anything at a fresh kill site, he doubted he'd find anything at an old one, but he refused to return to the castle empty-handed until he exhausted every lead he had. Not far from the unicorn corpse, a sad whimper floated through the trees. Creed whinnied, nudging toward the sound. Liam peered into the green gray of the woods but couldn't locate what had made the noise. He urged Creed forward, away from the sound, but the whine grew louder, and for some reason, Creed insisted they investigate. Sighing, Liam allowed the horse to lead him through a mess of goldenrod near a slender brook.

A live trap hid beneath a cluster of yellow blossoms. Inside, a vibrant orange fox circled, gnawing at the bars and squealing to be released. Liam pitied the creature. Live traps were used to catch foxes to train the hunting hounds—a steel trap would have been a quicker, cleaner death. Liam crouched in front of the cage, admiring how fervently the fox struggled to be free.

"You're fierce. I wish I could release you, but you're property of His Majesty now."

The fox whirled to face Liam the moment he spoke. Sticking his nose between the bars, the fox gazed at Liam as if to plead for his life. Liam stared at the fox's eyes. One was the deep, rich brown of dried anise sprinkled on Yuletide pastries; the other was a chilling, intense blue.

He'd known a boy, in his youth, with the exact same pair of eyes. He'd been a magician in the castle. Siegfried had been fond of him, allowing the magician to follow him around like a shadow. The young magician always hid his head beneath the hood of his robes, and kept his gaze on the floor, but whenever he would look upward—and he always glanced upward whenever Liam walked past—he'd stare at Liam with the same glorious mismatched eyes. His gaze could knock the cartilage from Liam's knees, turn his bones to jelly, fill his stomach with writhing, squirming snakes, and steal his breath until Liam was dizzy. The few rare times Liam snuck a word with the boy had been a thrill.

Then one day, he was gone. Liam never knew if he'd gotten sick, was sold, turned to sea foam like a maiden in a fairy tale. He'd simply vanished. Liam's hand reached out; his finger traced the crown embossed on the metal of the trap latch. Liam's gaze flicked toward the fox again. The fox whimpered and rested his paw on Liam's wrist, pleading.

"Tampering with a royal trap is a death sentence." Liam's hand flinched as if the latch was scalding.

He shouldn't. He shouldn't. He shouldn't. He shouldn't.

His entire life had been dedicated to serving the king, the very crown carved into the latch. This fox was for Seigfried. His life, like Liam's, was for Seigfried's whims and entertainment.

Maybe the boy…escaped?

The royal family had never been kind to magic users. They kept a dozen or so in court for entertainment, and the oracle lived in a shrine and predicted the best plans for crops, and how much of the harvest to save for the winter, or when to use diplomacy or go to war, but anyone caught practicing magic unlawfully was burned at the stake in the city square near the fountain of Saint Margaret.

Liam always assumed the royal mages were happy in their stations. They were able to practice magic, even if only to entertain the king, and lived in the palace. They ate better than most of the farmers in Phrophis and wore fine linen. Why would they ever escape?

The fox whimpered and licked Liam's fingers. His tongue was warm and wet and tickled.

"All right. This one time, but only because you remind me of an old friend." Liam shut his eyes, unable to witness his own crime as he lifted the latch and let the weight of the cage door propel it open.

The fox barked and dashed from the cage. He spun in a circle, dipping his front end low as if to bow, and disappeared into a cluster of goldenrods.

"I can't believe I'm risking my life because a fox reminded me of a boy who probably died of influenza twelve years ago." Liam smacked his face.

He reset the trap, making sure no one would notice it'd been tampered with, and rushed to the last site in his reports. Liam searched the entire area, even crawled on hands and knees for the slightest clue, but there was *nothing*.

There'd been fox tracks near the body.

Dread, cold and heavy, settled into the pit of Liam's stomach.

Maybe he escaped.

Had Liam's friend ever mentioned his familiar? Liam knew every sorcerer had an animal form. Seigfried often watched his own mages as bears or mountain lions performing tricks or complicated mazes.

He didn't think Seigfried's shadow ever transformed, suggesting his form might have been something small and common. But he *couldn't* be alive.

Liam never wanted to admit that he thought the mage had died, but when he stopped following the king, the most logical assumption was that he'd gotten sick and passed away. Liam always believed this in the back of his mind while never allowing himself to dwell on it because they hadn't had a chance to speak much as teenagers, only small, formal exchanges and a game of hide and seek, but it was still too painful to accept the death of the only person who'd ever caught Liam's fancy more than the king himself.

But now…

Liam sprinted toward Creed, mounting and going full gallop through the royal woods back toward Citadel. Because the forest was well-groomed, he didn't have to worry about Creed tripping over a hidden root and breaking his leg, so he urged the horse onward.

The oracle claimed there'd be two attacks. A hoard of shadow beasts stormed Citadel a week ago, and now five unicorns had been stripped of their ivory for a specific spell. Was Liam drawing conclusions based on coincidence? Did it matter if he was wrong? His instincts told him to return to Citadel. He passed the nameless hamlet and continued toward the city as fast as he could without hurting Creed. As soon as he crossed through the gates, Liam found a public stable and traded Creed for a borrowed horse in order to ride faster through Citadel's cobbled streets to the palace. Old Way to Huckleberry, left on Seller's Way, follow the King's Path to the castle gates—Liam leapt off the strange horse as soon as they reached the courtyard. He didn't bother searching for a worker to care for her. Instead, he ran in a straight line to the throne room. Liam shouldered the door open, freezing when he saw Seigfried sitting on his throne and discussing the tax budget with Chancellor Cole.

"What is the meaning of this?" Cole stood, his arms still at his side, but his facial features were livid.

"I… Is everything all right? Here?" Liam stuttered but kept quiet about foxes and probably dead mage boys.

"Until you burst in. Did you find anything in the Royal Wood?"

"Another body, but there were only animal tracks. Is it possible that—"

"That you failed? It seems so. I'll send the hunt master to the Royal Wood instead, like we should have from the beginning."

"Liam is the best tracker in the realm." Siegfried dismissed Cole's comment with a gesture. "The hunt master won't find anything Liam couldn't find. We'll send him to the oracle. Edeline can point him in the right direction."

"I don't trust her magic," Cole insisted.

"I don't need to trust it to use it to my advantage." Siegfried leaned into his throne.

Liam clenched his fist. His dread coursing through him almost vibrated. Perhaps it was soldier's nerves, the old fears of ambush from the war haunting him when there was no real danger. But Liam's heart was *pounding*. He couldn't risk meandering through the maze of the inner city to find the oracle's temple when a witch armed with unicorn ivory could attack at any moment. Valinsir said his men would *die* if they fought.

"I can't leave. What if you're attacked while I'm gone? I have to protect you, Seigfried. I—"

An explosion interrupted their conversation. Liam stumbled but maintained his balance. Cole clutched to the tapestry to keep upright while Seigfried clung to the arms of his throne.

Liam pivoted and pushed into the hallway searching for their attacker. Screams rang from farther along the hall. He followed the noise until he saw a witch in an iridescent, hooded robe wearing a fox mask carved from ivory.

"You." Liam clenched his fists and charged.

Chapter Three

The thud of Liam's footsteps against the floor pounded in his ears as he sprinted toward the witch. At least seven guards, two of them men from his personal company, lay scattered around the witch's feet. The hood and mask hid the sorcerer's eyes from view, but the fox mask and ivory couldn't be coincidences.

"How dare you!" Liam raised his fist, ready to punch the mask off the witch's face.

The witch raised his hand, and a blast of magenta fire spiraled toward Liam. Raising his shield, the flames disappeared in a cloud of smoke after crashing against the scales.

"Dragon scales. How could I forget?" The sorcerer snorted. "Then chase me, Stallion of Citadel!"

With a carefree laugh, the sorcerer spun in a circle before skipping down the hallway. He zigzagged through the halls, circling behind ceramic vases and lacquered walnut end tables. The witch reached out, grabbing a support pillar and swinging in a circle. As he faced Liam, he shot another burst of flame toward Liam, who ducked behind his shield, blocking the fire.

"Do you remember this game, good knight? During the harvest masquerade when you were a squire? You snuck away from the party and played with a lowly slave." The sorcerer danced more than ran, weaving between statues and art exhibits.

"Why are you doing this?" Liam shouted. His armor was light, but he'd ridden all the way from the Royal Wood, and he was stiff and clumsy as he chased the witch.

"Why? Why? Surely you know why!" His voice rose to a high, angry pitch.

"No, I don't." Liam spoke in earnest.

"Are you truly so stupid?" The witch spat.

"*Nothing* could justify slaughtering unicorns! They're innocent creatures! They heal the injured and keep the land fertile!"

"Whose land?" The witch continued to wear Liam down by running in circles. "Siegfried's land? His personal little playground to chase stags while his people's hunting grounds are cleared for quick gold?"

"Don't you dare call the king by name!" Liam threw his entire body toward the witch, reaching to capture him.

He missed and crashed into a vase as tall as he was. The ceramic shattered into plate-sized pieces as he tumbled to the floor. Liam groaned, holding a tear in his pants where a shard slashed through the leather and grazed his skin. He moved his hand to check the laceration. It was bleeding but was not so deep he couldn't stagger to his feet. Before he regained his bearings, however, the witch slammed him against the wall. Liam sucked in a breath. They were too close. The scent of bergamot surrounded him, and he could see the witch's enchanting dual-colored eyes through the holes in the fox mask.

"Or what? What will you do if I call your precious liege by his filthy fucking name?" the witch growled, still pressed against Liam.

Liam reached out to shove him back, but he grabbed Liam's wrist and slammed it over his head. He could have headbutted the stranger, or kneed him in the groin, or twisted out of his grip, but Liam's body ached, and he was struggling to catch his breath.

"Why are you here?" Liam asked, trying to distract the witch long enough to recover.

"Good question. Why? Before I answer you, let's play hide and seek. Somewhere in the castle is a secret room filled with secret treasures. Find the chamber, and you find me." The witch fingered the slit in Liam's leg.

Liam winced in pain, his body flushed from the heat of battle. The witch's fingers lingered a little too long as he examined the injury, and all Liam could do was squirm beneath his weight.

"Don't worry." The witch chuckled, his mask making the sound distant and muted. "It's not deep. You'll be fine. Count to ten, and no cheating."

The witch covered Liam's eyes with his palm. Liam blinked when darkness blocked his vision, and his eyelashes tickled against the sorcerer's hand. He felt the pressure and warmth leave his face, but the world was still black.

One. Two. Three.

Liam reached out his hands, panicked. His heartbeat throbbed in his ears. When he couldn't feel anything in front of him, he braced himself against the wall behind him.

Four. Five. Six.

"I'm going to find you!" Liam screamed, wanting to hear his own voice. His eyes watered from the nothingness filling his vision.

Seven. Eight. Nine.

Liam held his breath.

Ten.

Light seeped in one layer at a time. Silhouettes formed, then grayscale images, and finally, color washed over the room. His blood was stark and crimson against the leather a few shades lighter brown than Liam's skin. Deep-blue veins spread through the ceramic vase shards. Liam gasped deep breaths, touching a ceramic shard just because he could *see* the blue and white. He searched the room. The only entrance was the one they'd entered through, and he didn't think the sorcerer led him there to double back. Liam kept his path along the walls, feeling the smooth stones or the thick tapestries. Behind a tapestry of the Royal Wood, one of the stones depressed when Liam pushed against it. The marble slabs of floor ground together in the corner, sinking and revealing stairs.

Liam stepped as quickly as he dared but listened and searched around him in case the witch tried to ambush him. Torches spaced about six feet apart lead him to a hidden treasure chamber. Baubles and trinkets sat on long tables or on glass curios. Liam halted when he saw the treasures, then turned in a slow circle.

"These are…all magical," he muttered to himself as he noticed the faint glow that many of the items emitted in the soft lighting of the treasure room.

"Yes. Ironic, isn't it?" A voice spoke to Liam's left.

He jerked and saw the sorcerer leaning against one of the curios.

"Our glorious and mighty king hates sorcerers, keeps them locked up like pets. But he can't bear to part with our treasures." The witch gestured. "Remember this?"

"The coronation crown."

"Yes. Enchanted to give each king a boost to their health. He burns us to death but benefits from our powers. And over there is the legendary spear Sir Ragor used to slay the five harpy queens who'd managed to overrun the castle seven hundred years ago."

Liam averted his eyes. Sir Ragor had no heirs, and there were only fables of what had happened to his spear, but Liam had heard rumors of this treasure long before the sorcerer challenged him to a game of hide and seek. This was the very place he feared his own cloak and shield would rest after he died if he didn't adopt a successor.

"So, you knew about this place?" the sorcerer asked. "Your expression gives you away."

"Rumors," Liam confessed. "Rumors I hoped were not true."

"Don't you find it hypocritical?" He tilted his head, blue and brown eyes blinking behind his mask.

"It's not my duty to question the king—only serve him."

"What a convenient way not to have to rationalize any of the atrocities he commits!" The sorcerer shoved the curio beside him to the ground. Glass shattered, and Liam stepped backward to avoid the glinting fragments.

"The king is just!" Liam insisted.

"Oh really?"

"Yes."

"And the executions?"

"Don't commit crimes if you don't want to suffer the consequences!"

"Oh, please. You can't possibly believe everyone killed is a criminal." The witch marched closer. As he spoke, he gestured with his hands, but not for spells—he was simply the type to throw his entire body into a conversation.

"I can't speak on behalf of every single execution over the years, but I know that *you* are guilty of *murder*, so when *you* burn it will be *justice*."

"Justice." The witch sneered.

He was too close again, staring up at Liam. Had they been dancing instead of fighting, Liam would have sworn he was tilting his face upward to be kissed, but the ivory fox snout kept some distance between them.

"I swear to you, all I *want* is justice, and I don't care what sins I have to commit to have it." The sorcerer clenched his fists.

"The ends don't justify the means," Liam said.

"Then how do you defend a king who's also a murderer?"

"I've already told you—"

"No." The witch pressed a slender finger against Liam's lips. He shook his head. "No. I'm talking about…another death. Not an execution. A murder."

"Who?" Liam spoke although it made his lips brush against the witch's skin in a distracting way.

"You don't deserve to know."

The sorcerer's face was covered and his voice muffled, but Liam noticed the way his lower eyelid twitched and the sadness in his tone.

"I can't help you if you won't tell me," Liam whispered.

And he meant the words. Even a witch deserved redress for their own wrongs before they paid for their crimes. Plus, Liam had known him. They had played tag once during a festival and laughed until Liam's father decided it was time for them to return home so Liam could train in the morning. He wished he'd had more chances to get to know the young magician before he'd disappeared.

"Do you really want to help me?" the sorcerer asked, fluttering his lashes.

"If I can."

"Fight me." He shoved Liam into an oak curio.

Liam crashed hard enough to knock it onto its side. The glass broke and colored bottles tumbled onto the floor. Liam gritted his teeth, growling in frustration.

"I should have known you were scheming instead of actually asking for help."

Liam lunged, and this time he caught the witch. They crashed to the ground, rolling and struggling until Liam managed to pin him onto his stomach. He held each wrist so the witch couldn't cast any spells.

"That wasn't a lie! I'm here for vengeance!" the witch snarled.

"And I'm here to avenge the unicorns you killed!" Liam screamed at the back of the witch's hood.

"Personal friends of yours?" He glanced over his shoulder, but only his mask and a single brown eye showed when he turned.

"I don't have to know them to know what you did was wrong."

"But if their deaths hurt you, despite them being strangers, animals, how would you feel if it *was* someone close to you?"

"Is that a threat?"

"I'm trying to get you to understand me!"

"I don't need to understand you! I only have to drag you to the dungeons." Liam lifted the witch up and slung him over his shoulder, prepared to carry him to the throne room and lay him at Seigfried's feet.

"You're no different than the others!" The witch tugged at Liam's hair, but the locs were old and mature, and he wasn't tender headed, so he managed to march across the room despite the witch's struggles.

"You're no different than a common murderer on the streets! Don't hide behind a contrived cause to excuse your crimes."

With a wild twist of his body, the sorcerer managed to wrench himself free and smack into the rug below with a hard *thunk*. Liam grabbed him again, and they grappled, tugging at robes and riding leathers, until the sorcerer managed a solid kick to Liam's chest. Liam slammed into another shelf but caught his balance before lunging. As they crashed to the ground, Liam's shoulder hit a final curio, a tall, slender glass one displaying a single scarlet feather. Like the others, the display smashed to the floor. The feather rose into the air, bursting into flames the moment it lifted out of the case. Liam flinched away from the heat.

The witch laughed, loud and boisterous peals.

"You're easier to play than a tin whistle." Holding out his hand, the witch allowed the burning feather to rest in his palm before hiding it in the sleeve of his robe.

"What do you mean?" Liam held both the magician's shoulders to keep him from fleeing.

"That case was protected with a tricky enchantment. I couldn't touch it, but an oaf like you? Well, the spell was meant to protect the case from magic, not clumsiness. Thanks for the push."

"You—what?" Liam's gaze shifted between the witch, the case, the broken curios surrounding them, and back to the witch.

"You didn't notice because we'd broken several cases, but the phoenix feather was my goal all along. Now I have two of the three components I need to make Seigfried pay for everything he's done."

"Give the feather back!" Liam thrust his hand up the witch's sleeve, searching for the hidden pocket.

"It's magic, so you won't find anything I don't want you to, but I do enjoy a man with rough hands," the witch purred.

Liam pulled away at the comment, flushed from their struggle and the witch's words. Anger from being tricked mixed with the thrill of their proximity, and Liam never wanted to punch someone in the face as badly as he wanted to punch this witch.

"You're not escaping." Liam locked his arms around the witch's body, prepared to drag him to the dungeons.

"You're strong, but you're forgetting I'm magical," the witch whispered in Liam's ear, causing him to shiver.

The half second distraction was all the witch needed to free his hands and summon a pair of manacles formed out of light. He clamped the cuffs around Liam's wrists and chained him to the leg of a table.

"I wish we could play more." The witch nudged the tip of Liam's nose with the nose of his mask. "But I really must go."

"Wait!" Liam shouted as the witch dashed toward the exit.

Surprisingly, he stopped, turning and staring at Liam through his mask. Liam's cheeks were burning far more than the stolen feather had as it floated in the air. He tugged at the manacle, trying to break the table leg so he could hurl himself at the witch and capture him properly, using the ties Valinsir taught him to keep the mage from casting more magic. But the table held, and he was trapped much like the fox had been when they met in the Royal Woods. Defeated, Liam stared at the mysterious witch hiding behind robes and an ivory fox mask.

"I never knew your name," Liam said.

"Why would you want to now? To know who to curse?" The witch laughed. "Who to blame?"

"So I know who I played chase with as a teenager." Liam jerked at the chain again, but the magic held.

"Don't worry. Your chain will disappear in another minute. I won't wound your pride so much as to have you caught bound by such a simple spell. Although, I'm sure Cole will blame you for letting me slip away."

The witch secured his hood around his mask, as if suddenly self-conscious of it.

"I'll find you. I won't stop until I capture you and bring you to the throne for sentencing and execution."

"Every time, I think you might see me as a human instead of a cog in the machine." The witch sighed. "I really shouldn't tell you, but…Reynald."

"Reynald," Liam repeated. His chest fluttered despite the utter and sheer inappropriateness of the reaction.

"And you are Sir Liam Bord, the Stallion of Citadel. You get to be a hero because you scamper when your master calls, while I'm branded a criminal for no other reason than because I found a way out of my cage and fled."

"You're a poacher and a thief." Liam pulled at the chain again. The light was fading, and he felt the bonds stretch, though they didn't yet break.

"Cause and effect, Sir Bord. We'll have another chance to play chase in the future, but for now, I'd better take my leave before that spell wears off." Reynald slipped into the hallway.

Liam listened for his footsteps but couldn't hear anything as he escaped. The chain dimmed, and he was finally able to pull himself free. Inspecting the room, Liam grimaced at how many shelves and relics they'd broken during their childish wrestling. He'd let his emotions drive his actions—which was uncharacteristic of him—and now he regretted getting so carried away. Reynald wouldn't have been able to manipulate him had he stayed calm.

He also gave himself a quick look over. He was in worse condition than the room. He'd torn the cut more open, the entire top of his pant leg was dark from drying blood, and any area of exposed skin had been scraped or cut as they'd crashed into wood and glass. Without the adrenaline to keep Liam moving, he had to limp out of the hidden passageway and find the king, waiting in the war room.

"He escaped," the king said.

"Yes." Liam dropped to both hands and knees, guilty for letting his mark elude him.

"And he stole the phoenix feather."

"How did you know?" Liam raised his head.

"The oracle. She said the fox would elude the stallion with a feather clutched in his smirking muzzle. She also told me that if I send you to her, she'd tell you how to find him." Siegfried rose and walked toward Liam. He held out a coin with a dancing maiden etched into the gleaming, white metallic surface. "Place this offering at her shrine, and she'll appear."

"Perhaps we should assemble a team…"

"No. You must go. It's been foretold. Bring him back to me, my stallion, and I will grant you any reward you wish." Siegfried brushed his fingers along Liam's cheekbone. "Any reward at all."

Chapter Four

Liam unlaced his britches in the washroom. The king ordered him to leave for the oracle immediately, but he had to clean and bandage his cut before he was fit to ride. He had enough ointment in his field kit to treat the worst of his scrapes and could treat his injuries more thoroughly before he slept.

Patched up, Liam found his rented horse in the stables, despite having left her in the courtyard. He thanked the lad who'd stabled her, offered him a copper as a tip, and rode toward the shrine. The king's words echoed in his thoughts as he passed through the streets. *Any reward at all*, but Liam couldn't have what he wanted. The king's innuendo hadn't gone over Liam's head. Siegfried was willing to share his bed for a night, but a kiss, or even a night with a king, wasn't what Liam truly desired. He wanted to come home from battle to a partner already in his bed; he wanted conversation over dinner; he wanted a hand to clasp. Liam snorted, disgusted by both his own desire and the fact that he apparently hadn't done very well hiding his attraction to his liege.

How do you defend a king who's also a murderer?

Liam bit his bottom lip. What had Reynald meant? Throughout the history of Phrophis and its long line of kings, surely there were times where a man was sent to the gallows when he'd been innocent. Likewise, one or two of the magicians set to torch might not have been actual witches practicing wicked magic but victims of an imperfect system. That didn't mean Seigfried was a murderer, yet Reynald had conviction, if nothing else.

Shaking his head, Liam dismissed his thoughts. He was a knight, not a judge. It wasn't his duty to decide who was guilty or innocent, merely bring in the suspects so they could be tried. And despite the past, there was no question that Reynald was a poacher and thief and deserved the stake.

Deep purple orchids surrounded the circular building. The stained-glass windows depicted maidens dancing, some beneath the sun and others beneath the moon. Liam tied the horse to the appropriate post before frowning at the colorful images. For one to receive a reading from the oracle, they had to dance with her…and kiss her. He'd performed this rite once before, the evening before he was knighted, and he'd hated it. The oracle was beautiful, and men around the world would pay any cost for what he was about to do, but for Liam, this was another grim duty, not a pleasure.

It was night, so no light filtered through the stained glass as he entered the shrine. Incense smoke curled around the room. From somewhere in the back, the whine of a singing bowl reverberated through the air. Liam stripped himself of his soldier's gear, keeping only his riding clothes and cloak as he approached the altar. A platinum bowl sat in the center. From a skylight above, moonlight beamed onto the metal and illuminated it. He dropped the coin into the bowl; it circled three times before dropping to its side. Liam frowned at the disk until he saw a woman in the corner of his vision.

"I've been waiting for you."

She was black, dark, dark, dark, with almost black eyes and thick hair that rose from her scalp in spires. Her skin was smooth, her body was thick, and her features were broad and rounded. She was the most beautiful woman in the world, but Liam stepped away from her as she approached.

"My poor stallion." She laughed, her voice low and rich. "You don't want to kiss a soothsayer. You want to kiss a fox with dual-colored eyes."

"Capture a fox," Liam corrected.

"He was captured. You set him free."

Liam averted his gaze.

"Why didn't you tell Siegfried it was Reynald?"

"I... Didn't you tell him? He already knew I'd fail, so he sent me here."

"I told him his enemy was a fox. Both of us seemed to have forgotten to mention his name or the color of his eyes. How careless of us." Edeline held Liam's hands and waltzed with him around the shrine.

The floor was polished onyx, and their reflections danced with it. Edeline's usual dances were sultry and writhing. She'd grind against her clients, making their hearts race and blood rush through their bodies, but for Liam, she merely waltzed. It didn't matter. Liam's heart already rioted in his chest because he couldn't stop imagining kissing Reynald— why was he thinking of kissing the witch instead of capturing him?

No, not *the witch*. Reynald. The boy he'd chased through the castle during a party with no one around to lecture them. The boy with dual-colored eyes who used to shoot longing glances at Liam when they passed each other in the castle hallways.

Liam slammed his eyes closed and held his breath. His foolishness had to end. He had already allowed himself to become distracted, and Reynald had stolen a phoenix feather because of it. Liam was a knight; he had responsibilities to the king and country. Let the girls sitting in their sewing rooms and hiding risqué novels in their knitting work sigh and daydream about forbidden romances. Liam was going to find Reynald, capture him, and bring him to the castle for sentencing. He'd earn a king's kiss and gratitude afterward, but more importantly, he would have fulfilled his duty as a knight. Duty was all that mattered to Liam.

"You love how clever he is. You hate how he weaponized his cunning against you, but you love the razor edge of his mind all the same."

"He's horrible," Liam argued.

"You don't believe that."

"You see futures. You don't read minds."

"I don't have to read your mind. Your feelings are boldly written across your face."

"My feelings don't matter. Only my duty."

"Pity. Because you will fall in love with him over and over again. So many times, that you'll wonder what's wrong with you." The oracle laughed. "He is a fox, cunning and reckless, but he will be your fox."

"My prisoner. I'm going to bring him to Seigfried—to the king." Liam stared at the windows to avoid the oracle's gaze. Girls dancing under the sun. Girls dancing under the moon.

"Yes, you will capture him and give him to the king, and he will be put to the torch."

Her words dropped a weight into the pit of Liam's stomach. Unlawful as Reynald was, Liam really wished there was something he could do to help the sorcerer. He'd seemed so sad even when proclaiming his vengeance, Liam would at least give him a sentence less harsh than death, or if he had been wronged, justice.

Edeline plucked a quick kiss from Liam's top lip. He started, so lost in thought that he'd forgotten about her despite holding her in his arms.

"Sometimes we don't get to choose how our magic works, right?" She gave him an apologetic smile. Her lips were painted with a purple stain the same color of the orchids around her shrine.

"I understand."

"But I've seen quite a journey for you. We'll meet again after you return."

"My lady—"

"Lady!" Edeline laughed. "You're as bad as Tobyn. I'm not nobility, not according to the king, so don't insult me with formalities." She pressed her finger to his lips. "Just like my mother and your grandmother, we'll be friends one day. You'll come visit me when I wear orchids in my hair and laugh as we drink tea."

"Um…" Liam's face twisted.

"You don't believe me." Her belly shook with her laughter.

"They say you're never wrong," Liam hedged.

"I'm going to give you a map."

A slender dirk, not much wider than an awl, hung from Edeline's neck. She gripped the handle in one hand and Liam's wrist in the other. Pricking his finger, the oracle stretched his hand over the shrine and a drop of his blood splashed on a parchment stretched out beside the bowl. Like a drop of ink, the blood spread across the page, filling the little grooves of the parchment they couldn't see with their eyes. Further and further the red spread, until it was a rusty brown swirling across the page in the shape of roads and towns and mountain ranges.

"You'll find him here." Edeline pointed to a mountain far to the north of Citadel in the sparsely inhabited wild lands of Phrophis. "He's searching for dragon hide."

Liam smoothed his fingers over the map, as if he could slip into the paper like it was a bath and reach the dragon's lair more quickly.

"You're going to save the city in more ways than one," Edeline said.

"I'm leaving." Liam rolled the parchment into a tube and stuck it in his belt. "Thank you."

Liam glanced over his shoulder, wondering about her words, but he didn't have time to interpret her prophecy. He wasn't as cynical as

Cole when it came to magic, but he wasn't covetous of it like Seigfried either. He needed a map; she'd given him one. Now the task was to follow the parchment to his goal.

The late hour prevented him from traveling far, so Liam traded the mare for his own horse again and rode home. In his own room, he sat in a hot bath, allowing the water to soak the forming bruises and scratches. Liam toyed with the larger gash in his thigh, unable to forget the way Reynald had prodded the cut, checking to see if Liam was fit to chase him. What would have happened had he been too injured to chase? Would Reynald have found a different knight or guard to trick? Would he have bandaged Liam in order to get what he wanted?

Liam dunked his head below the hot water. Remaining submerged, he pretended he was drowned, a victim of Kelpie or a Jenny Greenteeth. The water distorted the sounds of the room. He broke the surface when his lungs burned. Gasping, Liam rested his head against the lip of the claw-foot tub and stared at the ceiling. He dozed, waking after his laundress came to collect his torn and bloodied riding leathers. Liam dressed in his night clothes after she left and crawled into his large, empty bed. Sleep evaded him as he tossed and turned. Well before dawn lightened the sky, Liam dressed and packed for the long journey north. A knock to his door startled him from his own thoughts.

"Enter," Liam called, checking each item he'd packed against the quest list he used before each journey.

"Good morning, Sir Bord, I heard from the men that you're off to capture a witch." Valinsir entered the room. He was weathered and scarred and was always a day or two behind on shaving, but he had the sort of smile that set men at ease and was an excellent teacher.

"Last night, the castle was attacked by an extremist." Liam searched for his waterproof pouch filled with matches and tinder.

"I have a gift for you. I hope this helps." Valinsir offered a rope.

"Is this unicorn hair?" Liam ran his fingers along the coils of shimmering silver glittering from the light cutting in from the open window beside them.

"Yes. With this, even simple binds will render the witch incapable of casting. I noticed you didn't care for the more complex rigging when I was training the others, so…" Valinsir shrugged.

"We used similar knots for interrogations during the war." Liam frowned. "I'd rather avoid torturing a prisoner."

"A necessary cruelty in both cases, no?" Valinsir always asked these questions in a way that made Liam feel like he was being tested.

"It was my duty to fight when the king commanded his knights to fight, and now it is my duty to capture the witch, but—witch or no, prisoner or no—he's only human. I don't want him to suffer."

"I agree." Valinsir scratched the day-old stubble growing on his face. "Too many of my kinsmen treat mages like animals. It's magic, not rabies—criminals need to be dealt with the same as any, but a magician is still a human. It pains me how easily society forgets magicians are people…even when they're children."

"They arrest children?" Liam almost dropped the rope as Valinsir's words sank into his mind.

"We are not sheriffs of Mascaria. We are hunters. They want all magicians controlled at any cost." Valinsir's shoulders slumped with his exhale. "Honestly? It's why I'm *retired,* and your father had a bit of a reputation of being a fair man, so I thought Prophis might suit me a little better."

"My father?" Liam packed the rope with the rest of his gear. "I didn't realize the stories they tell about the knights reach other kingdoms."

"Everyone loves a good story. But I'm keeping you from your own story, aren't I?" Valisir laughed. "I should let you pack. Are there any specific instructions you have for me while you're gone?"

"Keep training. Anything you can do to keep them alive. I fear…" Liam glanced out the window. The forest was all the horizon could hold, gorgeous sloping hills and trees and creatures with claws who loved to hunt. "The attacks will overwhelm the farmers if we're not prepared."

"Take care." Valinsir patted Liam's shoulder. "Try not to worry. By the time you return, I'll have these boys halfway competent and, dare I say, adept at protecting the roads and farms."

"I look forward to seeing their improvement." Liam nodded as he buckled the straps of his bags and carried all his gear to the stable where Creed waited, saddled and fed extra for the long journey.

Liam kept to the main roads, following the shortest route on his map. He stopped at the travel lodges when he needed supplies or a bath, but spent most nights in his single-person tent so he could wake early and hurry along the next stretch of miles.

After weeks of travel, the mountain peak on his map was white, intimidating, and real in the distance. The cloud line hid the mountaintop from view. Liam stopped near a stream to rub Creed's coat and allow him to drink and rest. As his horse nibbled on wild grasses growing along the river bank, Liam satisfied his own hunger with dried meat and chicory brewed over his campfire. The woody, bitter drink warmed him and gave him the motivation to ride three more miles before camping for the night. Liam wrapped his cloak around Creed's neck. The dragon scales would keep his horse from freezing while Liam slept in the tent. The tent was hide, treated to outlast the weather, watertight, yet not the warmest, but he had a thick fur covering to keep out the worst of the cold. Nevertheless, the howling wind rushing from the mountain slipped through, and Liam shivered. When he managed to sleep, he dreamed of arms holding him, warming him, but in the morning, there was only frozen earth and wailing wind to greet him as he stretched and prepared his body for another long day of riding.

No one lived beyond the rocky craigs leading upward, so Liam followed the caribou trails instead of cart paths. Signs of griffins and harpies littered the scenery. He found stray feathers tucked in bushes and between the long grass, and an entire griffon's nest nestled between three cone-shaped boulders. Recognizing the signs of the creatures enabled Liam to avoid them as he moved into higher elevations. Fog clung to the trails as he reached the cloud line. He spent another frozen night in his tent, miserable.

The fog thickened as he traveled. The caribou trail veered away suddenly, so Liam found a cave deep enough to fend off the worst of the wind's chill and left Creed wrapped in his fur tent cover to keep the horse warm while Liam explored on foot. Alone, Liam hiked up the mountainside of gray stones, following a littered path of bone shards to reach the den tucked just below the mountain peak. Liam exhaled when he entered the den. The air was warm and a little humid. Mushrooms, shinning bright as will-o-wisps, grew from the ground to the stalactites dripping from the ceiling. The fungus gave the entire lair an ambient, green-white glow. Quietly, Liam crept through the cave, searching for the dragon's nest and Reynald.

The dragon's form filled the bulk of the cavern. She rested curled in a spiral—much like a house cat—on a natural stone dais rising from the cave floor. Gold coins and trinkets filled her nest. The treasure helped camouflage the golden eggs hiding in the nest, while straw insulated the eggs even when the mother left to hunt. Reynald stood near the dragon's head. He looked small next to the huge creature, but no less sinister, a parasitic wasp preparing a poisoned stinger. At least, Liam assumed the needle-like blade in his hand was poisoned if he was going to fight a *dragon* with a mere *knife*. Crouching low, Liam inched behind Reynald. From his pack, he pulled the silver rope Valinsir had given him. Liam raised the cord, prepared to loop it around Reynald's chest, but the magician spun and aimed the long needle tip directly under Liam's jaw.

"Hello, Sir Bord. Your aftershave is intoxicating—I could smell you the moment you slipped into the cave. By the way, I'm impressed you were able to track me into the mountains."

"The oracle gave me a map."

"Of course, she did." A bitter laugh escaped Reynald's throat. "Seigfried isn't capable of anything without the assistance of magic, so he sent you to Edeline."

"Reynald, she has eggs," Liam said, too travel weary to debate the king's dependency on magic.

"Uh—"

"The dragon, not the oracle," Liam snapped, flustered about how sincerely confused Reynald looked as he twisted his lips and tilted his head to the side.

Cute. There was no other way to describe the expression. Cuter still when Reynald chuckled, clearly embarrassed by not understanding but keeping in character as 'the cunning villain.'

"So what? She's a dragon. Aren't the Bords famous dragon slayers?"

"She has *eggs*. This isn't how we hunt," Liam argued. "If you want to fight a dragon, find one attacking a village. Don't poison one in her own den while she sleeps."

"Mmm…yes. Indeed. Ever the noble storybook knight. Well, Sir Knight, you'd better be careful. If you keep fussing over every magical creature you come across, rumors that you're a magic sympathizer will spread, and you'll be tied to the stake with me when they light the match."

Liam winced because the statement was true. Any nobility convicted of sympathizing with witches, or abetting them in any way, had their lands and titles stripped and were forced into exile. Some of those of low birth, however, were burned.

"Besides." Reynald moved his blade enough to flick the cloak around Liam's shoulders. "If I skin her for her hide, we'll match."

"This is the hide of Kulvacc the Greedy. He kidnapped and ate children. It's not the same." Liam glanced at the sleeping mother coiled around her nest. "What did you do to her? She should wake at the sound of our voices."

"Nothing more harmful than a sleep spell. Don't worry. But I'm sorry to admit, I need a swath of draconic hide for my spell." Reynald batted his eyelashes behind his mask, even as he replaced the point beneath Liam's chin. "Unless you're willing to give me your cloak. If you do, I'll spare her. I only need a few yards, and I don't relish the killing, but my vengeance takes precedence over everything else, including morality."

"This is my grandfather's cloak. I refuse to shame his memory by giving it to a witch trying to assassinate the son of the woman Sir Linnel gave his eye protecting."

"It's adorable how strongly you believe in all this knight-in-shining-armor bullshit." Reynald snorted. "But if you won't give me what I need, then I'm afraid I'll have to carve a section of my own."

"I won't let you."

"You can't stop me."

"Yes, I can."

"You can certainly try."

Growling, Liam flung himself at Reynald. The recklessness of his action caught Reynald off guard because instead of stabbing him with the poisoned blade, Reynald only sucked in a sharp breath when he dropped his knife and was slammed onto his back. Crash-landing on top of Reynald, Liam froze for a moment, blinking like the fool he was and gazing into Reynald's eyes.

"Idiot! Be more careful! The rapier is poisoned!" Reynald punched

Liam's chest despite the metal mesh beneath his surcoat. "Had I even scratched you, you'd be dead!"

"I don't care! I can't fail again!"

"Get off me!" Reynald shoved Liam.

The force was enough to knock Liam off the dais. Liam reached out, grabbing Reynald and pulling them both over the edge. After their fall, the mask sat skewed on Reynald's face, and Liam slapped it off completely.

"Why would you even make something so awful?"

"Don't touch it!" Reynald cocked his fist and swung, but Liam caught Reynald's hand and tackled him to the ground again.

The force was enough to pull the hood away from Reynald's head. A burst of brilliant orange flowed out from the hood and spread around Reynald's face like a flaming halo. Liam stared at Reynald in wide-eyed shock, mouth ajar.

"What?" Reynald snarled.

"Sweet saints." Liam sucked in a breath. "You're beautiful."

"Oh? Am I?" Reynald grinned, lidding his eyes.

"I… You always were."

"Was I?"

Reynald's hungry gaze, with one brown eye and one blue, had Liam's stomach in a roiling boil, but he straddled Reynald and wrapped his wrists in a double bind with the silver rope. Reynald watched with an amused expression. Liam prepared for him to flee, but Reynald remained limp below him, his stare locked on Liam the entire time.

"I—I won't let you escape." Liam bit his lower lip, shoving his instincts away and reminding himself he was here *to arrest* Reynald.

"I don't think I could if I wanted to," Reynald said with a teasing lilt to his voice. "I can't change into a fox with this rope around my wrists. I suppose I'm at your mercy, Sir Bord."

"Don't say it like that." Liam blushed.

"Like what?" Reynald licked his lips.

"Doesn't matter." Liam shook his head. "I'm escorting you to Citadel where you'll receive a fair trial before being sent to your execution."

"*Listen* to yourself. Really listen. Fair trial before my execution? How is it fair if the outcome is preordained? Saints, you're pathetic." Reynald clenched his teeth.

Liam held Reynald's bound hands, focusing on the silver strands of rope so he didn't have to look at Reynald's high cheekbones, full lips, or mesmerizing eyes.

"I saw you in the woods near the dead unicorns. I caught you with your knife hovering over the dragon's neck. You're guilty. No defense will wash the blood from your hands."

"Killing a dragon isn't a crime."

"Hunting in the royal woods is."

"And the wise women of Balbraid Thicket dragged from their cottages in the dead of night and burned all three tied to the same stake? The traveling scholars who pass through to recruit Phrophis witches to the universities in Valen and Suzdal? Not to mention the children taken and raised in the palace like animals! Are they all guilty?"

"Quit complaining! Living in the castle is a privilege, not an injustice. There are children in huts crying themselves to sleep from cold and hunger every night, but you slept dry, warm, and well-fed in a palace!"

"Listen to yourself! Why are children going to bed hungry when Seigfried fills his coffers with coin from priceless exports! Yes! I killed unicorns! But I only took what I needed. Seigfried could have donated the literal fortune of the rest of the components to help his own people. But will he? No! He'll hoard it! He's worse than the dragon beside us! She hoards treasure to hide her eggs, but Seigfried wants to bleach his hair in lemon juice and rub shea butter on his skin every night and throw parties more expensive than an entire city's taxes!"

Reynald's expression twisted. He bucked in protest of Liam straddling him. The motion sent an embarrassing jolt through Liam's entire body, but he couldn't enjoy the sensation because of the rage-induced tears lining Reynald's eyes.

"Fair trial? Fair trial, my ass. It's only luck that I've done something wrong to deserve punishment. In Citadel, all witches are guilty, but fine! I'm your prisoner. Take me home." Reynald covered his face with his bound fists. "And give me my mask. I damned my soul for it; at least let me hide my face."

"Why hide?" Liam crawled off him.

Fetching the mask, Liam arranged it over Reynald's face. He fixed the flowing orange strands around the band, however, instead of pulling Reynalds hood up to hide the bright splash of color now framing the mask. It was the orange of a fox's coat, but much, much brighter.

"The king always treated me like a pet, an animal. Let me be one now." Reynald awkwardly pushed himself to his feet. "A demon's mask for the evil witch. Isn't it fitting?"

"If it suits you. Let's go." Liam stood with him and brushed the dust from both their clothes. He grabbed the lead on the rope and led Reynald out of the cave.

"Seigfried would do this, remember. Each magician wore a jeweled collar, and he'd personally lead his favorites down the hall."

Liam lowered his head. He remembered. He never paid much attention, always staring at Reynald's face instead.

"What will happen to the dragon?" Liam changed the subject. "She can't defend her eggs while in magical sleep."

"The spell is only an hour. I didn't blind you forever, and I didn't prick her finger with a poisoned spinning wheel spindle. I'm not as evil as you pretend I am."

"You were going to kill her."

"I was going to skin her tail, but only enough for my spell. She most likely would have survived."

"Most likely, unless the wound festered."

"It's freezing on this mountain, a horrible environment for infection, and I would have treated the area before leaving. Damn. I'm practical, not necessarily heartless."

"Have you even admitted to yourself that you killed those unicorns? I saw the last corpse. She did not survive. You did not treat *them.*"

"Of course, I couldn't treat the unicorns' injuries. I took their horns. There's no surviving or mending the loss of their horn." Reynald groaned in disgust. "I know it was wrong. Do you accept how much wrong you enable as a knight?"

"My horse is down this side of the mountain." Liam ignored Reynald.

He jumped down the first ledge of rock and glanced upward at his prisoner.

"Well?" Reynald snorted. "What do you expect me to do? I can't climb down with my hands bound."

"Jump into my arms. I'll catch you."

"For the love of—whatever. I'm sick of arguing." Reynald dropped.

Liam caught him. For all Reynald's wild, savage strength, he felt lithe and slender in Liam's arms. Their gazes locked, and Liam yearned to remove the mask from Reynald's face and touch his cheeks. Reynald chuckled low behind the mask, as if he could read Liam's thoughts.

"We…need to hurry." Liam set Reynald down so he could jump to the next section before helping Reynald down as well.

"Do we? Are you anxious to watch me burn?"

"No," Liam gasped but clamped his mouth shut and hardened his expression. "But the king is waiting."

"Oh yes. We mustn't allow Siegfried to wait. He's very impatient." Reynald snorted as he followed Liam down the rocks toward the path.

Chapter Five

Climbing their way down to the caribou trail was exhausting, and both men quit arguing as they focused on breathing the thin, cold mountain air. When they reached the cave where Liam had hidden Creed, stars glittered endlessly across the night sky.

"Better shelter here. The nights are too cold on the mountain," Liam said.

"Not with your cloak." Reynald snorted. "I'm sure you hardly notice."

"My cloak does protect from cold," Liam admitted. "But even I enjoy a fire."

"I suppose knights are humans after all." Reynald leaned against the cave wall.

"We are. Same as witches."

"I'm shocked you admit I'm human."

"Criminals are also humans." Liam arranged several stones in a circle to create a small firepit.

"Had to add the barb, didn't you?" Reynald glanced around. "I have to piss."

"Fine. I need to gather wood anyway." Liam grabbed the rope and led Reynald to an area with enough cedar trees for him to find a good amount of firewood.

"Are you going to hold my dick for me, or are you going to untie me?" Reynald asked.

"Your wrists are bound, not your hands. Manage."

"Surely, you're not going to keep me like this all the way to Citadel? Even on horseback it's close to a month's journey."

"You're not escaping. Now do your business or piss yourself. I don't care."

Liam hated his harsh tone, but he couldn't underestimate Reynald again, couldn't allow him to escape a second time. Liam's honor as a knight was on the line, and Edeline may have predicted he'd complete his mission, but she'd also claimed he'd fall in love—which was ridiculous—so he didn't trust her soothsaying and preferred to keep on guard instead of hoping destiny was on his side.

As Liam gathered wood, he glanced out of the corner of his vision and saw Reynald turned away from him with his robes lifted. Liam snorted. The mage had been capable of relieving himself the entire time but had been trying to find a chance to run. Liam filled his arms with cedar branches, and when Reynald was ready, they escaped the chill and tucked themselves deep within the cave where at least the wind couldn't cut through their clothes. The fire brightened the stone around them and kept their camp almost cozy. Liam unpacked a night's worth of rations for both of them and laid out his sleeping gear for them to rest on.

"I don't want this." Reynald pushed the food away.

"You need to eat something." Liam sat next to him, close enough to grab him if he fled.

"Starving is better than burning alive, so why should I eat?"

"I won't force you if you're going to be stubborn." Liam chewed on his jerky and stared at the fire, but the orange flames reminded him of Reynald's hair. He stole a glance at the sorcerer hiding behind his fox mask. "You look childish in a mask. Like you're pretending it's the All Saints' Eve festival."

"Says the man dressed up like a knight."

"I am a knight."

"Well, knights always look like they're ready for carnival, or perhaps it's a fool's motley you're imitating with your brightly colored surcoats."

Instead of replying to the insult, Liam offered Reynald a sip from his water skin. Reynald turned his face away as if Liam offered him a vile of poison.

"I don't need your empty gestures of care. I have my own water."

Reynald pulled a pouch from a hidden pocket and drank as if to spite Liam. He had to tilt the mask higher on his face as he did so, revealing his mouth. Liam turned away so he didn't stare.

"Do you still have the phoenix feather?" Liam asked.

"I'm not returning it, if that's what you're asking." The firelight played on the curves of ivory, giving the mask a lifelike quality.

"If you returned what you stole, we could beseech the king to reduce your sentence."

"If you think Seigfried would let me live because we asked nicely and gave him one of his toys back, you really don't know who your king is."

"I don't know him. I only serve him, but any reasonable monarch would—"

"It doesn't matter. The feather is in my tower in the Balbraid Thicket."

"Oh, you live in the Balbraid Thicket?" Liam leaned against a boulder and pulled his cloak around him for warmth. "We're practically neighbors."

"Then I've stolen apples and plums from your orchards before." Reynald glanced at Liam. "So, there's another reason to execute me."

"I've never stopped a hungry traveler from eating from my orchards." Liam shook his head.

"It infuriates me how close you can come to being decent. If you weren't always up your own ass with the laws, you might be okay company."

"It infuriates me how you have no reverence for the law." Liam shot Reynald a cross look.

"In a better world, we could temper each other's extremes, but in this one, neither of us is willing to change, so I guess I'm going to sleep." Reynald dropped onto his side, his back to Liam.

"If…you're cold," Liam stuttered," we can use my cloak as a blanket."

"Better to freeze to death than burn," Reynald said with a grunt.

"Suit yourself." Liam dropped on his side as well, facing in the opposite direction.

In the morning, he unbound one of Reynald's wrists and tied the other end of the rope to a tree so he could do his morning business. Liam packed their camp and prepared Creed for their journey home. When they stopped to eat, Reynald refused, consuming only water.

"I wish you wouldn't do this," Liam said.

"I wish you'd fall off the mountain and break your neck so I can get on with my life."

"This is going to be a long ride to Citadel." Liam rubbed his temples before hoisting Reynald onto Creed and mounting behind him.

Both of Reynald's wrists were bound again. He could hold onto the reins while Liam held onto him. He kept his grip light at Reynald's sides and didn't try to steer, allowing Reynald to guide them down the path leading away from the mountains. Reynald did so without complaining, probably too cold to stall their descent. The mountain scenery was breathtaking. The fir trees towered like giants above their heads. Ferns as large as Creed spread out between the red, brown, and gray trunks. The cold air muted the smells, but a faint hint of butterscotch-scented tree sap or pine needles would cut in and out of their path, and each time, Liam inhaled deeply, filling his lungs with the sweetness. He caught Reynald doing the same and had to stifle his laughter. He avoided arguing by not talking to Reynald.

By their third day of travel, though they'd left the mountain ridges, the fog continued to cling to the forest, and the sky peeking through the canopy was a flat, heavy gray. Liam prayed to Saint Barbara that the weather would break, but after another day of riding, a fat, damp snow drifted on top of their heads. Again, as they camped, Liam wrapped Creed in his cloak for the night and set up his tent.

"The horse?" Reynald laughed. "You're giving your cloak to the horse?"

"It'll be well below freezing tonight, and the tent is too small for him," Liam said as he arranged the fur cover over the hide.

"Why not the fur cover over your tent like before?"

"It's too cold tonight. The cloak is warmer."

"You actually love animals that much, don't you?" Reynald laughed so hard that he had to bring his bound hands behind his mask and to his face to wipe away a tear.

"I do. What of it?" Liam frowned at the tent. "Reynald…don't be stubborn. Don't argue. If you stay out tonight you may *actually* freeze to death. Lie in the tent."

"They say freezing to death is peaceful." Reynald shrugged.

"Please don't make me carry your corpse all the way to Citadel." Liam hugged himself, his long ropes of hair draping on either side of his shoulders.

"So even my death won't stop you from completing your little mission." Reynald dug his heel into the half-frozen ground. "Wouldn't want to disappoint Seigfried, would you?"

"Of course I don't, but that's not why… Reynald, *please*."

"Oh, that sounds pretty. Say it again."

"Please?"

"With my name. You have to say both."

"And then you'll sleep in the tent?" Liam asked.

"No." Reynald chuckled. "But I'll have a good time teasing you about how I made you beg."

"I'll untie you—in the tent only—if you quit being difficult."

Reynald stared at his bound wrists. A low growl hummed from the back of his throat before his shoulders slumped.

"I hate being bound." Reynald gritted his teeth.

"I would not tie you at all if I could trust you." Liam built the fire higher so it would last through the better part of the night. "But you're too dangerous."

"Yes," Reynald purred. "A frightening witch of the Balbraid Thicket."

"Reynald, please."

Liam knelt in front of him, using his name just as he'd asked. Liam didn't care if Reynald mocked him. Witch or no, Reynald was the closest thing to a friend Liam had ever known—although he'd hardly known him. He didn't want to see him burn, but worse still was the thought of him dying just a few feet away. Liam had no power to stop an execution, but he had a tent and a blanket to stop hypothermia. Reynald stared, unblinking, through the gruesome mask before exhaling loudly.

"Oh, sweet little knight who can't even stand to watch an animal freeze to death. Fine. I'll sleep in the tent if you untie me." Reynald slammed his fists into his lap before crawling toward the long but narrow tent.

Liam removed his mail shirt and crawled after Reynald. They had to lie on their sides in order to fit between the tawny hide surrounding them. An eerie glow from the fire filtered through the front of the tent, but it was hardly enough for Liam to see in front of himself.

"You're pretty close. Are you afraid?" Reynald asked.

"No."

"But I'm a dangerous and bloodthirsty witch," Reynald said in the sort of voice one used for ghost stories.

"You are," Liam agreed, blinking as his sight adjusted, and tried to catch Reynald's eyes. "And I'm a fool for trusting you, but you couldn't have slept well outside the last few nights, and is this not warmer? Even a wizard needs to rest."

"Just because we played hide-and-seek in our youth doesn't mean I'd spare you if I decided to escape."

"I'm not half as beautiful or breathtaking as a unicorn, so I have no delusions of being spared if you're set on murdering me in my sleep."

"Come now. Give yourself some credit. You're at least half as beautiful as those diminutive Royal Woods unicorns."

"You flatter me." Liam felt for Reynald's hands beneath the blanket. He worked at the knots, but the nose of Reynald's fox mask kept bumping into Liam's face. Liam huffed an irritated breath, trying to dodge the mask.

"Must you wear the mask in the tent?"

"I'll take it off after you untie me."

"I can't see *to* untie you." Liam pushed the mask higher so the nose pointed upward.

"Excuse you." Reynald's eyebrows furrowed as he scowled.

"Half a moment and I'll be finished." Liam managed to untie the knot. "There. See?"

"Capable of untying a knot. I'm very impressed."

"Does your skin feel chafed?" Unwinding the rope from Reynald's chilled arms, Liam brushed his fingers across Reynald's wrists, feeling for abrasions.

"Why do you care? I'm a prisoner."

"And a person. I want you to be as comfortable as possible."

"Yes. These accommodations are so luxurious." Reynald held up one of his palms.

A small fuchsia spark crackled above his hand to light the tent. Liam dragged himself closer and inspected Reynald's wrists. A few criss-cross lines indented the skin where the rope had sat. Liam pulled his herbal ointment from his pouch and rubbed the medicine along Reynald's pulse.

"Smells weak. I could make better." Reynald wrinkled his nose.

"You know how to make medicine?" Liam asked, focused on massaging Reynald's wrists.

"Not all my magic is bad," Reynald muttered.

"Were the three witch sisters of Balbraid Thicket really wise women? I always thought they were. The farmers thought so. People loved to sneak into the woods to give them corn dollies or fresh vegetables during harvest season." Liam spoke in a hushed tone, as if Siegfried, or, worse, Chancellor Cole, might overhear him if he didn't whisper.

"Sam would give them a bottle of brandy during the winter solstice."

"Sam?"

"My steward."

"Then why are you asking me if they're witches? If they were, you gave gifts to witches. If they're not, you stood by while Seigfried executed innocent women."

"Things were easier when Seigfried's father was king. The laws were there but loosely enforced. Now, Seigfried is always searching for the next witch, and Chancellor Cole stirs the king and other nobles' fears into a frenzy." Liam shifted, uncomfortable with his confession. He avoided thinking about how bad things had gotten over the last several years.

"Something isn't right about the chancellor. He moves like his joints are wooden, and I've seen…"

"Seen what?" Liam reached for Reynald when he stopped, realized it wasn't proper to do so, and let his own hands fall.

"It's stupid, so you'll dismiss whatever I say as my own paranoia." Reynald shook his head. His cheeks were flushed from the cold and from wearing the mask too long.

"No, I won't."

"Why wouldn't you?" Reynald flicked his gaze at Liam.

"I'm gullible." Liam grinned.

"At least you're self-aware?" Reynald laughed.

Liam's heart skipped. Reynald's laughter was what he'd been aiming for. Silence settled into the tent for a minute, before Reynald's mouth twisted in a frown and he finished speaking.

"When I lived in the palace, anytime he wasn't working, I'd see him sitting. It always scared me."

"Sitting? Scared you? That doesn't really make sense. Was he doing something strange while he sat?"

"No. *That's* what was scary." Reynald grabbed Liam's shoulder as if he wanted to physically push his point. "He didn't do *anything. Never* have I seen him read a novel, or whittle, or watch birds outside the window, or scratch his ass like a real person. He was like a toy unplayed with, just sitting unused on a shelf. It was creepy."

"I'll admit that sounds…unsettling."

"That entire palace is a curse. Be glad you don't know about some of the relics in that damn treasure room. You have no idea how careful I was about which curios we smashed. I didn't want either one of us to have to deal with the consequences of releasing the wrong object."

"That must be why Seigfried has them. To protect the public from negative side effects," Liam said.

"No." Reynald shook his head. "He hoards them, like Kulvacc the Greedy. Seigfried's eyes gleam when he sees magic. He *wants* it. Like some men want to own their wives, he wants anything or anyone with magic to be his property or to burn."

"Why do you even know so much about the king's treasures, anyway?" Liam propped himself up on his elbow.

"You're letting the cold in." Reynald tugged their blanket closer.

"Answer my question." Liam tucked the blanket fully around both their bodies.

"Because he showed me." Reynald flinched.

"Why?"

"Because I was his favorite pet, and he thought it was a *treat* to brag about his collection to his little pet mage." Reynald made a disgusted noise. "I don't want to talk about it."

"All right." Liam sank deeper into the covers and closed his eyes. "We probably shouldn't be talking about any of this."

"Why? Am I making you question your life?"

"Before you left your tower in Balbraid, did you notice anything…wrong, with the forest?" Liam asked.

"Like what? Magic? A curse?"

"My lands have been attacked. Ogres, dire wolves, hobgoblins, they've always harassed people who ventured *into* the thicket, but they stayed away from the fields and roads. Now they're fighting like caged animals. I keep telling myself it's because the new mills in the area have displaced them, but…" Liam bit his lip. He was about to admit something he hadn't said out loud, or even allowed himself to think much about.

"Tell me," Reynald said.

"I think they're terrified and desperate to flee. These are not deer frightened by the sounds of axes chopping wood. These are dire wolves who, if anything, should attack the woodcutters in their territory. Instead, they flee and attack anything in their path as if *panicked*, but I've been so busy doing damage control in the aftermath of all the battles—including *stryx,* which I thought were fairy tales—that I haven't been able to investigate the Thicket on my own."

"Fairy tales? Surprise, Liam, demons and their infernal realms are real. We've just forgotten half of what we knew about magic because, I don't know, scholars and mages keep getting *burned alive at the stake.*"

"That doesn't explain how these creatures are behaving. Did you summon any stryx in the Balbraid Thicket?"

"No! I love Balbraid!" Reynald sat upright, shivered, and dropped back to the covers. "I would never hurt the Thicket. Why do you think I went to the Royal Woods for unicorn ivory?"

"That's not really better." Liam winced. "You still killed—"

"Yes. Yes. Animals good. Witches bad. Good night, Liam." Reynald turned in the other direction.

Liam found himself staring at the firelight playing off the hide of the tent. He needed sleep, but his conversation with Reynald dug at his thoughts. When he finally managed, his sleep was worried with strange dreams. As the fire outside dwindled, the cold seeped into the tent. Liam shivered, searching for warmth. The only warmth available was Reynald sleeping two inches away. Too asleep to think of why he shouldn't, Liam pressed against Reynald's back. His half-asleep mind didn't consider the act might be rude, especially when Reynald groaned and rolled to his other side in order to curl into Liam's chest. Liam kept his eyes closed, wrapped his arms around Reynald, and pretended he was camping instead of bringing in a fugitive. They spent the night warm and comfortable. However, in the morning, Liam was careful to unwind from his captive, although it left him cold. Reynald whimpered, trying to grab for Liam's tunic, but his eyelashes fluttered, his eyes opened, and he hugged himself instead.

"You're going to tie me again."

"I have to." Liam flinched at Reynald's words. "You'll flee if I don't."

"I would never." Reynald smirked, accentuating the early morning crow's-feet around his eyes.

His hair scattered around his face, and his cheekbones rose a little as his lips stretched. He was so painfully beautiful that Liam almost choked. His fingers ached to reach out. His body screamed to stay beneath the covers and sleep curled together until the snow fused them into a single ice sculpture. He bit the inside of his cheek.

"You're staring at me," Reynald snapped.

"Hold out your wrists." Liam grabbed the silver rope.

"At least give me some gloves. My hands are freezing when I hold the reins." Reynald pouted.

"Here." Liam pulled his gloves from his tunic pocket and passed them over to Reynald.

"Not your gloves." Reynald blushed. "Don't you have a spare set? You seem like the type that checks off his gear on a list before he goes on a quest."

"It's practical! How else would I remember to bring everything?"

"Please tell me you're joking." Reynald held his stomach laughing. "Oh, Saints, you're serious, aren't you?"

"Forgetting matches or bandages could be the cause of my death while on an adventure. Naturally, I'm going to make sure everything is in order before I leave."

"Stop. You're going to kill me." Reynald flushed harder as his laughter intensified. "You have a list! Saints! It's too fitting!"

Enchanted by the sight and the sincere joy in Reynald's tone, Liam reached out to cup his cheek. He stopped midway, restrained himself, and pushed the gloves into Raynaud's hands.

"You have to hold the reins, so it makes more sense that you use the gloves. I'll have my cloak, so I'll be okay."

Reynald opened his mouth to speak, lips full and dark, but he closed his mouth and glanced to the side.

"Okay. Thanks."

"You're welcome." Liam pulled away from Reynald's hands before he did something stupid, like draw them to his lips and kiss them.

"Get it over with." Reynald slipped on the gloves before offering Liam his wrists.

"If I could trust you—"

"But you can't—"

"But I can't," Liam agreed. "I wish I could."

He tied Reynald's wrists in another bind and crawled out of the tent to restart the fire. A heavy, wet snow had fallen all night, and he had to find a dead log and peel away the damp, outer bark for wood dry enough to burn. As the chicory brewed in the fire, Liam gathered two fish for breakfast. He offered one to Reynald but didn't expect Reynald to eat. His eyebrows raised when Reynald surprised him by grabbing the plate.

"Is the hunger strike over?"

"I'm not going to freeze to death. Might as well eat."

A wave of relief made Liam forget the cold as he watched Reynald chew. He even offered the last half of his own plate, claiming not to be hungry. Reynald gave him a leery glance, not believing him, but accepted the food and continued eating as Liam packed their camp and prepared to travel. Liam waited until they were ready to mount before taking his cloak from Creed. He lifted Reynald onto the horse, set the reins in his gloved hands, and jumped behind him.

"Stick your hands in my pockets," Reynald said.

"What?" Liam asked.

"So they don't get cold."

"I'll be fine."

"Don't be stubborn. You have to hold on while we ride anyway." Reynald glanced over his shoulder.

"I don't even know exactly where…"

"Don't think. Act. They'll be there."

Used to following orders, Liam shoved his hands into two pockets that he was certain hadn't been there before. Liam almost jerked his hands away, not trusting the magical robe, but the pockets were warm, so Liam leaned closer and relaxed as Creed trotted forward.

"Thanks," Liam spoke in a low tone to Reynald's back. "For sharing your robe."

"Don't mention it." Reynald shrugged.

Chapter Six

They managed to travel three full days as the snow piled high around them. Each night, Liam would untie Reynald as they shared a tent, telling himself it was too cold for Reynald to escape. Each night, they'd cling together, desperate for any scrap of warmth, and each morning they pushed away and pretended they'd never touched. On the fourth morning, they crawled from their tent to blinding white. Most of the landmarks lay hidden beneath snowdrifts. New clumps fell onto their hair and melted on their cheeks. Creed marched in place, legs obviously cold despite the cloak wrapped around him. Their fire was lost beneath a fresh, white sheet.

"I can't navigate this." Reynald scanned the barren horizon before securing the mask to his face. "We have to find proper shelter and hope this blows over before we run out of rations."

Liam's lips drew into a tight line as he checked the oracle's map. He rolled the parchment and tucked the paper into his belt.

"Come on." Liam dug a ramp to help guide Creed out of the snow. He pulled his cape away from the horse, replacing it with his blanket, and slung the shimmering blue material over one shoulder.

"Where are we going?" Reynald asked when Liam lifted him onto Creed.

"There's a summer training camp for squires and new soldiers a mile from here." Liam offered his cloak to Reynald.

"Aren't you going to tie me?" Reynald asked as he surrounded himself in gleaming blue dragon scales.

"You're not escaping in this storm." Liam gave Reynald a single, humorless snort of laughter before spreading out the bottom end of the cloak so it covered part of Creed's back as well.

"You're going to freeze without this." Reynald touched the silver clasp of the cloak with his left, gloved fingertips.

"Moving will keep me warm." Liam grabbed the reins and marched through the snow in the direction of the fort.

Normally, he'd be able to find the area without a map, but because of the snow changing the landscape, he had to stop often and regain his bearings. After thirty minutes of struggling through knee-deep snow, the top of the fort peeked over the tree line. Having a goal motivated Liam, and he quickened his pace until they reached the log fence surrounding the small training ground. Unlocking the gate, Liam let them inside. He fed Creed first, making sure his horse had everything he'd need to wait out the storm, and once he was satisfied, he guided Reynald by the arm to the main barracks. Reynald tolerated Liam's grip, his eyes searching around the dim interior. Liam lit a lantern so he could see more than silhouettes.

"There are weapons everywhere," Reynald said.

"It's a fort for training soldiers." Liam kicked as much snow off his boots as he could before unlacing them. He built a fire and laid most of his outer clothes near the hearth to dry, wearing his woolen garments and wrapping a blanket over his shoulders. His body shook from the mile trek through deep snow.

"What's to stop me from cutting your throat?"

"Aren't you cold?" Liam dropped onto the nearest bunk, his teeth chattering.

"Not in your cloak." Reynald smirked as he grabbed a spear and marched toward Liam. He pointed the tip beneath Liam's jaw. "Not even a little afraid?"

"You're holding it wrong," Liam said.

"Oh, come on, be a good sport and beg for your life."

"You have an odd fixation about me begging."

"If I do"—Reynald tossed the spear aside like a toy and wrapped the dragon-skinned cloak around Liam's shoulders—"it's because I was a prisoner in the palace for half my life and picked up some bad habits from Seigfried."

"I would have loved to live in the palace, even as a servant."

"So you could pine for your valiant prince?" Reynald mocked as he set the mask onto the top bunk and stripped the robes from his body so they could dry. He wore nothing beneath, and Liam averted his gaze.

"He wasn't the *only* one I'd admired as a lad."

Liam clenched his hands into fists after he'd spoken. It was stupid to say—he was dragging Reynald against his will to Citadel for an execution! What was wrong with him? Had the snow frozen his brain senseless?

Or was it because Reynald was crouched naked in front of the fire, his hair swerving around him like a second set of flames.

"I was ugly when I lived in the castle." Reynald stared at his feet.

"No, you weren't."

"Siegfried was jealous. Can you believe it?" Reynald laughed, but he sounded sad. "His hair is dull and sandy without the treatments, but mine's bright, and he thought I was prettier, so he sheared me."

"N-no." Liam's jaw dropped. He sat, staring at Reynald not to admire him, but to give Reynald his full attention.

"Of course you don't believe me." Reynald clenched his knees with both hands.

"I'm not saying I don't believe you. I remember your head was shaved." Liam stood, but he stared at the bunk beds lining the room. "You were no less beautiful for it."

He hesitated, but shook his head and marched toward Reynald. Liam wrapped the blanket and cloak around Reynald's shoulders before untucking the hair and combing it with his fingers over the blanket.

"You're shaking." Reynald rolled his eyes. "Take your cloak and warm yourself."

"I… We've all done shameful things in youth." Liam left his cloak wrapped around Reynald. "I'm sure the prince was…immature but meant no malice."

"Yeah? What shameful things have you done? Did you throw a stone at a bird? Pour salt on a slug? See if you could raise the temperature of water slowly enough to watch a frog boil alive without noticing his peril?"

"Of course not." Liam gasped. "I would never hurt anything unless I had to for food or was ordered to."

"You're right. *You wouldn't.* You're the knight who swoops in and saves dragons even when your grandfather slayed them. You cry when you find a unicorn dead in the forest when any other noble would have quietly removed the body to sell for parts on the black market."

"They wouldn't," Liam insisted.

"You believe the best in people, don't you?" Reynald glanced into Liam's eyes.

"I know the other knights. They're good men."

"They're men on your side." Reynald shook his head. "You'd feel differently if you had to fight them in a battle."

"That's human nature." Liam shrugged, shoulders still shivering.

"Fool. I told you to take this." Reynald tugged Liam to the floor until they were side by side.

"What?"

Before Liam could finish the question, Reynald swooped the blanket and the cloak over both of them. Their shoulders pressed together, and the fire licked across their faces. They sat in front of the fire, bodies thawing. Liam told himself not to lean closer to Reynald, but his body was warm, and Liam was so cold he hurt.

"Did Seigfried do those things? Pour salt on slugs and boil frogs?"

"You don't want to know." Reynald shook his head. "He made me heat the water. The frogs always jumped out, no matter how slowly I warmed it. Siegfried accused me of doing it too fast on purpose and locked me in my cell without food for an entire day."

"Cell?"

"Have you never seen the magicians' quarters?"

"Honestly? I haven't."

"They're better than the dungeons." Reynald shrugged. "Similar to monks' chambers. Clean with a bed, but *small*. Not a pleasant place to be locked away. They're in the center of the palace, so there's no windows and every hour feels like a day."

"I'm sorry." Liam maneuvered his hand beneath the blanket and rested his palm against Reynald's back.

"Your hand is cold because I stole your gloves." Reynald's head dipped low, his hair spilling around his face, but Liam caught a tired smile on his lips.

"*Those* you didn't steal." Liam bumped their shoulders together before standing and swaddling the material around Reynald's body. "Stay near the fire. I'll prepare supper."

"You need to get warm." Reynald grabbed his wrist.

"I'm a soldier. I'm tough." Liam shrugged, but he grabbed another blanket from one of the bunks to wrap around his woolen clothes. "And I'm hungry."

"Whatever. Suit yourself." Reynald snorted.

"I don't have a squire, so I always suit myself." Liam grinned at his own joke as he left to find the mess hall.

Salted beef, dried fruit, and legumes filled the pantry along with large wheels of wax-sealed cheese and a small container of pepper for any knights or nobility visiting the fort. Liam boiled a pot of lentils and salted beef for a stew, using a generous amount of pepper and dried rosemary. He carried the soup pot into the sleeping quarters and set the iron cauldron near the hearth so it could stay warm while they ate.

"I like rosemary," Reynald said.

"It grows around my manor like a weed. Charity adds it in everything she serves."

"Your wife?" Reynald gave him a sly grin.

"My chef." Liam ladled the stew into two bowls and handed one to Reynald.

"Your horse is Creed. I can imagine you with a wife named Charity."

"If my father had lived long enough to arrange a marriage, perhaps." Liam grabbed another blanket before sitting beside the hearth with some space between him and Reynald.

"I'll never marry either." Reynald tasted his soup.

He didn't say the rest, but the *because I won't live long enough to marry* was implied and weighed on Liam's consciousness. A lot of boys tormented birds and cats and whatever bugs they found in the mud, didn't they? They were trained with swords almost as soon as they could stand; was it any wonder their curiosity led them to mischief when immersed in the life of a soldier? It didn't actually mean Siegfried was cruel. Adults grew out of such petty, boyish meanness. Or, even if Seigfried had a callous streak, he was still the king. It was still Liam's duty to bring the witch to trial—regardless of other circumstances. Nothing Seigfried did absolved Reynald of poaching and theft.

They finished their meal in silence. A few times, Liam glanced over at Reynald, wanting to break the dead air between them, but only the noise of flames cracking wedges of cedar filled the room.

After dinner, Liam explored the building because he hadn't been here since right before the war. There were four separate barracks, the mess hall, and an indoor training area. Liam used the empty training room for sword practice and did his stretches. Sweat dampened his wool underclothes by the time he finished. He heated water in a wash basin and bathed himself with a towel, before going back to their room and dressing in dry linen.

"Could I borrow my cloak for a few minutes?"

"It's yours." Reynald slipped from the shining material. "But where are you going during a snowstorm?" Reynald asked.

"I wanted to check Creed one last time before bed."

A timid smile played on Reynald's face. "Need help?"

"I can manage, but thank you."

"Don't leave me alone too long. I might open a portal to another world and escape."

"Can you?" Liam tilted his head.

"With the right grimoire and components." Reynald gestured. "Don't you think I would've already escaped if I could step through a portal by waving my hands?"

"I, um, well, yes. Of course. I was too distracted daydreaming about other worlds to think about the practical application of magic."

"Other worlds…are dangerous. I've read a few accounts from books in Siegfried's library, and I wouldn't risk it unless I had no other options." Reynald's brow wrinkled. "Darius's world burns the very air, Erinyis lives in a cold void, and anyone who's ever peeked into Malphas's dimension went too mad to describe what they'd seen. Not to mention, there seem to be a high number of worlds underwater."

"What about other lands? Could you travel to Mascaria or Suzdal without a ship?"

"Theoretically, but the greater the spell, the greater the risk, or the higher the cost of the ingredients—like the life of a unicorn. It's better to stick with simple spells."

"What about enchanted items? My nurse once told me a story about a crow-shaped pin that allowed a witch to send out shadow crows to spy for him, but he could only use the magic during certain phases of the moon. Why not simply make the object work whenever the user wants?"

"Why can't humans run on all fours like wolves and go faster when it'd be more convenient? Because nature doesn't work that way." Reynald flung his hands in the air for added emphasis. "Besides, no sorcerer ever woke up and decided: today I'll make a crow pin that's only useful in very specific circumstances. It's more like you wake up in a cold sweat at three in the morning not knowing where you are and muttering about the coming of the murder and all the while you're digging through your rock collection looking for onyx and dried brown-eyed Susans."

"Sounds awful."

"Sometimes. It's like getting shit-faced drunk. You'll either dance and sing and kiss a stranger, or you'll vomit and wake up half naked in your own piss. There's not much moderation in magicians."

"I've noticed."

"Why are you asking about magic? You're begging to be charged with treason. Go tend to your horse." Reynald waved the conversation away.

"Right." Liam ran his fingers through the coils of his hair. "Right, we're not allowed— I need to check the horse."

Outside, the snow cut at his face in a diagonal sheet. He could barely fight his way to the stable where he added more coal to the stoves in the corners and made sure no ice had formed in Creed's water trough. He gave Creed an extra blanket and more oats before fighting through the storm to return to Reynald.

In the barracks, Reynald had stretched out on top of one of the mattresses, which he'd dragged from the nearest bunk bed to the edge of the hearth. He lay beneath a pile of blankets. His finger teased the empty pillow beside him.

"Look. Even with the fire, it's pretty cold in these empty barracks, and this bed is three times wider than your tent, so there's more than enough room."

"The snowstorm has become a full blizzard." Liam shook the snow from his cloak before laying it on top of the other blankets and removing his clothes, except his thin linen tunic, near the fire. "Fortunately, the pantry is stocked, so if we're stuck here for a few days, we won't starve. I…can sleep in one of the other beds."

"Right. You could. I'm just saying, there are plenty of beds, but *this* mattress is closer to the fire."

"Sure. Why not?" Liam waved off Reynald's words. "Huddling together is how soldiers sleep in the field when the weather is dangerous."

"Exactly. This is about survival. Nothing else." Reynald turned away from Liam. "Good night."

"Good night." Liam crawled in beside him.

The mattress was far more comfortable than the single-person tent, and the extra blankets kept them decently warm. There was no reason for Liam to roll onto his side, his nose touching Reynald's spine. He flushed when his skin brushed Reynald's naked back. Reynald cooed in his sleep before settling. Liam dug his fingers into the mattress to prevent himself from resting his hand on Reynald's hip. He had slept beside fellow soldiers during battles, but this was different. He and his troops had never exchanged longing looks from across the palace halls when they were younger. When sleeping together outside, everyone wore as many layers as they could swaddle around themselves, but Reynald was naked beneath the blankets, and Liam only wore a thin top. Even an accidental shift would brush the bare skin of their legs together. Liam had to think about each breath as he stared at the slopes of Reynald sleeping so close. Had this happened when Liam was younger, he probably would have thrown up from nervousness. Despite his frenzied imagination, Liam soon dropped into a hard sleep, warmer than he'd been in over a week.

Something woke him in the middle of the night, a draft or a noise. He ground his fist into his eyes, ready to add wood to the fire. In the dim light, he saw Reynald propped on his hands and knees hovering over him. His eyes were wide and gleaming. Shadows covered half his face, but there was enough light to see his expression twisted in emotional pain, and Liam was sure Reynald wasn't looking *at* him, but rather seeing something from long ago. It was the look soldiers often had after battle when the death keens still rang in their ears. The sickness was called soldier's nerves, and all the soldiers had it to some extent after the war, but he couldn't understand why *Reynald* would.

"Reynald? We're safe." Liam held Reynald's arm. Sometimes a light touch was enough to ground a soldier.

"Safe? Safe? How are you so gullible? Don't you realize how powerful I am? How dangerous?" Reynald's expression twisted into a grimace before he covered Liam's eyes with his palm. "I don't need a knife. I can blind you for a day, or week, or permanently. I could steal your gear, your cloak, your horse, and escape while you stumbled sightless through the snow until you died. Yet every night this week you've untied me and let me lie beside you. *Why?* Are you simple?"

"I'm not afraid of you hurting me. I'm only afraid you'll run away, and I'd have to track you down again." Liam kept his hand on Reynald's arm, squeezing but not gripping.

This wasn't the first time a panicked fighter had put a knife to his throat or aimed a crossbow at his chest. In time, the terror would fade and leave Reynald exhausted. Then they could go back to sleep and ignore the incident in the morning like the other knights always did. Liam only had to wait.

"Chase me because it's your *duty*?" Reynald sneered.

"Of course." Liam held his breath.

"I hate you… I hate you…" Reynald's hand fell away.

Liam blinked at him. Reynald was slender, not scrawny, but lean, but that wasn't what caught Liam's gaze. Reynald remained hunched over Liam's body, his breaths shallow but rapid. The fire was bright enough for Liam to catch the stark white scars dappling Reynald's body in endless crescents. He touched Reynald's stomach, studying the marks.

"Bite marks?"

"Dogs." Reynald wrapped one of the blankets around himself to hide the scars.

"Dire wolf." Liam exposed his stomach and showed the larger line of teeth marks on his skin. His scars were the angry pink of a recently healed wound.

"What happened?" Reynald teased each tooth mark. His fingers shook as they glided across Liam's brown stomach.

"I told you, everything in the Thicket has gone wild. This was from the last attack. Their alpha was going to maul a family, so I jumped in the way."

"Of course, you did." Reynald dashed to his robes and searched the pockets until he pulled out a small bottle.

Uncapping the flask, the scent of lavender rose into the air. He dabbed his fingers and treated the marks on Liam's stomach.

"Smells nice."

"Lavender is good for the skin. It's not magic, but it will have to do. How's the cut on your thigh?"

"Uh, it's fine," Liam muttered.

"Don't trust me with a fresh wound?"

"I'm shy."

"Are you shy around all your doctors?"

Reynald slipped his hand to the exact spot where the vase had stabbed Liam's thigh. Liam had stopped bandaging it a day or two ago because it had closed and scabbed over. He hitched on instinct with the touch.

"You're no doctor." Liam forced his body to lay still.

"All done." Reynald capped the flask and stored it in his robes again.

"What about you? You have scars."

"Mine are old. They're as healed as they'll ever get."

"Would you really kill someone whose wounds you've treated?" Liam examined the gleaming marks on his skin before lowering his shirt.

"If I needed to."

"Why *haven't* you blinded me?" Liam asked.

"I wouldn't get far in a blizzard." Reynald dropped to the bed, on his side but facing Liam so they could talk.

"What about the first night?"

"I was too cold." Reynald shrugged.

"Speaking of, the fire is dying." Liam rose to add wood to the blaze.

Liam hugged himself once the covers fell away from his body, shivering from the chill. He added fresh wood to the coals and stoked the bottom half of the fire until the flames caught and the smell of burning cedar perfumed the air along with the lavender oil on their skin. Eager to be under the blankets, he jumped onto the mattress and squirmed into position.

"Here." Reynald held Liam's hands to heat them.

"You don't have to." Liam spoke in a steady voice despite his thudding chest.

"You gave me your gloves. This is the least I can do."

His gloves were spread near the rest of their clothes around the fire. Nothing was stopping Liam from wearing them now, but he didn't pull away. Giddiness scrambled Liam's thoughts as Reynald teased the calluses on Liam's hands.

"I must be a fool." Liam lidded his gaze. "For letting my guard down like this."

"You must be." Reynald spoke in a dry, controlled voice. He snuck a glance at Liam, however. "But what makes you admit it? Most knights are too proud."

"I don't think you'll hurt me." Liam couldn't stop memorizing all the details of Reynald's face. "You liked it better when we were friends. I did too."

"You are, indeed, a fool." Reynald's thumbs halted, pressing deep into Liam's palms, but no longer caressing them.

"Despite our current circumstances, I feel like we're still friends," Liam confessed.

"You're insane." Reynald laughed.

"You've had dozens of chances to kill me."

"I'm tired," Reynald interrupted. "I'm going to sleep."

"Why'd you wake up?" Liam asked. "Was something wrong?"

"Nightmares," Reynald whispered.

Liam opened his mouth to say he'd watch over Reynald, realized the hypocrisy, exhaled, and nodded. Reynald wasn't paying attention to him, however; he was already curled on his side and breathing heavily in sleep.

Chapter Seven

By morning, they were locked in each other's arms. Liam woke by slow degrees. The fire had smoldered to a pile of glowing coals, but he wasn't cold beneath the stack of blankets. Reynald's arms clamped around Liam in a stubborn grip. Liam's gaze swung around the room. The walls, roof, and support beams were unfinished logs cut from the surrounding forest. A thick film of dust coated the floor, except the spots where they'd left footprints. The windows had been shuttered and bolted for winter, so what little glow remained from the hearth carved deep shadows, and the room was slightly smoky from the fire.

Behind Liam, Reynald nuzzled between his shoulder blades. Liam's breath caught in his chest as the subtle movement sent a warm tingle through his body. The night before flashed in Liam's mind: how panicked Reynald had looked. Now he clung to Liam like he was driftwood and murmured something in his sleep. Liam remained still. The embrace was comfortable, and guilt needled Liam at the thought of waking Reynald after he'd had such a rough night, but Liam needed to separate them. This, what they were doing, wasn't right. This was the fox in the cage all over again—Liam breaking rules because of a few brief moments over fifteen years ago. Sharing heat during a blizzard to survive was one matter, but cuddling near a hearth? This was not how one treated a prisoner.

Reynald nudged his hips forward. His morning wood found Liam's backside and the mild warmth pulsing through Liam's body became an electrifying jolt. Liam's eyes slammed shut; he held his breath. Reynald settled, face buried in Liam's linen undershirt. Liam released a slow, hesitant breath, willing his flushed body to calm itself. After he regulated his breathing, Liam tried to pry Reynald's grip away from his belly. Whimpering, Reynald latched on more tightly.

Liam sighed in defeat. He didn't want out of the hold enough to force himself free. The room would be cold once he snuck out from the covers. Why would he ever want to move? Reynald hitched his hips a second time, and Liam muzzled himself with his hand to hold in a moan.

"R-Reynald," he whispered, but Reynald only made a "don't disturb me" grunt.

Liam controlled his inhales and exhales, but he couldn't control his heartbeat. His cock throbbed each time Reynald moved. Reynald's hand lay low on Liam's stomach, the slightest shift downward and…

He couldn't.

"Reynald."

"Your hair is scratchy." Reynald released Liam's belly and leaned away from his locs.

Liam gripped the mattress. He wanted to scream and thrust Reynald's hands on his body again, only lower. He could flip on his other side and hold them flushed together, cocks pressing.

Kiss him.

Embarrassed, Liam scurried out of bed and stacked more wood in the fire. He rushed about and cleaned to distract himself, sweeping the dust from the floor and redressing in his clothes, armor, and surcoat. While he kept busy, Reynald stayed in bed and watched without speaking. His face made a better mask than the ivory, because no matter how many times Liam glanced at Reynald, he couldn't figure out what the mage was thinking or feeling.

"I'll make breakfast and check on Creed." Liam grabbed his cloak and headed toward the stable before Reynald could respond.

Creed was content and feasting on hay. The storm had broken in the night, and the sky was a sharp, crisp blue. Although snow piled high, past Liam's boots as he walked, the air was warm enough that the snow would melt. Liam sent a prayer up to all fourteen saints that the snowbanks would sink fast because he did not think he'd survive much longer sheltering with Reynald and sleeping naked near the fire. After tending to Creed, Liam spent as long as he could making skillet bread for their breakfast. He brought the loaf and a jar of boysenberry preserves to the bunks and split the loaf with Reynald.

"The blizzard has passed," Liam said.

"So we can go?"

"It was a struggle to dig my way to the stables. In a day or two, there should be enough melt to forge forward as long as no new storms come along."

"Maybe I could try walking up front and blasting fire from my hands to melt everything," Reynald teased with a slight chuckle.

"I couldn't allow you to openly use magic. Not even to assist me." Liam used his spoon to re-smooth the jam back and forth across his already covered bread.

"I wasn't serious. Magic, like the Balbraid Thicket, isn't an unlimited resource. Even if I wanted to help, it'd be impossible to do for longer than several minutes."

"It's not that I didn't understand the joke, but the issue felt important enough to clarify."

"Mm-hmm, you've made yourself very clear. Excuse me." Reynald stood. "I'm no longer hungry."

Liam didn't stop Reynald from leaving. There weren't too many places for him to go. Liam himself finished eating and spent the day training or going through routine inspections of the quality of the gear and the barracks itself. He made a list of maintenance suggestions to be completed next spring. By evening, however, they both ended up in front of the hearth again, eating reheated stew. The silence between them was somehow louder than the crackling fire beside them. Liam wished he'd brought a bestiary to read, but he hadn't planned for leisure time during his quest. With a heavy sigh, Liam stood and began dressing in extra layers to keep things as formal as possible between them while they slept. The second day passed by in the same way as the first. Liam marched around the courtyard perimeter, trying to convince himself it wouldn't be so bad to leave a day early, but by the time he went back inside to dry his clothes, his chattering teeth and burning skin convinced him otherwise. So they continued to wait as nature went at her own pace.

When enough snow melted that Liam could at least make out the tree branches against the skyline, he decided the journey was worth the risk and made the necessary preparations. In the kitchen, Liam sliced salami and cheese for their breakfast, packing extra to restock their travel rations, and brought a plate to where Reynald was dressed, masked and staring at the fire with his arms crossed over his chest.

"The snow has settled enough that Creed can stomp through what's left. We'll eat, clean up, and head out again."

"Great." Reynald didn't hide the irony in his tone.

"Next town we come across, I'll buy a bigger tent so we're not crushed at night."

"Great," Reynald repeated. He sounded more cheerful that time, but his tone had a strained quality.

Liam didn't acknowledge Reynald's curt mannerisms. Instead, he restored all the blankets and the mattress to their proper beds, and carried last night's pot to the kitchen to be scrubbed. Normally, a servant would see to cleaning, but Liam refused to leave the fort until everything was in place and tidy. He waited until the last second to grab the rope. He fidgeted with the fibers at the end of the cord. Reynald turned away from the fire and stared at Liam before thrusting out his hands.

"I'm sorry this is necessary," Liam muttered.

Was it though? What was the point of tying Reynald if they shared a blanket at night? He wasn't afraid of Reynald—cautious around him, but not afraid. So, what *was* he afraid of? Being seen riding with a witch and laughing out loud? Was the rope nothing but a prop to maintain the illusion of prisoner and captor?

"Stop. I don't want to hear your half-assed apologies."

After tying Reynald, Liam kept a hand on Reynald's arm to guide him through the barracks and into the high snow. Creed waited saddled and ready in the courtyard, and Liam lifted Reynald onto the saddle before grabbing the reins and leading them out of the fort.

"Aren't you going to ride?" Reynald asked.

"Tomorrow, after more of the snow melts." Liam stepped high through the drifts. He'd be exhausted in an hour, but he was good at pushing through.

Also, the cold would help distract him. He couldn't think about spooning while he trudged through snow.

"Then I should walk as well."

"I'd rather you stay on the horse. The snow's deep." Liam wrapped his cloak on Reynald, trying to spread it behind him so Creed had some of the warmth as well.

"You're a living martyr, Liam." Reynald rolled his eyes behind his mask. "Any other knight would make *me* walk while *they* stayed mounted."

"You're trying to frustrate me, but I'm going to take that as a compliment."

"Take it however you want."

Liam smiled despite himself. He wanted to keep the conversation going but knew he wasn't supposed to be fraternizing with his prisoner, so they fell silent as they traveled. Snow clung to Liam's clothes and made him shiver. Without his cloak, the movement alone wasn't enough to keep him warm. His exposed skin stung after an hour. He thought about borrowing his own cloak for a moment to thaw, but stubbornness and chivalry prevented him. Desperate for something else to focus on, Liam rambled about his bestiary lessons. It wasn't fraternizing if it was educational, right?

"You know a lot about the creatures in the Thicket," Reynald said.

"All I wanted to do as a boy was study everything I saw. From the bears to the dire wolves. I wish I'd been born a kennel master instead of a knight." Liam sighed. "Then I could at least raise and train the dogs. Or maybe work in the stables with the horses. Although, I'd never have learned to ride, and that would be a lost joy."

"One would think after being torn into by a dire wolf, you'd be more bitter."

"I don't blame the dire wolves we fought, nor the ogres. Actions have consequences, and we're destroying their territory."

"Exactly," Reynald agreed. "But Siegfried doesn't care if a few farmers are mauled to death. He would *not* jump in the way to save them."

"Because that's my job. I've hired a beast specialist to train my men on the regular animals, and a Mascarian to train them to fight the magical creatures. We'll defend the farms and city as best we can, although I'd rather find a way to rehome the displaced creatures. It's…" The words *not right* almost left his lips, but he swallowed them. "It's a shame to kill them."

"When you murder magical creatures because Seigfried destroyed their homes, it's 'a shame,' but when I murder them to stop the very king causing the problem, it's 'poaching' and I deserve to die."

"Those unicorns weren't attacking anyone," Liam snapped, avoiding the rest of what Reynald said.

"For what it's worth, I hated it." Reynald hugged himself. "Killing them made me sick. Makes me sick to wring a chicken's neck as well, but we do what we must to eat."

"You didn't kill the unicorns to feed yourself," Liam said.

"At the end of the day, I can live with myself after killing the unicorns. I could not live with myself if I allowed Seigfried to breathe."

"What did he do to you?" Liam stopped in the snow, turning to stare at Reynald.

"You mean besides shaving my head, keeping me on a leash, and punishing me when I failed to use my magic to boil a frog alive?" The mask hid Reynald's expression, but his voice was angry.

"Those are all horrible things, but they don't drive the sort of extreme vengeance you're committed to. There's something you're not telling me."

"What are you, a priest? Want to hear my confession? Will you tell me to pray to all fourteen Holy Helpers for each life I took and then my soul will be clear before I burn to death?"

"You're hedging my ques—"

"Shh." Reynald pressed a finger to his mask. "Do you hear that?"

"Fine. Don't tell me." Liam fought his way through another few feet of snow.

"Wait. Stop." Reynald tugged on Creed's mane. "I hear crying."

Liam halted, listening. The wind scooped a few dead leaves from nearby branches and swirled them in the air, but there was no other sound. Reynald dropped to his feet, sinking to his knees in snow and stumbled to Liam. He pushed his bound wrists outward.

"Untie me. I need to go find her."

Liam blinked at the ropes, then at Reynald. "You can't think I'm stupid enough to untie you simply because you're pretending to hear someone cry."

"You're naive. Not stupid. But this would be too obvious a ploy if I were escaping, which means I'm being serious."

"Which is what you would say if you were trying to convince me to let you escape."

"You're overthinking."

"Am I?"

"Liam, listen to me." Reynald pushed his mask onto the top of his head so he could lock their gazes together. "I am a witch, yes, but that doesn't only mean I know how to shoot fire and lightning at my victims. Even in human form, I keep some of my fox senses, and it's not my fault you can't hear what I hear, but you need to trust me when I tell you someone is crying in the forest east of us. You're a knight, be heroic, and let me go help her."

Liam stared into Reynald's face. His cheeks were red with cold, like holly berries in the snow, both eyes gleamed in the sunlight, though they were completely different. The orange hair was a salvation of color in the monotonous landscape, and his expression was earnest, so completely earnest. Liam's hand reached out to untie him, but he jerked his hand to the scale symbol on his surcoat.

"I…can't."

"Fine. I gave you a chance, but you're a jackass." Reynald dislocated his wrists and slipped out of his binds.

The sickening crack of his bones was enough of a shock to freeze Liam in place. The rope dropped in the snow, and an orange fox leapt from drift to drift toward the forest.

"You're insane! Come back here!" Liam shouted, snatching the rope and jumping onto Creed's back.

Reynald reached the tree line first and disappeared amongst the evergreens and holly. He was easy to track, however, and Liam spent the next hour following his trail through the snow. Coughing echoed through the cold, still air. Liam rode farther and his jaw dropped when he saw a girl with braided hair curled beside a bright-orange fox near a leafless oak. Liam's dragon scale cloak swaddled around the girl, keeping her warm in the snow. Liam winced at the fox's smug "I told you so" expression.

"All right." Liam jumped to his feet, Creed's rein clenched in his fist. "I owe you an apology. I'm sorry, and you were right to run off when I didn't listen to you. I'm sorry, Reynald."

"Naturally." Reynald stood where the fox had been.

The change was too quick for Liam to register. In other circumstances, he would have asked Reynald a dozen questions about transformation, but the girl coughed again. Stooping low, Liam cradled her in his arms and carried her to Creed.

"Don't worry. We'll get you home," Liam promised.

"My village is on the edge of the woods on the southern side." The girl clung to Creed's neck.

"How did you end up here?"

"I got caught in the storm. I found a cave, and when it stopped snowing, I tried to find my way home, but I got lost." The girl, twelve or so, pressed her face into Creed's coiled mane. "I can't believe I was stupid enough to get lost."

"The best of us can lose our way in the middle of a storm. Don't be hard on yourself."

She nodded, glancing at Reynald. "Are you the steward of this wood?"

"I'm from Balbraid," Reynald answered her question without really answering.

"Mama always told me if I was ever in trouble, I should find the local witch and she'd keep me safe until they found me, but I couldn't find her hut, just a cave, but you found me." She smiled. "Thank you, steward."

"Of course." Reynald pulled his hood over his mask. "Think nothing of it."

Liam bit his lower lip at Reynald's bashful behavior. He was surprised the girl had mentioned the *local witch*, instead of using the term "wise woman." Closer to Citadel, where news traveled easier to the palace, no one would have ever used the term "witch." That had become synonymous with "criminal." However, wise women and stewards were supposed to be left in peace, as long as they didn't break any laws or practice openly in the cities. Liam had believed this to be the case… hoped it to be so, until recently. His stomach cramped at the thought of the three sisters from Balbraid. They traded salt for medicine, and Liam never heard a single rumor about them doing anything other than healing. So why *were* they arrested? Did it have to do with Seigfried wanting to harvest the entire Thicket? Had their magic been…protecting the area somehow?

Well before they left the wood, they heard dogs barking and people calling, "Mary, Mary." Reynald flinched at the sound of the dogs. Liam laid his hand on the curve of Reynald's trembling shoulder.

"Rescue dogs," Liam whispered in his ear. "Searching for Mary. They won't bite."

"I smell of fox." Reynald stepped forward but stumbled in the snow, and Liam had to brace him.

"I'd jump in the way and let them bite me before you. I promise, they won't hurt you."

Reynald examined Liam before moving faster. "I wish you were lying. I actively disdain you, but you're too candid, and you make my job difficult."

"Again. Compliment."

"It's really not." The tension in Reynald's shoulders slackened.

"Mary!" A man rushed toward their horse.

"Uncle Stephen!" Mary slipped from Creed's back and teetered through the snow until she was embracing her uncle.

They spoke in quick clips. Stephen asked a barrage of questions, and Mary tried to recount her harrowing night in the woods, and how a fox saved her. At the mention of a fox, Stephen glanced at Reynald and bowed.

"We're fortunate that a—" He glanced at Liam. "—a steward was in the area…and a knight?"

"Yes. We're traveling to Citadel," Liam said.

"Oh." Stephen frowned. "I'm sorry, but you both must be cold. My son is…in school. His room is free if you'd like a place to stay."

"We would. Thank you." Liam nodded his head, his hands throbbing without his gloves.

"Come on, Mary. Your mother cried herself sick every night you've been gone. We need to show her you're okay."

The sign near the road leading into the village read Elktrail. It was small but had an inn, a travel lodge, and three general stores besides the grocer. The forest most likely lured in enough hunters to allow the town a bit of commerce. Mary's parents thanked both Reynald and Liam. They returned Liam's cloak to him and showered them with small gifts as was custom for heroic deeds. They gave Liam a pair of fur-lined gloves and a hunting knife. They gave Reynald a wooden box filled with coarse ground black salt.

"This is a wonderful gift. I can't accept it." He handed it back to Mary's mother.

"You must." She pushed the box back into his hands. "I insist."

"I'm being escorted to Citadel. Most of this will be wasted." Reynald kept his eyes on the ground as he spoke.

"Use it on the way." She squeezed his hands tightly. "I'm sorry."

Liam stood off to the side and pretended to be fascinated with the finish on the knife handle. He gave Reynald some time to say goodbye to the girl and her parents before Stephen showed them where he lived. It was the house closest to the travel lodge. Music hummed from next door, smoke rose from three separate chimneys, and laughter rolled to them in waves as people came and went. In Stephen's home, the aroma of smoked duck filled the kitchen. A single servant greeted them, led them to their room, and offered them a basin of warm water to wash in before supper. Reynald removed his mask and washed his face.

"Why the salt?" Liam asked. "Is it for a spell?"

"You're clueless, aren't you?" Reynald laughed.

"Apparently." Liam washed his hands and face after Reynald finished.

"Yes. Salt is used in many rituals, but mostly it's for the cravings."

"Cravings?"

"Don't look at me like I'm a vampire. Magicians crave salt, and the salt she gave me is smoky. It's a treat, not an escape hatch." Reynald brushed his hair away from his eyes. "Not that I need a spell to escape you."

"Yes. You've proven you can flee if you really want to, so why are you here?"

"I wanted to see the girl home safely."

"Honorable." Liam dried his hands. "And tomorrow?"

"Are you going to tie us together at the hip to keep me in tow?" Reynald asked.

"If I must."

"I'm looking forward to the experience." Reynald stashed his mask in one of his magic pockets and went downstairs to eat.

Liam stayed behind. What would he do if Reynald escaped again? Valinsir taught him binds Reynald would not be able to wiggle out of, but the thought of using them made Liam sick. They were torture binds, and Reynald wasn't a simple poacher. As much as Liam wanted to hide behind Reynald's crimes, his situation was more complicated. He'd saved a child whom Liam would have left to freeze because he hadn't heard her, and the village clearly had experience with benevolent magic users. The girl trusted Reynald without question, and the town treated him with more reverence than they did Liam… Was it only the nobility and soldiers who feared witches?

Liam tabled his internal debate to eat. The duck was served with whipped potatoes and roasted carrots. The meal was far better than their travel rations, and they both ate two plates. Reynald sprinkled a generous amount of the smoked salt onto his food, and he moaned after taking a bite of the potatoes.

"These are amazing."

"My wife loved these potatoes. She could skip the rest of the meal and eat a pot of potatoes by herself." Stephen laughed as he stirred the potatoes on his plate, but he didn't take a bite.

"I'm sorry," Reynald whispered.

"What's important is Zach's in school. He writes me every week." Stephen offered them a sad smile.

Liam nodded and emptied his mug of beer. There was a conversation within their conversation. A mother dragged away for the stake and a son sent to Valen to avoid the same fate, but any condolences Liam could have offered would have been insults. Never before had he questioned whether the executed were anything less than deserving of their fate. Tormented by the unspoken grief between Stephen and Reynald, Liam excused himself from supper as soon as it was polite and paced near the bed. Liam started when Reynald entered the room.

"Are you sick? I told you, you shouldn't have walked in the snow all day long."

"Why haven't you run? Why haven't you escaped?"

"In this snow? I'm not daft. You'd track me before breakfast." Reynald sat on the bed.

"Everyone in town knows why we're traveling together, and I'm sure any of them would assist you. They look at you as if you were one of the fourteen Holy Helpers."

"Don't be ridiculous. Aiding and abetting a fugitive witch is a death sentence." Reynald's jaw clenched. "I'd rather burn than drag these people to the stake in my place."

"I don't understand." Liam clenched his hands into fists. "How can you be so heroic in one breath and so sinister in another?"

"Am I sinister?" Reynald laced his fingers behind his head, reclining against the pillows behind him.

"Did you know these people?" Liam leaned against the wall, peering out the window and watching travelers gather near the entrance of the lodge to smoke and chat.

"No, but I like people—when they're not royal puppets—so I try to help when I can. What good is being magical if you can't be helpful?"

"Stephen's wife…"

"You're not stupid. It's clear they burned her, so he sent his magical son to a sorcerer's university in Valen. Because they *hire* sorcerers instead of murder them."

"Once I return, I'm going to investigate the burnings. See if there's any records, any proof—"

"You'll be accused of heresy within a year and stripped of your title." Reynald shook his head.

"I'll be discreet."

"You don't have the personality for espionage." Reynald snorted. "You'd blow your cover the first night."

"I can't protect people if I don't know what I need to protect them *from*." Liam grit his teeth.

"I can't believe this…" Reynald covered his face with his hand. His laughter was low, bitter, dark…pained. "Don't you understand? You can't serve the king and protect his people. Siegfried *is* the threat. He's the only one with sinister plans for the future of Phrophis."

"If what you say is true, then there has to be proof. Documentation. I'll find something no matter the danger. I have to try to learn the truth." Liam pressed his cheek against the cold window pane. "Regardless of the consequences."

"If every knight were like you, maybe this world wouldn't be such a pit." Reynald scooted over and patted the empty half of the bed.

"You sleep. I'll stand guard."

"Guard from what? The townsfolk? Just because they respect witches doesn't mean they'll pull out the torches and rebel against the king for me. Get some sleep.”

Liam was aware there was no danger, but he couldn't endure another night in Reynald's arms. Sweat glazed his palms as memories from the morning haunted him.

“You're too resourceful. I need to be vigilant.” Liam hugged himself as he kept his gaze fixed on the travel lodge. It didn't help, Reynald's reflection lingered in the glass, so beautiful that Liam's fingers ached.

“Are you serious?” Reynald's expression twisted in disbelief.

“Am I laughing?”

“Suit yourself. I'm going to bed.” Reynald threw the covers over his head.

Chapter Eight

The snow melted as they traveled. High banks remained around the trees and near ledges, anywhere the shade kept the ground cold, but the sun melted everything off the roads, and they were able to make better time as they left the northern wilds and returned to proper roads scattered with towns and villages. Liam purchased a larger tent. They still shared each night, neither of them mentioning the fact, but there was enough room for them to have some distance. Liam didn't bother tying Reynald after his escape. Whenever Liam asked why Reynald never escaped, Reynald always had an excuse ready. Liam didn't trust any of his reasons, continuously watching Reynald for clues to his true motivations.

Not that he could resist watching Reynald anyway. Reynald moved with a mesmerizing grace. The way he held a spoon as he sipped on the broth, the tilt of his head when he listened to Liam speak, how he mounted Creed without his hands bound and his hair whipping like flames behind him. The more time they spent together, the more Liam couldn't get Reynald out of his thoughts. Every dawn was a waking daydream of Reynald's smirk and half-amused chuckles.

"I need a bath." Reynald rubbed his neck. "A real bath, not a rag dipped into the river."

"The snow already delayed us by a week." Liam pursed his lips. Eventually, he checked his map. "Another half day can't hurt. I can check our supplies. The closest village doesn't look large enough for a travel lodge, but they should at least have an inn with a bathhouse."

"Yes. Bath. Praise the saints." Reynald slumped forward. "I'm so sore from riding. Have you ever tried changing into an animal and running yourself? Much more freeing."

"Sounds wonderful, but I'll have to take you at your word." Liam chuckled.

"Take me at my word? You've been believing me more easily these days." Reynald smirked. "Careful. I might be charming you."

"After Mary, I feel I owe you some trust." Liam's answer was serious, despite Reynald's teasing.

"About this much." Reynald used his thumb and pointer finger to demonstrate about an inch of space.

"And not an ounce more," Liam agreed. "I can't lose my reputation as a knight."

"Is that the village up ahead?" Reynald pointed to the horizon.

Liam glanced over Reynald's shoulder. He had to lean forward and squint to see the steeple of the local church.

"Your sight is as keen as your ears."

"My sense of smell too. Why do you think I'm dying for a bath?" Reynald laughed.

Liam joined him but leaned away, self-conscious. The town was barely large enough for the inn to have a stable and a bathhouse. Liam paid extra to make sure they fed Creed oats and apples on top of his regular meal. He rented a room, stored their gear, and removed his armor for the night. Reynald stood near the door, mask hiding his face.

"Well? Aren't you going to escort your dangerous prisoner?" Reynald leaned against the frame, hitching the snout of his mask toward the exit.

"I figured I'd start a fire in the stove so the room will be warm by the time you—"

"Sir Bord, if you do not keep a *close* eye on me tonight, I *will* flee to teach you a lesson on watching your quarry."

"You…*want* me to prevent you from escaping?" Liam dusted the stove ash off his hands and stood.

"I want some conversation as I bathe." Reynald waved his hand in the air, as if it were only common courtesy for knights escorting witches to their deaths to keep them company in the bathhouse.

Too tired to analyze Reynald's whims, Liam followed him. A row of round, tiled well-like tubs lined the back wall of the bathhouse. To their side, steam escaped from the sauna door, and the fragrance of lavender and bergamot filled the humid air. Reynald pulled a cord near one of the empty tubs, and a spigot released steaming mineral water into the large basin. As the bath filled, Reynald removed his clothes.

"They have screens." Liam pulled the sliding, fogged glass so Reynald had some privacy.

"Then you come here." Reynald pulled Liam into the private cubicle created by the screen.

"Reynald." Liam swallowed, body clammy despite the steam rising from the bath beside them.

"Knights bathe together, right?"

"Yes, it's common, but…*I* never have." Liam stared at the shelf of scented oils and bath salts behind Reynald.

"They're going to have to rename you Liam the Shy." Reynald pulled the tunic and woolen undershirt from Liam's chest.

"You're doing this to annoy me, aren't you?" Liam forced his voice to sound as casual as possible.

Ha-ha, not a seduction, only Reynald being Reynald. Guys roughhousing and bathing together like chums. Not sexy. Not sexy. Not sexy.

"I'd be lying if I said I didn't enjoy watching you squirm." Reynald removed the final layer of linen from Liam's chest before he hooked his finger in the lacing of Liam's britches, pulling the knot free. "You can manage these on your own, I'm assuming?"

"Yes." Liam only removed his shoes and pants to prevent Reynald from doing so.

His cock couldn't handle Reynald's dexterous hands unlacing his pants. Liam hurried into the water to hide the length he'd added to his dick with the mere thought of Reynald touching him. He grunted as the hot water surrounded him. Only when the heat loosened some of the tightness in his back did he realize how tense he was. Liam sighed, sinking a little lower and reclining against the edge.

"See? This is nice." Reynald dipped in across from Liam.

The pool was large, made for at least four grown men. Liam closed his eyes, blocking out the last week of travel. He submerged his entire body and let himself float in the void of heat. For a glorious moment Liam was weightless and free of concern, but Reynald grabbed him and jerked him above the surface.

"What's wrong?" Liam wiped water from his eyes, confused at the stress wrinkling Reynald's brow.

"You were under a long time." Reynald frowned. "I thought something was wrong."

"No. I'm sorry. I always submerge in the bath—I didn't think you'd be worried."

"I-I wasn't," Reynald lied.

Reynald didn't often lie, preferring to answer carefully instead, but his expression gave him away. The way his pupils darted as he examined Liam, the twist of his lips, the tightness of his jaw. For the first time, Reynald's expression wasn't hard to read.

"Thank you for saving me." Liam diverted the subject instead of pressing the issue.

"They say after you save a life, you're responsible for them because you stole them from fate."

"Then be sure to take good care of me." Liam grinned, sitting on the ledge circling around the tub.

"I could." Reynald sighed, dropping into his own seat again. "I'd love to."

Liam's nerves alternated between freezing and burning. They way Reynald bit his lower lip after speaking, and the glaze in his eyes as his gaze flicked toward Liam's chest then away. Liam held his knees to keep his hands away from his cock—or Reynald's. Reynald jolted Liam from his fantasy with a splash of water to the face.

"You don't have to be so aggravating." Liam returned the splash.

"Trust me. I do."

"Do you need help washing your hair?"

"Oh? Going to treat me like a lord in a manor?" Reynald glided across the tub, layering his hands on top of Liam's.

"It's so long, I imagine it's a hassle to manage." Liam held his breath after speaking, too aware of the heat and Reynald's touch.

"I make do." Reynald sat next to Liam and tossed a wet strip of orange into his face.

"You're impossible." Liam sputtered, laughed, and collected all the strands before lathering shampoo from root to tip.

"You really shouldn't pamper me. I'm going to enjoy this too much. What will I do next time when I have to wash my own hair?" Reynald purred as Liam massaged his scalp.

"Suffer," Liam said.

"Story of my life," Reynald groaned.

"I'm going to dip you." Liam cradled Reynald's head and lowered his hair into the water to rinse the bubbles.

The suds scattered around them. Reynald kept his eyes closed. His face was calm, serene. Liam admired the way his lips parted and how his hair danced in the water. A force pulled Liam closer; he caught himself and lifted Reynald to sitting.

"There."

"How do you wash your hair, Sir Stallion?" Reynald rolled one of the coils between his palms.

"I treat the scalp with oils most days. I have a special soak I use for a deeper cleansing." Liam squeezed the excess water from the bottom of his locs. "I shouldn't be so careless with them. I'll have to sit by the fire to let them dry."

"Hmm…" Reynald hummed to acknowledge Liam's words, but his gaze kept lowering to Liam's chest.

"Better start drying them now." Liam soaped his body, washed in a rush, rinsed, and pulled himself out of the water.

"Fine. A bath's only good when the water stings anyway." Reynald lathered soap on one of the washcloths in a basket at the edge of the bath.

Time slowed as Reynald washed himself. The bubbles slid along the curves of his body, and Reynald was thorough in covering every inch. When he caught Liam staring, a smirk curled on his lips, and he dropped the washcloth. With bare fingers, he worked the suds along his body, breathing hard.

"If we hurry, we can catch dinner before the kitchen closes for the night," Liam murmured, but he didn't look away.

"It's early." Reynald splashed water onto his chest to rinse his skin.

"Oh, r-right. I forgot we stopped early."

"Yes. For the bath. And wasn't it worth it?" Reynald stood, the waterline cutting right at his Adonis belt. Liam almost audibly whimpered.

"Here." Liam offered him a towel, praying he'd cover himself.

Reynald sighed, shoulders slumping, but he accepted the towel and dried before dressing. They helped each other with their hair. Liam showed Reynald how to roll each coil so the towel could soak up as much water as possible. Afterward, he gave his locs a preliminary dry by the fire while Reynald talked about the Balbraid Thicket.

"Have you ever seen a Balbraid unicorn?" Reynald asked.

"No. I've seen tracks, but they avoid people."

"Wild creatures for a wild forest. Unicorns in the Royal Wood are stunted… That's why I went there. I…" Reynald's face twisted. He paced behind Liam. "I couldn't bring myself to hurt the ones in my own forest, and I don't give a shit about poaching laws. How stupid is it to keep an entire woods as a garden? The monarchy disgusts me."

"What do Balbraid unicorns look like?" Liam asked.

He couldn't bring himself to argue with Reynald about poaching and theft. The fire was warm; they smelled of rose and basil. Arguments could wait for Reynald's trial—though sentencing was a more honest word. Then he could scream about the obscenity of poaching laws, and Liam would watch them drag Reynald away…loathing himself as he stood silent and obedient before his king.

"We're the same. I'm such a hypocrite." Liam held his head with both hands before Reynald had a chance to answer his question about unicorns.

"What do you mean?" Reynald stopped pacing.

"I judged you for killing an innocent creature, but now I fear I might be equally guilty by bringing you to Citadel."

"You're not like me, because I'm not innocent." Reynald crouched next to Liam. "Not like they were."

"You're still a hero despite being a thief," Liam said, thinking of Mary.

"Balbraid unicorns are taller than Creed. Their manes are twice as thick and crimped, a little like your hair. They have shaggy coats and feathered hooves. If a Balbraid unicorn lashed you with his tail, he'd knock you plumb on your ass." Reynald chuckled. "And their horns are textured, almost like petrified wood. Balbraid is my forest, so using their ivory would have made a far more potent mask, but…I couldn't."

"I often hear about stewards of the forest, do witches have a distinct connection to nature in general? Or is it more specific to the woods?"

"Have you never heard of a sorcerer's Place?" Reynald asked.

"No. Well…" Liam paused in thought. "I suppose I have heard the term used frequently with mages, but I feel like there's a meaning I'm not catching."

"Magic and nature—they're more or less connected. Magic is the intuitive understanding of nature. So I would say witches do tend to have a general love of nature, but each of us has a Place we're magically connected to."

"Like the oracle's temple?"

"Exactly. Her Place is the temple and gardens. My Place is a clearing in the Balbraid Thicket and my tower. I lived most of my youth in the palace, but when I escaped—" Reynald held out his hands in a helpless shrug. "It calls you, your Place. Witches might share a wood, but they'd have their own territories. A Place doesn't have to be a forest, a hill, a river, or a single tree, but the Balbraid Thicket holds old, strong magic, so there are over a dozen spots mages are connected to. Most are empty, though. Seigfried's caught or killed most of us over the last few years."

"And we're destroying those sacred places as we clear-cut the forest." Liam shook his head, wrenching the last stray drops of water from his locs before he stood. Liam paced in front of the fire.

"You look like you're about to march to the palace and give Seigfried a piece of your mind." Reynald raised an eyebrow.

"Nothing so bold. He'd arrest me, but there must be a way to use my station and privilege to save some of the land. It borders my own, perhaps…"

Liam dropped the sentence.

I will grant you any reward you wish.

He thought he wanted a kiss, but the king's mouth would taste of ash and tears if Liam kissed him after all he'd learned. Seigfried's beauty meant nothing compared to the sadness in Stephen's eyes as he stirred the potatoes on his plate and spoke of his son.

Was Reynald's life worth a hundred acres?

Liam was a knight. He had to fulfill his duty. Reynald was condemned—Liam couldn't change that—but he could make Reynald's execution mean something. Liam unrolled his map onto the table.

"Show me where your tower is."

"Absolutely not." Reynald planted his hands on his hips. "A wizard's tower isn't a safe place to root around."

"Please. I wish I could convince Seigfried to show mercy and save your life, but we both know a witch has never been declared innocent in a trial, but he promised me a boon. I could ask for an expansion to my land, and if I can protect your meadow…isn't that something?"

"You…would keep my Place safe?" Reynald's face softened.

"I feel it isn't nearly enough." Liam traced the border of the map where the forest hugged close to his own lands. "But I'm not sure what else I could actually *do*."

"Ask me again before we reach Citadel." Reynald bit his bottom lip. "Maybe I'll tell you. Maybe I won't."

"We really don't trust each other, do we?" Liam rubbed the top of his head.

"I suppose not." Reynald shrugged.

"Let's forget this for now and get something to eat, okay?"

"Sounds good." Reynald laced his hand with Liam's as they walked.

"Reynald, w-why are you holding my hand?"

"Well, you don't want me escaping, right?"

"You're not trying to escape. You're trying to fluster me." Liam pulled his hand away.

"Don't make it so easy, and it won't be so fun." Reynald grinned.

They found a corner table, and Liam had an idea so he excused himself and returned with two mugs. Reynald accepted the drink, pulling a face when he noticed the steam rising from the mug. Cautiously, Reynald sniffed the cup.

"This isn't beer, it's…chicken broth?"

"Yes."

"Why did you hand me broth?" Reynald chuckled.

"Don't you like it?" Liam frowned.

"Sure. Broth's actually my favorite drink, but how did you know?"

"The salt." Liam shrugged.

"Dammit, Liam." Reynald leaned into his seat and blew on the top before taking a sip.

"What?" Liam blushed.

"Nothing."

"Should I not have?"

"It's good." Reynald sighed. "What's on the menu?"

The conversation died as they examined their options. They ate stew in a trencher, listened to the music playing from the stage, and Liam watched as Reynald joined in a few card games before they both turned in for the night. They walked close enough for their shoulders to bump, and Liam wished he hadn't drunk two extra beers during the card games. He wasn't drunk, but he was relaxed, which was arguably worse. Especially when Reynald elbowed him in the ribs and grinned with a booze-flushed face.

"Better watch me closely. If you go to sleep, I might turn into a bird and fly away."

"Your familiar shape is a fox, so you can't become a bird." Liam fumbled with the key to get into their room. "I know that much about magic."

"How do you know?" Reynald snorted.

"You told me, once, while we rode."

"Dammit. This is exactly why we shouldn't be fraternizing. I'll divulge all my best secrets." Reynald licked his lips, as if he were eager to share an extra secret or two.

"You're right. We really shouldn't be so informal with each other." Liam sat near the stove. "I should finish drying my hair."

"It's dry. You should stop playing valiant knight and actually sleep." Reynald folded the covers over his lap. "See how comfy?"

"Maybe it'd be better if I stood guard." Liam kept his hands near the heat of the stove. His plan was to sit there until his buzz faded.

"I'm sorry… In the fort, I wasn't going to blind you again."

"When you darkened my vision at the palace, I was afraid it'd never return," Liam admitted. "I've never been as terrified as those ten seconds."

"I don't blame you for avoiding me since then, but…it's a long journey, and…"

"And?" Liam glanced at Reynald.

"You might as well sleep. We're back on the road tomorrow, right? Don't let a good bed go to waste."

Liam massaged his temples. Reynald thought Liam was avoiding him because Liam was afraid of him. The problem was entirely the opposite—Liam wasn't afraid enough and was going to hurt them both if he didn't rein in his loneliness and keep his distance. Liam raked his hands through his locs. They were dry; he was a coward. Everything was an excuse to keep from holding Reynald at night. He was going mad from want.

"I'm sorry," Reynald repeated, head hanging low in shame.

"Don't be. I know you wouldn't hurt me now."

"You know nothing of the sort," Reynald argued.

"Do I not?" Liam jumped to his feet and marched toward the bed with his gaze locked on Reynald. He crawled on top of the mattress and hovered an inch away from Reynald's unmasked nose.

"What are you trying to prove?" Reynald didn't flinch or blink.

"That I'm safe around you."

"I could summon lightning directly into your heart. Do you call that safe?"

Reynald pushed the tip of his finger to Liam's chest. His words were more apt than he realized. Liam floated a little closer but forced himself not to close the gap between them.

"What are you waiting for? I'm defenseless."

"I'm tired," Reynald said. "It's too late to bother with spells."

"Told you. I'm safe with you," Liam whispered against Reynald's lips before dropping away and pulling the covers over himself.

"Out of all the knights in Seigfried's court, why did Edeline have to send you?" Reynald gripped the sheets on each side of him.

"I wish she hadn't," Liam confessed at the dark ceiling lit only by the firelight slipping through the grate of the stove. "The world was so simple before, but now I'm questioning everything I stood for."

"You *should*. You stood for badly constructed lies you only believed so you could sleep at night."

"So how do I sleep now?" Liam asked.

"Like this." Reynald locked his arms around Liam's chest, using him as a pillow.

"Are you cold? Do I need to add wood to the fire in the stove?" Liam stiffened at the sudden contact.

"I'll be fine right here." Reynald nuzzled his chest the same way he'd nuzzled against him the last time they'd shared a bed.

"You're not drunk, are you?" Liam frowned.

They'd had a little extra beer, yes, but not enough for this. But why else would Reynald act so affectionate if not for alcohol?

"Yes. I'm drunk. I won't remember any of this in the morning, so do whatever you want with me tonight."

Liam choked back a groan. His resolve shattered, and he returned the embrace. Their skin was soft from the bath, and their hair freshly washed, and it was the most comfortable Liam could ever remember being in his life. Yet it was an agony to endure, a sweet, delicious agony. This experience wasn't his to keep. Any feelings they had were doomed to be temporary. Liam was stupid to indulge in something so ludicrous, but he could not pull his arms away if he tried.

But he didn't try.

Instead, he settled deeper into their tangled arms and relaxed. He listened to Reynald's breath and heartbeat, pretended *this* could be his life.

"You're too noble." Reynald's voice sounded choked.

"I'm too weak." Liam closed his eyes.

If he was noble, he wouldn't be wrapped up with his enemy. If he was noble, they'd be closer to Citadel instead of wasting time in a village for baths and beds. He fell asleep lost in the bliss of Reynald's arms around him and woke up with Reynald sprawled on top of him. A bare leg was slung across Liam's body, and Reynald's chest rose and fell as he breathed heavily. Liam teased along the outline of Reynald's knee. The gesture woke Reynald, who gasped at the light touch and jerked upright.

"Sorry." Liam blushed.

"No tickling." Reynald shoved a pillow over Liam's face.

"No pillow fights." Liam tucked the pillow under his head.

"I slept too hard." Reynald rubbed his face. "Still tired. Can't we sleep in?"

"Yeah, let's sleep in." Liam stared at the ceiling.

"Really?" Reynald leaned over him, grin as mischievous as ever.

Saints, he was beautiful. Liam's chest hurt at the sight of Reynald without his mask.

"We could get lost. Maybe end up in Suzdal for a year," Liam said.

"Sounds great. I'm in." Reynald combed his hair with his fingers.

"Could you so easily give up your vengeance?" Liam asked, half tempted to race to the nearest coastal city and buy passage on the first boat.

"Could you so easily give up your duty?"

"Maybe not." Liam shook his head, not really believing his words.

"Didn't think so. Guess it's another grueling day of riding and arguing politics after all."

"I'm right, aren't I?" Liam shoved himself out of bed to dress. The stove had burned cold in the night, and the wooden floor was icy below his feet.

"About what? Exactly?"

"Your vengeance. You have a plan. That's why you're not escaping. I'm delivering you directly to your target. I'm your armed guard, not your captor."

"My armed guard? Sounds lovely." Reynald hummed.

"Are you as good at dancing with your feet as you are with your words?" Liam pulled his mesh mail shirt over his head and overlaid his surcoat on top of his armor.

"Ask me to dance and find out." Reynald covered his face with the fox mask, and lifted his hood, though several orange wisps of his hair framed the ivory.

"You're such a mess." Liam arranged the little flames of hair around the mask so they wouldn't obstruct his vision.

"You seem like the type who likes to tidy a mess." Reynald shoved at Liam's chest.

They stood face-to-face, gazing at each other. All their japes and snarky comments lost, leaving only a knight in his armor and a wizard with a magical robe and mask. Liam's throat tightened. The room offered little distraction. The bed was plain with brown woolen blankets, the pipe leading out of the stove was rusty at the seams, the floorboards were swept but scratched from an endless rotation of travelers scuffing the boards with their worn boots. None of these things were a fraction as interesting as Reynald. Possessed by too many urges, Liam chose to do something ridiculous and poke the tip of the mask's nose.

"Boop."

"What is wrong with you?" Reynald rubbed the snout as if he'd felt the gesture.

The only thing wrong with Liam was that he wanted to kiss Reynald but knew it was a horrible idea. He gathered his travel bags and checked out. The innkeeper's wife winked at him when she saw Reynald. Liam blushed but didn't correct her either. If only this was a secret getaway between lovers, but that was another fantasy for Liam to crush and bury.

Creed greeted them both with a shake of his head before they mounted and found the road out of town.

Chapter Nine

Another week passed by without incident. Liam was an expert at quick travel, but he stopped too often for supplies, or to get a properly cooked meal instead of camping fare, anything to stall the journey. When Reynald mentioned his inefficiency, Liam insisted they were already so behind schedule because of the blizzard that he didn't see why he should rush. Reynald laughed and suggested they stop for cider and pies before the sunset, and Liam agreed without argument. The nearest town was large enough for a proper travel lodge, and they bathed and found a cozy public house for drinks and sweets. Liam laughed when Reynald salted his pie, but Reynald shoved a bit into Liam's mouth, and the flavors complimented each other. Reynald pulled his fork from between Liam's lips. Their gazes locked. Time moved like syrup dripping down a maple trunk. Liam licked his lips, reaching his hand toward

Reynald's unmasked face, but Reynald dropped back in his seat and teased Liam for being right about the pie.

Each extra day they traveled was an extra day Reynald was alive, and Liam wanted him alive.

"You can't avoid the inevitable." Reynald sipped from his mug on a different night. "We'll run out of inns eventually, and Siegfried will be waiting."

"How do you plan to kill him?" Liam stared at his cider.

"Why should I tell you? So you can thwart me?" Reynald chuckled.

Would he? Probably? Despite everything else, Liam was still a knight. Did Seigfried deserve to be assassinated? Other kings were selfish and greedy, and their knights stood beside them. Liam couldn't watch Seigfried murdered, murder was always wrong.

Although that meant execution was also wrong.

Liam's head hurt.

The next day, while searching for either a village or a place to camp, they saw a sign with a skull painted onto the wood nailed over the original

WELCOME TO BIRCHSHIRE.

Painted in black letters, the words on the second sign read:

PLAGUE: DO NOT ENTER.

Reynald dropped to the ground and stood a few inches from the sign.

"Birchshire was bustling when I came through this way before."
Liam shook his head. "No one was sick."

"They probably were. Illness is like a seed. It sprouts roots inside
the body before you can see the leaves of the symptoms."

"I wish I could help somehow." Liam remained on Creed's back,
waiting for Reynald to climb on so they could circle around Birchshire
and set up their tent somewhere distant.

"I know a lot about medicine." Reynald glanced up so he could
stare at Liam. "Maybe I *can*."

"I think these people need more than some herbs." Liam shook his
head.

"Serious question, Liam. I want you to think before you answer.
When you were sick as a boy, did your father fetch a doctor? Or did he
summon someone from the Thicket?"

"He'd ask for my grandmother to look after me," Liam said.

"Your grandmother?"

"She was good with nursing fevers. She'd cook a chicken soup
that'd have me back in the training yard before I could enjoy the extra
time in my bed."

"You think that soup might have had some healing herbs from the
Thicket in the broth?" Reynald pressed both hands to his hips.

"Probably." Liam sighed in defeat.

"I know how to make medicine. I might be able to save someone."
Reynald pulled off his mask. "What good is being magical if you can't
be helpful?"

"Okay." Liam dismounted and held Creed's reins in his hand.

"Let's try."

"Really?" Reynald asked.

"If we can save even one person, then it's our duty to help."

"For me, helping is more compulsion than duty, but at least we agree on our course of action. Let's go." Reynald beelined through the town toward the church.

Tents surrounded the churchyard. Women in white smocks and veils rushed from cot to cot. They all wore medallions of St. Pantaleon around their necks. The nauseating smell of fever sweat and damp linen clung to the area despite being outdoors. A doctor in a bird mask saw them approach and held out her hands.

"Why are you here? This fever is extremely contagious. Didn't you read the sign?"

"My name is Reynald Egesgrima, and this is Sir Liam Bord. We did see the sign. Let me examine the sick," Reynald said. "I'm a steward of the Balbraid Thicket, and I want to help."

"Oh, a steward." The doctor bowed. "We'd appreciate your skills. My name is Doctor Euphrosina. I've treated the sick the best I can, but I'm running out of supplies. I've had to ration the laudanum for the dying because we don't have enough for everyone."

"I'll see what I can do." Reynald knelt near the closest patient.

Scarlet splotches covered the patients' faces. The red traveled up their noses and across their foreheads and cheeks. Little white blisters poxed the corners of their mouths, and their clothes stuck to them because of the sweat. Reynald examined a handful of patients before washing his hands in a basin outside and pacing between the tents.

"Liam, may I see your map?" Reynald asked after about thirty seconds.

Liam unrolled the parchment and laid the paper on the grass. Reynald lowered himself to his hands and knees, eyes darting across the lines. He jabbed his finger to an area a few miles north.

"The Tangled Grove. Here. Should be similar to Balbraid with similar herbs. I need you to gather the materials while I set up a workstation. I'm going to write a list. I can draw examples if you're not sure what something is."

"Leave you here alone?" Liam asked, instinct driving the question out of his mouth. "That'd be the same as abandoning my post."

"I'm not leaving these people, so don't worry about me escaping." Reynald rested his hands on top of Liam's. "Whatever else you might suspect of me, I can promise you right now, I'm here to help them, but I need fresh ingredients for medicine."

"You summoned monsters to attack Citadel. You didn't care for civilian lives *then*." Liam shook his head. "But now you do?"

"This town doesn't burn witches—Citadel does," Reynald hissed in a low whisper. "We don't have time for a debate on morality or human nature. Liam, *please*. I thought all knights were Seigfried's dogs. Prove me wrong. Do the right thing and not the lawful thing."

"This once…I *will* trust you. Write a list, and I promise I'll find every ingredient on it and bring them to you before sunset." Liam nodded, thumb glancing across Reynald's knuckles.

"I need a pen and paper." Reynald called to one of the nurses.

Reynald wrote instructions with each ingredient. Giving specific details as to which tubers to dig between the oak roots, and precisely which fungus to collect from the underside of a dead log, and which moss to gather on the shady side of the creek bank. The nurses had given Liam special envelopes to store various herbs so nothing would be damaged or contaminated during travel, and he stored everything in a knapsack.

Liam cantered past the town, crossing the grasslands and reaching the woods after an hour's ride. He dismounted and walked Creed once beneath the canopy to keep Creed safe from injuring his legs. Liam followed Reynald's notes meticulously, double and sometimes triple reading each section before collecting specimens. Growling interrupted his work as he peeled inner bark away from a slippery elm. Liam stood upright, glancing toward the noise.

A dire wolf stood eye level with Liam. His silver coat shimmered in the rays of sunlight trickling through the canopy. Liam held up his shield, but left his sword in his scabbard. He stood between the wolf and Creed, who was most likely the wolf's target. Creed tugged at his rein, but Liam had secured it to a birch trunk before gathering ingredients. The horse's nostrils flared and his eyes were wide with raw instinct.

"Calm down, Creed. We'll just show him we're not easy prey." Liam stood tall, trying to match the wolf's height.

In the dabbled patches of light cutting through the leaves, Liam's cloak flashed as brightly as the dire wolf's silver fur. Liam took a single step forward, crunching leaves and a branch to make noise. The wolf crouched low, eyes wary. Sniffing the air, the wolf sneezed after catching the mix of herbs in Liam's bag.

"Go!" Liam shouted in a stern voice, thrusting his shield outward. "Go!"

To their right, an elk crossed the stream, spooked by either Liam's or the wolf's scent. The dire wolf caught sight of the frightened creature, pivoted, and sprang toward the elk, deciding he was an easier meal. Liam fell against the birch trunk. He gave himself some time for his heartbeat to slow. The knuckles gripping his shield were white-capped, and his free hand clutched at the scars below his surcoat.

His scar burned with the memory, but those wolves had been driven out of their hunting grounds by axes and mills. Liam couldn't hate them for the attack any more than he hated Reynald for summoning the stryx. Actions had consequences. Liam always took the phrase to mean one's own actions had consequences, but a king was his kingdom. Thus, the consequences of Siegfried's actions were far-reaching. Exhaling, Liam focused on gathering the slippery elm and one last type of mushroom before making his way out of the Tangled Grove. He escaped the forest just before sunset when other predators would begin their nightly hunts.

Reentering Birchshire, Liam saw a musseri, a creature resembling a dog-sized rat but with teeth that looked far too human in the rodent's grinning mouth. Liam stopped Creed, dismounted, pulled the hunting knife Mary's parents had gifted him, and punctured the creature's throat before it caught his scent. The musseri squealed, blood gurgling and drowning the noise. With a final twist, the musseri curled on its side, dying as its paws twitched in the dirt. Liam wrapped the rodent in a piece of cloth and carried the corpse with him until he found Reynald and

Euphrosina in a makeshift medical station near the sick tents. Musseri made burrows in ogre and goblin dens, scavenging off the larger predators. Liam had never seen one; few humans had. He only knew they existed because he read about them in his bestiary studies.

He'd also read that they carried various diseases from the carrion they ate.

"I found a musseri scurrying near the general store." He told Reynald when he entered the tent.

"Did you see signs of goblins in the Tangled Grove?" Reynald ignored the wrapped bundle in Liam's arms and stole Liam's knapsack slung over his shoulder. Reynald then sorted the packets at a table.

"Neither goblins nor ogres. These shouldn't be native to this area."

"It's the caravans carrying wood to the coast to ship to Suzdal." The doctor grabbed her mortar and pestle to ground the small blue-green snail shells Liam had gathered from beneath forest rocks. "They brought musseri and little jacks into town as the drivers stopped in the inn. We've been trying to exterminate them, but people were struck with this fever before we could manage the infestation."

Reynald and Liam exchanged a long glance. They didn't have to say out loud what was obvious: Siegfried clearing the Balbraid Thicket and exporting the wood was the cause of the plague. Reynald shook his head, tearing open packets, boiling some of the ingredients, crushing others, and submerging the moss in a vial of grain alcohol for an extraction.

"Birchshire is within the fiefdom of Sir Pines, have you sent a message to him requesting supplies?" Liam asked.

"We sent pigeons and a rider. The rider was refused entrance because they feared he'd bring fever with him, and the pigeon replies promised aid two weeks ago, but we've yet to see any." One of the nurses answered for Doctor Euphrosina. Euphrosina nodded to confirm what she'd said.

"I see. I will write to my steward and have him make arrangements." Liam stormed toward the back of the church where he burned the rodent corpse.

Finished, he consulted the nurses for a list of the foods and medicines they needed. Then he borrowed Dr. Euphrosina's writing desk and penned a letter instructing his steward to gather and send the items as soon as possible while stockpiling extra supplies in case any similar epidemics broke out in his own fiefdom. All the while, Reynald brewed his potions—his medicine. To give the sick some relief, the nurses gave them tea and broth and smoothed herbal mud masks over the fevered victims' burning faces as they waited, but it was three in the morning before Reynald finished condensing the other ingredients into a sap-thick syrup. The moment the medicine cooled, Reynald helped administer his concoction to everyone in the church sick beds and the surrounding tents. With the sheer number of infected, Reynald didn't have a chance to sit until the sun crested over Birchshire's roofs.

"I've taught Doctor Euphrosina how to synthesize the medicinal syrup. Most of the ill should recover in three to five days." Reynald dropped onto a stool and rubbed his shoulders.

"You make an exemplary field nurse." Liam offered Reynald another mug of hot broth he'd salted with Reynald's smoked salt.

"Thank you." Reynald slipped his mask over his face and drank deeply from the cup, sighing. "Give me a few minutes to rest before we ride out."

"Betty offered us her home so we can rest before we leave."

"Betty?" Reynald scowled.

Liam pointed to one of the nurses making rounds throughout the sick camp. She was tall and broad-shouldered, and her hair sat on top of her hair in a meticulous twist. She had the bulldogged look of a woman children hid from when she entered a room, but she'd handled the patients with a delicate and practiced care and answered all Liam's supply questions without snapping, despite her visible exhaustion.

"Ah. Well, I'm not going to refuse a chance to sleep." Reynald yawned to punctuate his sentence.

"I could use some sleep as well." Liam nodded.

"It was smart of you to write your personal steward instead of Sir Pines."

"I do not regret my decisions. Helping these people…traveling at our own pace…but it would not serve to announce our location to one of the other knights. Siegfried would expect our return within two weeks if he knew how close we were." Liam offered Reynald a sheepish smile. "But who knows? We may need to stop and help others yet."

"Perhaps you're more suited for espionage than I'd given you credit for, but only when it's for the sake of charity."

"Of course. Do you think this is my first time skirting the rules? I've spent my entire life hiding myself from my country. The common folk are free to marry whom they wish, but nobility exists to create heirs and pass estates from father to son, and I've been avoiding that expectation for ten years.”

“Royal magicians aren't allowed to marry or bear children.”

Without his mask, Reynald's hurt expression was exposed. Liam crouched in front of him, resting both his hands on Reynald's bent knees.

“Did you—”

“No.” Reynald shook his head. “But it made the women sad.”

“Of course. Sorry I assumed.” Liam stood. “We should get some sleep.”

“Yeah.”

Reynald finished his broth, and they found the small cottage house surrounded by autumn mums. A key lay beneath one of the flowerpots, and Liam let them inside. The room smelled of dry violets. Tiny saint statues or hand-carved wooden animals guarded all the tables and shelves. The white lace curtains were pristine, no yellow edges or dust.

“You'd fit right in here.” Reynald grinned as he looked around.

“What do you mean?” Liam noticed one of the glass cat figurines on the mantel was a little off center from the other three. With his finger, he nudged the cat back into her proper place.

“Exactly.” Reynald pointed to the cat. "Everything's so clean and organized."

“What do you do? Throw all your belongings on the floor?” Liam raised an eyebrow.

“I keep a few things on the floor.” Reynald shrugged before exploring the rest of the house.

They found an extra room. It was decorated like a guest room, but the tiny bed suggested it was once a child's room. Neither argued as they climbed into the twin-sized bed, though they had to press together to both fit.

"Reminds me of your first tent." Reynald grinned.

"Softer though."

"Yes. Softer." Reynald lidded his gaze.

Liam halfway leaned in, paused, and lowered his head. Reynald unapologetically used Liam's chest as a pillow. The birds on the wallpaper watched, accusing Liam of being stupid after all, of not seeing the obvious.

"You...*like* this, don't you?" Liam's mouth parted as he figured out why Reynald was always insisting they lay cuddled together.

They'd been out of the mountains for some time. The autumn air was cool, but not as bitter or life-threatening as sleeping in the snow. Originally, he thought Reynald was mocking him, but each night, as Reynald slept, his grip tightened as if he were afraid Liam would slip away from him as he slept.

"I like flustering you. Keeps you on your toes. I might stab you with your own knife, or I might kiss you. You can only guess."

"I dare you."

"Kiss you or stab you? Be more specific."

"Either."

"If I choose, you'll call me a criminal for acting out my choice. You must request which one you *want*."

"Stab me," Liam said.

"Shut up." Reynald smacked his chest. "You're not serious at all."

"You wouldn't hurt me. You're either growing fond of me, or I'm still too useful to you."

"The second one. I assure you."

"Then kiss me."

Reynald dragged himself higher, leaned forward, and pressed his lips to Liam's forehead. In the center, where a unicorn's horn would sit. Liam felt as if he were being cleaved in half by a great ax. Half of him was still angry at Reynald for killing. But the other half…

"Good night." Reynald bumped their noses together.

"Good night." Liam roped his arms around Reynald and held him until they both snored in the guest bedroom.

Liam dreamed he was tied to a stake, burning. He struggled against his binds but couldn't escape the burning pressing against his body. When he awoke, he realized fever radiated from Reynald's body.

"Reynald." Liam pressed his palm to Reynald's forehead.

The heat was almost too much to endure. Liam scooped Reynald into his arms and carried him across town and to the medical camp. He found Betty, the first familiar face, and held Reynald out to her as if he were a doll.

"He's burning."

"Poor dear was too close to the sick beds. Come on. We'll clear a space inside the church for him."

They set up a cot in the corner of the church, near a fountain glorifying Saint Giles. Betty fetched a vial of Reynald's medicine, and Liam held his mouth open so she could administer it. Afterward, she offered a bowl of cool water and a cloth to Liam.

"Bathe his face. His fever should break, but it will take some time for the medicine to work."

Liam bowed before wringing the towel and following her instructions. He bathed Reynald's face, neck, and arms. Reynald shied away from the cool cloth, shivering.

"Shh, shh, don't worry." Liam tied Reynald's hair away from his face and bathed the sweat from his brow.

"Joan," Reynald cried.

Liam's hand stopped. He studied Reynald's crimson face, but there was no way to ask who Joan was. Liam ignored the mysterious name and kept cooling Reynald's skin as best he could. Reynald twisted away from the cloth and muttered he was cold. Liam wrapped his cloak around Reynald, tucking it to his chin. Blue light filtered from the stained glass surrounding them. Triangles of red, green, and yellow sliced through the various shades of blue. The light struck Liam's cloak, and the dragon skin gleamed with hidden pinks, whites, and lavenders scintillating along each curved scale. All the rainbows surrounded Reynald, transforming him into an angel. Liam stroked his fevered brow and cheek.

At some point, Liam dozed on the stool beside Reynald's bed. A light, delicate touch along the curve of his lips woke him. He opened his eyes to Reynald's smile.

"Did you stay here the entire time and watch over me?"

"Of course."

"I'm a lot of trouble, aren't I?" Reynald kept his hand cupping Liam's face.

"Not really." Liam brushed a loose strand of hair behind Reynald's ear.

"I'll repay you one day for this and for letting me out of that trap."

"The trap. You're going to be my ruin." Liam groaned, shoving his face in his hands. "All my life I've followed the rules and guidelines set before me, and you've somehow managed to make me step off the path again and again."

"I'm taking that as a compliment." Reynald struggled to stand.

"Careful." Liam braced Reynald's back and arm.

"I'm okay. Thirsty."

"Rest. I'll bring you a drink."

Liam fetched water and broth for Reynald. One of the other nurses brought them two bowls of chicken soup, and they ate quietly, too hungry to interrupt the meal with conversation. Afterward, Reynald patted the space on the cot beside him.

"It'd be more cramped than the tent." Liam shook his head.

"So what? You haven't slept in almost two days, and I need at least a day to recover before I travel." Reynald wrinkled his nose with a mischievous grin. "You know you want to."

"We're in the middle of a makeshift hospital." Liam glanced around, at the patients in their beds—some waking as the medicine helped them recover—and at the nurses rushing to feed and care for them.

"Your point?"

"This is exactly what I was talking about. You drag me down into your lechery constantly."

"Are you thinking of lechery? I was thinking about a nap." Reynald resettled onto the cot, but the lidded gaze he fixed on Liam simmered with desire.

And Liam's body moved before he convinced himself not to. He stretched out on the cot and allowed Reynald to use him as a pillow again. The same way they'd been before his fever. He held his breath and waited for one of the nurses to gasp at the sight of them, or at least shoot a disapproving look their way, but no one in the church cared. A few of the sick and families who'd contracted the fever at the same time sat in clusters, hugging and thanking the saints for their recovery. In the farthest corner, someone wailed, mostly likely learning of a loved one who hadn't survived. In all the general emotional chaos, Reynald and Liam were simply two more people, and the relief of being so unimportant flooded through Liam as he fell into a deep sleep with Reynald curled against him.

Chapter Ten

By the next day, people were getting out of their sick beds and trying to return to their homes. The nurses chased after them, physically leading the most stubborn ones to their sick beds.

"Once again, I find myself having to admit you were right." Liam sat on the little stool beside Reynald's cot. He watched the chaos, a happier chaos than before since it was proof people were on the mend.

"Mmm, I do so love when you say those words." Reynald hummed.

"This is the second time I would have kept going, while you insisted we stay and try to make things better." Liam stared at the hunting knife he'd been gifted for his *heroism*. A gift wholly unearned. "Next time, I need to be less stubborn and listen to you."

"Seriously, Liam, you keep talking about listening to me and me being right, and I'm going to throw my clothes off right in the middle of this church."

"I've seen you naked. I don't think even the saints could consider the sight a sin unless they're also liars." Liam spoke in a distracted voice, tired, *mentally tired.* He stood. "I'm going to the general store for supplies."

"Liam." Reynald sat upright.

"Rest. You look a little fevered again." Liam tucked a strip of orange behind Reynald's ear.

Liam rushed out of the church to the general store he had seen. He didn't need supplies, and Reynald had been flushed, not fevered. Which was all the more reason for Liam to get away before he said something else stupid. Liam pulled out the inventory he kept of their supplies, deciding it wouldn't hurt to buy some cooking oil while he was pretending to shop. As he stared at bins full of nails and jars and sacks of milled flour, Euphrosina walked beside him. Her mask hung from her belt. Her dark eyes twinkled from the morning sun angling into her face from a nearby open shutter.

"Good morning," she greeted Liam with a slight nod.

"Good morning." Liam returned the gesture.

"It's difficult being a doctor, knowing there's medicine that wise women and stewards have access to, but I don't. We haven't had a steward in the Tangled Grove for over a generation. Even if one did live there, writing down the recipes of any tinctures or salves is illegal. I could be sent to the stake because I kept a *scientific record* of medicines."

"I will bring up these concerns to the palace as gently and anonymously as I can, good doctor, but…" Liam kept his expression neutral, but his throat burned with acid. "I must disclose that the king considers me a sword, not a councilman."

"I understand." Euphrosina stared out the open window. "And I understand why a knight travels with a mage."

"I don't relish this duty." Liam stared at the vinegars in their dark glass bottles.

"I imagine not. You cared for him last night like his life meant something to you."

"Every life means something to me," Liam said.

"Are we going to be coy? You shared a cot."

Liam touched the nearest label of a jar of preserves, intent on reading and re-reading *strawberry jam.*

"The king will kill him."

Strawberry jam.

"And once he's gone, all his knowledge of medicine is gone. And he's a far more adept healer than *me.* Do you know in Valen and Suzdal almost no one dies from a fever? They have alchemists who combine magic and science and have refined the herbal remedies into even more potent medicines, but countries like Phrophis and Mascaria refuse to import them because they're *magic and evil.*"

Strawberry jam.

"I know you have the authority to arrest me for everything I'm saying now, but I don't care anymore."

"I wouldn't." Liam shook his head. "I wouldn't dare. Nothing you've said has been wrong, but the king has *ordered me* to bring this witch to him directly."

"And you're going to obey? Because I believe *you* want Reynald to flee."

Liam grunted. Reynald could flee anytime he wanted. Each morning Liam woke hoping Reynald would be gone, but he was set to get to Citadel.

"Sir Bord, have you heard of the Salt Merchant's Path?" Euphrosina asked.

"Is that the caravan trail that brings pepper and other rare spices into Phrophis?" Liam muttered. He'd heard Sam mentioning something about salt merchants a few times when they needed more supplies.

"You don't have a clue. How strange, considering." Euphrosina gave him a weary smile. "But I'm glad. The path isn't the sort of thing a knight should know about, but…"

Euphrosina hesitated, and Liam frowned. This was like Reynald explaining a mage's Place all over again. He'd probably heard plenty while people talked around him, but he never listened to the real meaning of the words. Salt was a common seasoning like pepper, but why would there be a path for it when there were local salt mines? People did tend to favor the smoked and colored salts from Suzdal, but those they often gave as gifts to—Liam's eyes widened as several facts clicked into place all at once.

"Ah, you must be talking about an underground system to smuggle witches out of Phrophis." Liam nodded to himself, even as he wrapped a bottle of cooking oil into cloth so it didn't break as they rode. He went to the counter to pay for the oil.

"You figured out the meaning rather quickly." Euphrosina raised an eyebrow at him. "Have you heard of it, after all?"

"Probably. Salt isn't something a knight pays attention to."

"Which is how many of us are still alive." Euphrosina folded her hands in front of her. "Most sorcerers refuse to leave. Their sacred Places are so connected to them that the risk of death is worth staying, but when one *does* wish to escape, the path is the best option for them. I have a contact…if you don't?"

"Trust me, Reynald won't leave. He's powerful enough to escape whenever he wants, but doesn't. Don't share your contact's name. The less I know, the better." Liam exited the store.

"Try to talk to him." Euphrosina chased after Liam. "Convince him to flee with you."

"With me." Liam chuckled. The doctor's comment wounded him deep in his chest. "I'm the last person he'd escape with."

"Are you a fool? You're both clearly in love."

"No. He's playing a sorcerer's game." Liam shook his head.

"Is that what you tell yourself so you don't have to take responsibility for your actions? Your feelings?"

Liam halted midstep. She sounded a bit like Reynald. Euphrosina folded her hands again, physically restraining herself though she was visibly angry.

"All right. I'll ask him. If he agrees, we'll seek you out for information about your contact, but if we leave Birchshire without saying goodbye, please don't take it personally. The king is not a patient man, and we've already taken too long to reach Citadel."

Euphrosina pursed her lips, then nodded, bowed, and walked back to the sick tents surrounding the church. A few had been disassembled, a good sign people were recovering enough to be transferred to their own beds.

Liam found Reynald at the church, making rounds for the remaining patients. Candles and saint statues surrounded all the beds. Reynald currently lectured an older man about his smoking habit as he prescribed a list of greens for the man to start eating to help strengthen his lungs. Liam couldn't hold in his laughter.

"What?" Reynald noticed Liam and followed him to their own private corner away from the recovering patients.

"You lecturing anyone for a bad habit is a little hypocritical."

"His heart and lungs are weak, and he smokes a pouch of tobacco a day."

"Why did the nurses let you leave your bed? You should be recovering."

"Oh that? Well…" Reynald pressed a finger to his lips. "I'm a wise steward with magic, so of course *I* don't need to follow those rules."

"See? Hypocrite."

"You are in no position to lecture me on the vise of hypocrisy, *Sir Bord.*"

"Euphrosina spoke with me." Liam changed the subject.

"Did she?"

"She asked if you needed to find a salt merchant before we left." Liam wasn't exactly sure why he phrased his statement the way he did, but he was oddly certain this was the proper way to ask Reynald if he wanted to leave Prophis.

"Oh, I'm sure you gathered all the supplies we need for the trip."

"Do you understand what I'm asking you?" Liam dropped his hands to his sides in frustration.

"You didn't even know witches craved salt until I told you. Don't presume to know more about these things than I do." Reynald scoffed.

"Then why don't you go and talk to her?"

"What if I slipped away from your grasp after talking to her?" Reynald mocked him. "I was under the impression you'd hunt me down to the end of my days. What's the point of going?"

"I could chase you forever," Liam teased. "Think of all the adventures we could have."

"You would grow tired of that, I assure you." Reynald went back to his cot where their things sat on top of his folded blanket. "I'm ready to go when you are."

"To buy salt?"

"You need to be careful throwing that word around." Reynald sent a sharp, warning glance over his shoulder. "You could get good people killed with your carelessness."

"Not here. You saved these people. How many gifts have you gotten?"

"A few." Reynald smirked.

"I'm sure you have more than a few." Liam reached for Reynald's hand. "Reynald, please."

"There you go with that delicious, traitorous mouth of yours again.

Saying please to a witch. Tell me, Sir Bord, where would you hide your dragon scale cloak and shield? They'd give you away and make us both easy to track if we fled."

"You act as if luggage doesn't exist?"

"That shield isn't exactly travel-sized. What if we had to abandon our luggage? Would you throw your prized heirloom to the ground and so easily forsake all your responsibilities?"

Liam touched the shield resting on his back by a sling as he thought. The legends of his grandfather were the first stories he'd heard in the cradle. He'd striven his entire life to become exactly like Linnel Bord: strong and courageous enough to fight a dragon, heroic enough to rescue anyone in need, proud and chivalrous and honorable. Could he throw the symbol of all that into a lake and run away?

If he was with Reynald? Could he?

"You're a silly little boy playing pretend. Grow up." Reynald snapped his mask in place, hiding his face and leaving Liam behind. "If you want to help me, get me to Citadel *faster*."

Once they reached the church stable, Reynald mounted Creed as if they were going for a casual ride instead of continuing toward his death. Liam stared at him, but with the mask on, there was no chance of gleaning any information from his facial features. However, of one thing Liam was certain, whatever Euphrosina saw when she saw them together—she was wrong.

"You call me a silly boy, but you'd rather die playing vengeance than escape?" Liam led Creed out of the stables and mounted.

They rode out of town without finding Euphrosina.

"Playing? Oh, sweet little knight. You don't have a clue."

"I obviously don't." Liam rested his hands on his outer thighs instead of Reynald's waist. It took more effort to balance, but he didn't care.

Silence swallowed the journey. Creed's hooves clopped along the road. Liam made a note to get him reshod the next time they were at a travel lodge. He also realized he'd gotten wound up in his fight with Reynald, and they hadn't had breakfast. Liam clamped his jaw tight, furious—mostly at himself. He didn't really *need* Reynald to abscond. If he had any true guts, he'd throw down his sword and run away on his own, but who would that help? The Thicket would still be destroyed. Reynald would continue to Citadel on his own. Perhaps it was better if Liam stayed and tried to influence policy—because *that* had worked so well the last time he'd asked Seigfried to halt the clear cutting.

"I need a flute. Traveling would be better with some music," Reynald announced as they rode.

"We'll reach Bridge's Crossing by nightfall tomorrow. I'm sure they'll have something at the general store." Liam spoke but was more lost in thought than listening.

"A sorcerer does not *buy* an instrument. I'll have to make my own," Reynald said.

"Didn't you want to reach Citadel *quicker*?"

"Yeah. I do." Reynald shrugged. "But this is boring, and if you're not going to entertain me, I need something distracting. I don't want to be bored for the last days of my life. That's worse than dying."

"I swear to all fourteen saints, you make my head hurt," Liam snapped.

"Testy. What's wrong? You can't be *that* upset that I didn't run away." Reynald chuckled.

"What's wrong? What's wrong? My life wasn't great before I met you, but at least it made sense, and at least I had purpose. Now, I'm exhausted because I was up all night tending to you, hungry because you decided to storm out of Birchshire before we had breakfast, and, and you're annoying," Liam snapped at Reynald so he didn't cry.

And you're going to die.

And you'd rather die than escape with me.

And I don't know what I'm going to do with the rest of my life if you're not with me.

"I didn't realize all it took to break a knight was to have him skip a meal." Reynald pulled a loaf of oat and honey bread from one of his pockets. "Here. You've fed me this entire trip. I figure I owe you at least one meal."

"I don't want your bread."

"Don't be stubborn. It's just a snack."

"You mean a gift from one of the villagers, because you saved their life when I would have passed them by."

"I only saved their lives because you went to the Tangled Grove for the ingredients I needed. Even a fetch quest deserves a small reward, yeah?"

"No, thank you."

"Okay, then, I guess we're on a hunger strike again." Reynald shoved the bread into his robe. "This wasn't the entertainment I was seeking, but I'm game. Let's see who can last longer without food. Not to brag, but Seigfried used to deny me food for days at a time, so I'm really good at this game."

"I'll eat the bread." Liam flinched at the thought of Reynald not eating. His hand reached out to hold Reynald's shoulder so he didn't fall off the horse from the movement.

"Wonderful. Enjoy." Reynald passed the little loaf to him.

"I won't eat this alone. We have to share." Liam tore the bread in half and gave Reynald the larger chunk.

"All right." Reynald sighed. "We'll share. Just don't blame me when you're hungry again in an hour."

Chapter Eleven

While Liam set up camp for the evening, Reynald changed into a fox to hunt rabbits. Liam didn't protest. He was grateful to have some time to himself. After Reynald returned, Liam skinned and processed the meat. He slipped the chunks onto a spit and set them over the fire to roast. Reynald remained as a fox, curled into a crescent and watching Liam like a nervous house cat.

Sighing, Liam lay on his cloak with his travel bag behind his head as a pillow. A Sycamore tree stood near the camp, gold leaves shivering whenever a breeze caressed them. Creed cropped grass near the trunk.

"Creed likes you." Liam spoke to the fire. "He's particular, but he likes you."

Reynald flicked an ear in Liam's direction, listening but not changing. Liam ignored him and continued to watch the dusk-blushed sky slowly darken. By the time the boldest stars revealed themselves, Liam couldn't stand the silence, so he spoke out loud about whatever came to mind.

"We're still a way from our home, but the stars are the same. Survival trainings were my favorite times as a child, going into the Thicket and learning what tracks were animals and what tracks were dangerous, camping in a glade and watching the stars. If I could have brought a book it would have been perfect, but Old Mac would have caned me for bringing something so frivolous."

"They wouldn't let you read?"

Liam jerked to the side. He hadn't noticed Reynald changing, but now Reynald sat cross-legged, the ends of his hair pooling on the ground behind him.

"Training manuals. War strategy. Old finance logs to practice math and accounting. But bestiaries? Legends? Anything interesting? No. They thought my time was better spent on *useful* knowledge."

"Useful knowledge is a redundant term."

"I'll let Old Mac know the next time he goes into the Thicket for training exercises." Liam's face crumpled at the thought. "What am I saying? There isn't going to be a Thicket left after Seigfried's had his way."

"Do you still plan on using your boon to reserve some of the Thicket?"

"As much as I can, but what's a hundred acres compared to an entire forest?"

"You're assuming my tower is that close?" Reynald raised an eyebrow.

"I assumed nothing of the sort, that's why I asked to see it on the map. Instead of asking for a set number, I could outline a section on the map and ask for the section."

"In hopes that Seigfried can't count if you get greedy?"

"In hopes he would be in an indulgent mood." Liam flicked his gaze at the stars. "At the rate we're traveling? I keenly doubt it."

"Poor little knight." Reynald stretched on his side, eying Liam. "No matter how hard you try, you can't figure out a way to salvage this adventure and still feel like the hero."

"I'm open to suggestions."

"Sorry, your morality crisis isn't my concern." Reynald sniffed the air. "Better check the meat before it burns."

"Dammit," Liam swore as he tended the fire and their meal.

They ate, found a stream, washed, dried near the fire, and crawled into Liam's tent once it was late. Reynald spoke in a quiet voice in the dark.

"Seigfried has a lot of books. I'd sneak pages out of the magic ones, study everything I could. That's why I know so much about medicine."

"If only he'd share the books. Euphrosina was desperate for the medical knowledge of a wise woman."

"He only sees the cities and towns of Prophis as little toy models for him to play with. He doesn't care if people have medicine."

"Not just the cities, the forests and mountains and rivers are all commodities," Liam added.

"Yes. You're beginning to understand."

"Take me hostage, Reynald. Make a blade of light like you made manacles and drag me to Valen."

"Take you hostage?" Reynald laughed. "So you don't have to make decisions anymore?"

"I don't make decisions. Seigfried does."

"So, you'll trade one master for another? Why don't you act on your own?"

"Because everything I think of is wrong somehow."

"If you could do anything right now, without consequence, what would you do?" Reynald asked.

Liam sought out Reynald's face in the dim light seeping through the tent. He almost reached out, held Reynald's face, and kissed him. *That* was exactly what he'd do if he lived a life without consequences. Instead, he spoke.

"Carry you to Birchshire and put you on a wagon down the Salt Merchant's Path."

"Carry me bridal style? Or slung over your shoulder like a sack of grain?"

"That question is a trap."

"Your defensive response gives away to the fact that you were day-dreaming about carrying me bridal style." Reynald laughed.

"I'm going to sleep now." Liam closed his eyes.

"I'm cold." Reynald curled close.

Liam stared at the ceiling of his tent as soon as Reynald's weight settled on top of him. He supposed even Reynald didn't want to be alone before he died, so Liam let him curl close until they both snored in each other's arms.

In the morning, the spell was broken, and they milled around camp, performing the morning routines out of habit but otherwise ignoring each other. As Liam doused the fire and stirred the ashes, he spoke in a hushed, tense voice.

"What if everything goes well and he dies? He has no heir."

"Seigfried has a bastard uncle hiding somewhere." Reynald waved his hand. "Or his legitimate aunt. There's always someone to fill in a position of power."

"Right, a legitimate aunt and a bastard uncle on his father's side. Not to mention a cousin on his mother's side. None of these people are any better than Seigfried. They won't rule the kingdom more justly, and they won't spare the Thicket. What they will do is start a civil war over who claims the crown."

"And you, a poor knight, will be stuck right in the middle. Shame." Reynald found a moth cocoon beneath a fallen sycamore leaf and stuck both in one of his hidden pockets. "At least you'll still have someone to give you orders after the war, and you can spend your entire life never making a difficult decision."

"If I survive." Liam broke down the tent, rolling the fur and hide into tight coils and securing them with leather ties.

"You'll survive."

"You're an oracle as well as a wizard now?" Liam bit his inside cheek after he made the remark. All his time with Reynald was giving him some bad lessons in the art of facetious retorts.

"You're Liam Bord, the Mighty Stallion of Citadel. There's no way a little skirmish over the throne could kill you."

"Most of us are dead from the last war. The few left are crippled by soldier's nerves."

"I can't afford to feel sorry for you or regret my decision." Reynald balled his hands into fists. "The stupid war was also Seigfried's fault. If anything, I'm getting justice for all of us."

"It doesn't bring back the dead," Liam said, thinking of his father.

"I'm aware."

Reynald mounted Creed despite Liam still having to double-check all their gear to make sure everything was packed before they left. Liam shot Reynald an annoyed glance.

"I'm not ready to go yet."

"Forget your checklist. I watched you pack everything. Let's go." Reynald teased Creed's plaited mane.

"Which pocket has the moth cocoon?" Liam asked, distracting Reynald so he could finish his task.

"What are you on about now?"

"You stuck a leaf with a cocoon attached to it into your pocket not fifteen minutes ago. Which pocket?"

"What…does it matter?" Reynald began digging through several pockets, pulling out ribbon, corn dollies, a cat skull, and a deck of playing cards with naughty satyr artwork on each card—but no yellow leaf.

"Okay, I'm finished. Now we can go." Liam hoisted himself behind Reynald.

"Why did you need the cocoon?"

"I didn't."

"Then why did you ask about it?"

"So you'd focus on how you manage *your* things instead of lecturing me on how I manage mine." Liam tapped a spot below Reynald's left hip. "You placed the leaf here, by the way."

Reynald grabbed his wrist. Liam jerked on instinct, but Reynald held tightly.

"Don't move. The pockets wander. Let's see…" Reynald hooked their fingers into the fold of cloth, checking within. "Hells, you're right."

Reynald pulled the leaf from his pocket and showed Liam the moth cocoon.

"These become moths that love the wild flowers near your estate every fall." Reynald gave the fuzzy patch a sad smile. "I probably won't see my tower again where I could put him in a safe jar and watch him emerge, but habit is a bitch."

"Yeah," Liam said.

"I'm surprised you were paying attention to what I was doing."

"I always do."

"So I don't escape?" Reynald grinned.

"I dare you to escape." Liam rolled his eyes.

"So far, you've dared me to stab you, kiss you, and escape. In that order, I should add. Not to mention last night when you asked me to kidnap you." Reynald slipped the leaf back into his pocket.

"The last one's my favorite because then I don't have to ever see the king again." Liam sighed. "I don't think I can stomach the sight of him now."

"In my defense, I never imagined you'd listen to a word I said, let alone start to agree with me." Reynald glanced over his shoulder, letting Creed follow the road.

"You're not wearing your mask today." Liam lifted his hand from Reynald's hip to touch his bare cheek.

"Too heavy." Reynald frowned before turning away. "Does your sword and shield ever get too heavy?"

"Yes. When I've been fighting for too long."

Reynald hummed at the statement but didn't verbally reply. Liam glanced to their left and right, but there was only farmland on either side. People combed through the fields with scythes, bundling wheat and hay to stockpile for the long winter ahead.

"What's with the mask anyway?"

"It's for the All Saints' Eve Festival," Reynald muttered.

"Did the ivory have to be a mask? Could you have fashioned something else? The magical plate of doom or a nice music box?"

"The symbolism does matter. I carved the mask in the image of the demon, Darius."

"Right. The demon Saint Margaret fought. He swallowed her whole, and she burst from his belly, unburned."

"He is *many* things. A fox, a boar, a dragon, lord of the stryx and the hunt. I chose the fox symbol because that's my familiar."

"Fair. You're a fox, one of his images is a fox. But you killed *unicorns* in order to carve a mask in the visage of a *demon*, and you're okay with this?"

"Why wouldn't I be?" Reynald asked.

"I'm not religious, but demons being bad is the general rule."

"Didn't you feel that way about witches?"

"Witches are people and demons are demons."

"He's the demon of revenge." Reynald shrugged. "Who else would I choose on my own path of vengeance?"

"There are dozens of fables explaining why this is a bad idea. Demon pacts never end well."

"Fascinating. Tell me more."

"Yes. Yes. I have no right to try to explain the fairy tales I've only read to an actual wizard who could open portals to their realms if he wanted to."

"How do you even know so much about demons? I thought you weren't allowed to read for fun?"

"As a squire, my elders chose my studies. Now I'm lord of the manor. Who's going to pull the books from my hands?" Liam chuckled.

"Fair." Reynald laughed with him.

They rode until Creed needed to drink and rest. The sun dropped to the western horizon as they traveled. The lanterns in the streets were lit by the time they reached Bridge's Crossing. They checked into a three-storied travel lodge with laundry service and the option to have food delivered directly to the rooms. Liam ordered chicken, greens, and candied sweet potatoes. He missed Charity's cooking and felt homesick. Or maybe what he really missed was his old life where everything had been simply "right" and "wrong" instead of the gray bog he found himself drowning in the longer he stayed with Reynald.

"I need a bath," Reynald said.

"Go ahead. I'll catch up." Liam sat crossed-legged on the bed, his plate in his lap.

"You expect me to go alone? Unsupervised?"

"I doubt you'll be harassed. And if someone was foolish enough, you're more powerful than any of the soldiers or hunters here."

"What if *I* cause mischief?"

"I've already arrested you. One crime or seven, the punishment is the same." Liam set his plate aside and unpacked his travel bag to sort his laundry for the overnight laundry service.

"You were more fun when you were easily flustered." Reynald stomped out of the room.

Liam groaned as soon as Reynald left and flung himself face-first against the mattress. He gave himself three luscious minutes to sulk and pity himself before he pushed himself to his feet and finished sorting the laundry. He kept himself busy until Reynald returned, flinging his pearlescent robe into the basket and sitting in a chair in one of the courtesy robes left in their rooms.

"What happens to the things in your pockets when they wash the robe?" Liam asked, too curious to resist.

"They're fine." Reynald waved away the concern. "They're not really there. They're both in the robe and somewhere else entirely."

"Where?"

"The trick of the magic is not to think about it much. Concentrating on objects tends to lock them in place, which is how you find them again." Reynald made a face. "If I can focus enough."

"Is this sort of magic…normal?" Liam glanced at Reynald.

"Normal by what standards?"

"Everyone knows stewards can change form, brew potions, summon the elements. Oracles have soothsaying. Legends tell of powerful wizards summoning demons or making enchanted weapons. Your pockets seem…unique?"

"Is it any different than a cloak of invisibility?" Reynald shrugged. "I can't really compare my powers to others, considering the circumstances."

Liam pinched the bridge of his nose. Even trying to ask a simple question curved back to the inevitable fact of "No one knows the answers because they were erasing everyone who might."

"You're right. Sorry I asked." Liam grabbed the other bathrobe and went downstairs to wash himself.

Liam submerged himself as soon as he was in the hot water. He tended to forget how many aches and pains he had from old battle wounds and a lifetime of rigorous training until he floated in a hot bath and those pains eased enough to bring his attention to them. Liam's fingers traced the wolf bite around his stomach. He'd been riding, the night of the attack, in leathers, but not his mail, so the teeth had sunk into the softness of his middle. He pushed above the bath's surface for air, wringing the water out of his locs.

When he went upstairs, Reynald lounged on the bed with his deck of cards. Liam sat near the fire to finish drying his hair, and Reynald didn't hide how many times his gaze wandered to Liam's chest peeking through the opened bathrobe. Liam ignored the attention, though it made his skin tingle each time he caught Reynald staring.

"You're boring. I'm going to sleep." Reynald tossed the cards next to his mask, which he'd set on the stool near the bed.

Liam waited until his hair was dry before joining him in the room's only bed, but he couldn't sleep. After a few hours of listening to Reynald's steady, sleeping breaths and battling his own constant, whirring thoughts, Liam decided to build up the fire. Once he left the bed, Reynald whimpered, reaching out. Liam placed a pillow in his arms, but he shoved it away and rolled to his other side. After the fire crackled, Liam paced the room. He'd never felt so out of control in his life. Law, duty, honor, these concepts had guided him from day to day, helping him endure the long, lonely nights, but how would he serve Seigfried after Reynald's dying screams scarred the city square? How would Liam ever sleep again without Reynald draped over him?

"Joan—" Reynald twisted in sleep, huge tears rolling down his cheek. His chest wracked with sobs.

"Reynald?" Liam sat on the edge of the bed, shaking his shoulder.

"No!" Reynald jerked away from Liam's touch, startling awake.

Reynald scrambled to the far edge of the bed, pressing his back to the wall and searching the room. Reynald's face contorted in confusion. Gradually, he came around, wiping the tears away from his face. Reynald moaned and curled into a ball, hiding himself from the world.

"Who's Joan?" Liam asked, scooting closer to where Reynald sat on the mattress.

Reynald shook his head no, still coiled into a knot. The bathrobe half slipped off his shoulder when he struggled out from the covers, and his legs jutted on either side of him—a little bony, angular, incredibly fragile-looking.

"Tell me," Liam pleaded.

"I don't…want to talk…about…" Reynald's breathing thinned.

Rounded as he was with the robe skewed, each vertebra in his spine poked from his skin. He trembled, clawing at his hair and coiling tighter into himself. The same wild panic from their night at the fort radiated from Reynald's body. Liam grabbed him and tugged him close, preparing for Reynald to punch and shove away from him, but Reynald dove closer. He crawled into Liam's lap and clawed at his shoulders, as if he physically couldn't get close enough. Liam stroked his hair and crushed their bodies together. When Reynald raised his head, eyes desperate and pleading for them to somehow squeeze tighter together, Liam did the only thing he could: he kissed Reynald. Reynald fisted his hands into Liam's locs and deepened the kiss. Their lips mashed together, taking several rough starts before they relaxed enough to get the pressure right for it to feel like a kiss instead of an attack. Neither broke until they had to pant for air. Tears lined Reynald's eyes.

"Don't cry." Liam shook his head, pressing Reynald's cheek to his shoulder.

"My sister. She was my sister." Reynald did cry, limbs twisted around Liam as he sat in Liam's lap. "She fell in love with one of the guards who watched over the mage quarters and got pregnant. There's maiden's friend in the palace garden, and the women chew the petals to keep from getting pregnant, but she didn't, because she wanted the baby. They decided to run away together, so I went with her."

Liam explored the bite-shaped scars dappling Reynald's body. He shuddered as the dark truth seeped into him.

"Seigfried sent hounds after you?"

"They tore her to shreds. I watched them." Reynald sobbed. "They fought over us like scraps, but I managed to change into my fox form and flee. I made it to the river, flinging myself into the water. It was spring, and the cold from the snow melt sliced into me, but the current was strong enough to whisk me away from the dogs and they lost my trail. I passed out and woke up in my meadow near the ruins of a tower. My Place."

Liam held his breath. His body tensed, but he couldn't hold back the stream of scorching tears slipping down his own face. He swallowed the sobs. He had no right to cry; he'd suffered none of this pain himself. Instead, he held Reynald, continued to stroke his hair, and considered regicide. But no, it wasn't his justice to take any more than they were his tears to shed.

"You don't have to do this. We can still turn around. Backtrack to Birchshire. Find Doctor Euphrosina—"

"No." Reynald lifted his face. "Siegfried murdered my family and now he's trying to murder my forest. I'd rather burn at the stake than run away!"

"*This* isn't the answer!" Liam grabbed the fox mask and held it to Reynald's face. "*This* won't help you."

"I don't expect you to understand." Reynald shook his head.

"Dammit." Liam dropped the mask.

The ivory clattered to the rug beside the bed. Liam grabbed Reynald, and they rocked in each other's arms, their conversation over. Somehow, they fell asleep, mangled together like carriage wreckage. In the morning, Liam's throat stung and salt crusted his eyes. They moved slowly, washing their faces and milling around the room with blankets over their shoulders. Liam retrieved their clothes from the hallway, but neither dressed. Instead, they sat side by side on the bed and stared at the rug. Liam spoke first.

"My mother died in childbirth. My father didn't remarry. He was respectful and admirable, but not affectionate. My servants are obedient and pleasant. My own soldiers tell me jokes and stories about the girls they've wooed. The other knights invite me to celebrations and hunts. I think of them as friends, but not family. I don't think I've had any true family. Not the sort I'd grieve for the way you grieve for your sister. I've never loved someone strongly enough to jeopardize my very soul for them, though I would gladly die for anyone in Citadel. I cannot insult you by claiming to have empathy, but I understand you now."

Reynald laced their fingers together but didn't speak. The fox mask lay near Liam's feet from the night before. The ivory snout sneered at Liam. He shoved it further away with his toes.

"Did you know the baker on Cherry Street is a witch?" Reynald asked.

"No. Of course I didn't." Liam shook his head, ashamed at how little he truly knew.

"He's an acquaintance of the oracle and snuck me into her shrine.

I'm not quite as clever as you think I am. I've been following her design this entire time."

"So, you're letting her move you like a chess piece to assassinate the king because it suits your vengeance." Liam shook his head.

"If I'm her rook, you're her knight. Don't you think?" Reynald asked.

"True. Seigfried sent me to her, and she gave me a map to find you. What do you think her endgame is? To escape in the resulting chaos?"

"I never gave her any real thought. She dangled a carrot in front of me, and I chased after the bait like a hungry mule."

"I suppose prophecy is much easier when you're offering everyone exactly what they want if they follow your plans." Liam's gaze shifted from the floor to Reynald. "Have you ever tried flat-out changing one of her predictions?"

"Does the mule ever veer off the road to search for an apple?"

"But what if we tried? Hypothetically, what's to stop us from going south until we reach the mountains bordering Prophis, and then crossing them to either die in the wilderness or be the first to discover a new kingdom?"

"Besides common sense?"

"I said hypothetically."

"I suppose nothing's stopping you. But I'm still on a quest even if you've given up on yours."

"Okay." Liam stood as if he were going to march barefoot in his robe.

"You're not going anywhere," Reynald said.

"You mocked me for not making my own decisions, and now you're teasing me for trying."

Liam checked outside their door. The laundry basket sat with all Liam's clean clothes and Reynald's shimmering robe. He brought the basket to the bed, folding his extra linens and packing them.

"Would you really?" Reynald laughed.

"I'm sincerely weighing my options." Liam placed Reynald's folded robe in his lap. Reynald rested both of his hands on top of Liam's.

"Don't."

"Don't…go?" Liam flicked his gaze to Reynald's, a twinge of hope crawled across his heart, hope that Reynald might admit he cared.

"Don't make me go to Citadel alone. If another knight finds me, he'll hog-tie me and throw me in the back of a cart."

"You can turn into a fox. You don't need me." Liam pulled his hands away.

Reynald's expression twisted in pain. "I…don't want to be alone. I've been alone for years. Riding with you and Creed is more fun."

"Are you sure you wouldn't rather find the Salt Merchant's Path?" Liam laid his travel clothes aside so he could change after packing.

"I'm sure. I don't care if this is Edeline's game of chess. The point of chess is to take out a king." Reynald lifted the fox mask off the floor and ran his fingers over the carved detail work.

"It's beautiful craftsmanship, even if I hate it." Liam changed into his clothes and laced his boots.

"I'm very good with my hands." Reynald attempted a smile. He covered his face with the ivory. "I've never told anyone what happened before, about Joan."

Liam wasn't sure what to say, so he sat beside Reynald, allowing Reynald to rest his head on Liam's shoulder. They stayed that way, not speaking, but pressed together.

Chapter Twelve

The day was long and silent. Liam started a conversation a few times, but whenever he tried to talk, they'd stumble over their own words until the quiet would stretch between them again. They rode past a thicket too small to have a name on the map, although the locals probably had a nickname for the expanse of pines and bramble. Liam nudged Creed toward the tree cover, veering off the road.

"Where are we going?" Reynald asked.

"Let's hunt."

"You're not even being subtle about stalling anymore." Reynald dropped to the shrubs below.

"I thought you might enjoy a chance to run around—as a fox."

"Really?" Reynald asked.

"Sure."

Reynald turned away. Liam couldn't see his face, but he suspected Reynald was blushing.

"Only if you want to." Liam fidgeted with the pommel of his sword.

"I love being a fox, actually."

"Flush out the game, and I'll take the shot." Liam unpacked a foldable compact crossbow he used for hunting.

"Don't shoot me by mistake." Reynald winked before changing.

The fox dashed through the foliage. Reynald was harder to track without snow leaving obvious prints, but Liam was experienced and found his trail. They wound deeper into the thicket, across a creek, and between two sloping, tree-covered hills. The air was a little chilly in the shade, but Liam had his cloak and Reynald had fur, so neither minded. An hour later, Reynald yipped. Liam waited with the crossbow raised. A deer as big as Creed ran through the trees to where Liam stood. He had at least sixteen points on his antlers. Liam made his shot; the bolt penetrated where the deer's chest and neck met. The deer managed to push through a cluster of trees, but a dark red trail followed him. Liam steadied his breath, giving the deer time to bleed out. He'd never enjoyed the moment of the kill, but the shot had pierced the buck's heart, so he'd at least die quickly.

"Are you all right? You look pale." Reynald stood beside him. The mask was pressed to the top of his head, and his face was flushed from the hunt.

"I'm fine," Liam said.

"I'm surprised you manage to eat meat, as softhearted as you are when it comes to animals." Reynald patted his shoulder.

"I was expected to track, hunt, and process my own game by the time I was eight as part of my training." Liam followed the dark trail into a dense grove of aspen.

"I suppose neither one of us had a choice in who we became. Did we?" Reynald knelt beside the buck and whispered a prayer into his ear.

"Thank you," Liam said.

"I didn't do it for you." Reynald shook his head. His fingers shook as he touched the buck's antlers.

"Did you pray for the unicorns?"

"For what it was worth." Reynald pulled down his mask.

Liam nodded but didn't dwell on the topic. He fetched his hunting knife from his belt to skin the deer. It took the better part of the day to hang the hide to dry and smoke the meat for travel. While Liam worked, Reynald built a fire and stripped a section of the buck's antler for a flute.

"Will you play for me after you finish?" Liam asked.

"Yes." Reynald smiled. "Do you like music?"

"Who doesn't?"

"Knights who write inventory lists when they pack their gear," Reynald teased.

"You know why I'm so fond of animals? Because they don't talk."

"You *hate* when I'm quiet." Reynald snorted.

"I do. You're chatty when you're happy, so…" Liam shrugged.

"I always wanted to speak with you, when I saw you in the castle." Reynald blew away dust from the carved section of horn. "But I wasn't allowed to address anyone."

"That's awful." Liam paused in scraping the deer hide to glance at Reynald.

He raised up a hand and shook his head. "I wasn't trying to needle you. I was thinking how nice it would be if we could have gotten to know each other better before."

"I would have enjoyed talking to you."

"Yeah, you're not so bad."

The conversation eased back and forth. Talking and busy work helped keep Liam's thoughts away from the future he dreaded more with each passing day. Reynald finished his flute, admiring the instrument.

"Is it magical?" Liam asked.

"No. Some things are good without magic. Still want me to play?"

"Of course."

Reynald played until the moon was high enough to shine down on them through the gaps in the canopy. Afterward, they sat near the fire and stared at the stars together until weariness forced them into the tent. Liam stretched his toes, glad to be rid of his boots for a few hours. Reynald slipped beneath the blanket, facing Liam.

"You look thoughtful." Liam traced his fingers along Reynald's cheekbone.

"What are you doing?" Reynald giggled as if the caress tickled.

"You're always wearing that stupid mask, but I like your face."

"Do you?" Reynald held his hand on top of Liam's.

"I do."

"You make it hard for me to hate the rest of the world." Reynald touched Liam's lips.

Reynald's eyes fluttered shut. Their mouths drew close, breath washing over each other's faces. Yet their lips never connected. Instead, their noses brushed along each other's cheeks, around their jaws, along the sinew of their necks. They caressed everywhere but their mouths, too afraid to bridge the gap. Trembling in each other's arms, they gasped against each other's skin.

"Please, Reynald." Liam met his gaze. His heart couldn't maintain a rhythm and skipped several beats.

"I can't." Reynald untangled himself from the blankets.

"Reynald?" Liam reached out his hand.

"I can't breathe. I need fresh air." He fled the tent.

"Don't go," Liam whispered, but he didn't think Reynald heard him.

Liam lay on his back and stared at the firelight playing against the hide of their tent. Music drifted through the air. Clenching his jaw, Liam listened to the flute and the night insects. The melody lulled Liam to sleep, but in the morning, the same as every morning, Reynald was sprawled on top of him. Liam combed his fingers through Reynald's orange hair. Outside, the dawn sun burnished the sky in saturated, vibrant orange, but it was dull compared to Reynald. Liam refused to move. As long as he could, he lay there until Reynald woke, made excuses to use the loo, and ran from the tent a second time.

With plenty of meat, they rode along the smaller cart-paths and avoided the roads and cities, but they eventually had to swing onto the main road to purchase salt and a few other staples. Since they were in town, Liam decided to rent a room and spend a night in a bed. The town was small. The only inn was a combination of inn/tavern and their room stank of cigar smoke. Face wrinkled, Reynald cracked open the window, but the rusted coal stove couldn't keep the room warm enough, and even after they closed the window, the chill lingered.

"We should have saved your money and stayed in the tent." Reynald buried himself beneath the blankets before popping his head up again. "Grab the extras. These are as thin as the soup they served for dinner."

Liam nodded as he unrolled the fur blanket from his gear. He smoothed the extra blanket over Reynald before lying beside him.

"Better?"

"Much." Reynald nodded.

"No music tonight?" Liam smirked.

"Saints, you've been spending too much time with me." Reynald groaned. "You're becoming sardonic."

"Now you know how much I suffer traveling with you."

"Do you suffer?" Reynald traced Liam's knuckles.

"Greatly." Liam's attempt to sound sarcastic failed. The yearning in his voice was raw and exposed.

Again, they moved in as if to kiss but paused and turned away from each other. It wouldn't stop them from waking up in a pile, but they fought their instincts with every fiber of their wills. Yet, when Liam did sleep, he dreamed. In his dreams, he held Reynald in his arms without reservation, and by all the saints, Reynald's mouth was warm as they kissed and his cock was hard and thick in Liam's hand.

Liam groaned. He didn't want the dream to end, but the feel of a buck against him caused him to jerk awake. In his sleep, he'd flung a leg around Reynald's side and twisted his arms around him until they were chest to chest. Liam tried to untangle himself, but Reynald hooked his arms around Liam's neck.

"It's okay. You can." Reynald nudged his tented cock between Liam's legs.

"I-I was dreaming," Liam stuttered.

"Yeah? Show me what you were doing to me in your dream." Reynald's voice was rough.

"We really shouldn't."

"Maybe not, but I can't stand it anymore." Reynald dragged his lips along the curve of Liam's ear. "Please, please, please, Liam. Touch me."

The stove only cast the faintest hint of red light into the room. They were little more than silhouettes beneath the covers, but Liam could see Reynald's mixed brown and blue eyes blown out with lust. He was fully awake, lips parted as he added a few more *pleases*. Succumbing to his invitation, Liam groped beneath Reynald's robes until his hand found warm, smooth skin. Liam moaned as he touched Reynald, his hand meandering higher until Reynald's shaft was secure in his grip.

"Saints," Reynald swore. "Liam."

"Reynald," Liam spoke Reynald's name against his lips as he pumped his fist up and down.

Reynald's breathing filled the room, raspy and frantic. Liam's bicep bulged as he stroked Reynald. He nudged his own hips forward. Precum leaked into his underclothes, but he couldn't stop as Reynald bucked into his clenched hand.

"Is this good?" Liam whispered.

"*Mmm.*" Reynald grunted.

"I love how thick you are in my hand."

"*Ngh*! Liam…Liam…Liam…Liam!"

Reynald bit Liam's neck as he came. Liam growled, encouraged by the flash of mild pain. Reynald rode out his orgasm before sinking boneless in Liam's grip.

"I can't think when I'm around you," Reynald moaned. "Dammit, Liam, why do you have to be so sincere?"

"It's my nature," he panted, still excited and hard as steel.

"You're maddening." Reynald licked his way into Liam's mouth.

Liam tilted his head to give Reynald a proper angle. His other hand slipped beneath Reynald's robe, and he squeezed Reynald's ass with both palms. Reynald grunted, breaking their kiss so he could work his way lower. He tugged down Liam's wool pants, freeing Liam's cock. Liam whimpered, thrusting his hips high when Reynald gripped his base.

He is a fox, cunning and reckless, but he will be your fox.

Liam thanked all fourteen saints as the flat of Reynald's tongue dragged up Liam's shaft. He licked Liam's tip clean of precum before sealing his lips just beneath the hood of his cock and sliding down to the base. The sensation was a lightning bolt striking Liam's spine. He arched and wailed, unconcerned about noise in their shabby rented room.

Reynald's tongue worked along Liam's cock. He toyed with him for a minute before plunging deep and bobbing his head. Liam clawed at the mattress. Razor-sharp bliss skinned Liam alive, revealing all his nerves and laying them bare for Reynald to play with as he saw fit. As the pleasure swelled, tears lined Liam's eyes, and he came with a roar. Reynald swallowed before throwing the blankets away and popping up for air.

"That was warmer than I thought it'd be." He held his hand over his mouth.

"I'm sorry." Liam's face couldn't grow hotter.

"It wasn't bad, just surprising." Reynald laughed, giddy.

Liam joined him. They lay in each other's arms, giggling and exchanging quick kisses along each other's shoulders. The afterglow wrapped around Liam like a bath, and as he fell asleep, he was excited to exist.

But in the morning, he lay in an empty bed. Liam blinked, confused, hands searching for a stray limb or Reynald's familiar mess of orange hair, but Reynald wasn't beside him. Searching the room, he saw Reynald sitting on a stool near the stove, fully dressed—including his mask.

"Do you have to wear the mask today?" Liam rolled onto his side so he could admire Reynald as he made a few last, decorative, flourishes to the flute.

"Yes. I do."

"But I really like to look at your face." Liam's smile was warm.

His brain was still sleepy and a little fuzzy from the happiness the night before had brought. The relief coursing through him was overwhelming. They didn't have to pretend anymore. No more hiding behind the roles of witch and knight; they could be two people. They could kiss and whisper little affectionate observations into each other's ears and hold each other freely and run away from everything.

"I think it's best if we don't get sentimental over this." Reynald spoke with a cool, formal tone.

The force of the statement wasn't physical, but Liam dropped onto his back as if shoved away. He laid his arm over his eyes, not wanting to see the room or Reynald.

"Do you regret what happened?" Liam asked once he found his voice at the bottom of his crushed chest.

"No, but we shouldn't make more of it than necessary."

"You're a coward." Liam screwed his eyes shut, blocking out the entire world.

"Liam, I enjoy your company, but—"

"But you don't care about anything except killing Seigfried." Liam jerked from the bed and suited himself in his armor, surcoat, and cloak. He kept focused on small goals. No feelings. No thoughts. Only safe, miniscule tasks.

"Don't make this more painful than it has to be." Reynald kept his eyes glued to the floor.

"Trust me, I can't hurt more than I already do. Let's go. We can skip breakfast. There's plenty of venison left for us to eat while we ride. If this is how it's going to be, I'd rather get our journey over with."

"You'll have your wish in ten days or so if you stop stalling," Reynald said.

"Sorry for trying to keep you in the world for a little longer." Liam stormed out of the room.

He spent a few extra minutes checking all the straps and buckles on Creed's saddle and bags. It didn't take long for Reynald to meet him in the stable. Liam mounted first, so he could hold the reins this time while Reynald sat behind *him*. Liam needed to watch the scenery, look ahead, do anything but stare at Reynald.

They went back to silent travel, and wasn't that always the case? They'd slip, talk, laugh, grow closer, but in the end, the rift between them was too wide. No matter how far Liam reached out his hand, Reynald would never clasp his in return.

Evenings were the worst. They'd sit near the fire, eating venison, mushrooms, and wild greens, but after their meal, Reynald would play his flute to avoid conversation. The songs were melancholy and full of yearning, or perhaps Liam was projecting his own emotions onto the notes. He'd crawl into the tent and pretend to sleep long before Reynald turned in. He kept his shield strapped to his back so he couldn't roll in the night in search of Reynald. The irony of using a physical shield as an emotional one didn't go unnoticed, but joking about it would only make him and Reynald laugh and share another moment. Liam's heart would burst if they laughed, for there would eventually be a pause, and they'd gaze into each other's eyes, and Liam would wish Reynald would carry through on his earlier threat and fucking blind him permanently.

Three days wasn't long for Liam to travel without a break. As a knight, he'd led men through marches lasting weeks on end, but he could see it wore Reynald down. His iridescent, magical robes never ripped or stained, but his hair was tangled, and he constantly rubbed his legs and shoulders from riding stiffness. Upset as he was, Liam wasn't angry with

Reynald—if anything, he was angry on Reynald's behalf—so he decided to check his map and navigate toward a city, though all the larger ones were out of their way.

"Where are we going?" Reynald asked once they'd veered off course enough for him to notice.

"St. George. The city should have travel lodges far nicer than the hovel we stayed in last time we rented a room."

"I thought you were done stalling?"

"I thought you'd enjoy a bath."

"Oh? For me?" Reynald couldn't douse the warmth or humor in his voice. "Are you sure you're simply not longing to see me naked again?"

"I'll rent a room with two beds. We can bathe in shifts." Liam stared at the birch trees going gold from autumn.

"You're still angry with me."

"I was never angry. Not at you."

"You're acting like you're angry."

"I'm upset because I don't want you to die."

"But I still have the phoenix feather."

"What?" Liam blinked, so much had happened. He'd forgotten about the feather.

"I lied when I told you it was in my tower. Seigfried doesn't know about my pockets, so as long as he executes me in my robe, I should be able to survive—one way or another."

"You could have told *me* you weren't going to die."

"I didn't think you cared." Reynald laughed. "Not at first. Neither of us trusted each other until… I'm not even sure when I started trusting you. It was an accident."

"We can't really go too long without speaking to each other, can we?" Liam sighed.

"It's a long journey. It's easier when you share it with someone." Reynald pressed his face against Liam's shoulder, the ivory snout jabbing Liam's shoulder blade.

"Then I yield. Talk to me." Liam pressed into Reynald's weight.

"How do you know I have anything to say?"

"Make something up."

"Well, you know if musseri eat too many berries, they turn pink, right?"

"Yeah." Liam smiled. "I've heard the washwoman whisper stories about pink musseri stealing their bloomers."

"So *that's* why my bloomers disappear," Reynald gasped.

"Tell me another story."

"No. You tell me one instead."

They spent the afternoon trying to outdo each other with spectacular tales. Liam invented a dragon who demanded sweet rolls instead of virgins. Reynald shared some of the actual stories he'd read about sorcerers traveling the other worlds.

"What about the saints?" Liam asked. "Were they sorcerers? The church insists their acts are *miracles*, not magic, but I've always wondered if the fourteen helpers were simply powerful wizards."

"Seigfried has a good deal of old books where the historians agree with you, but it would be heresy to share their opinions, so they're hidden."

"I really want to raid this secret library you keep talking about."

"We covet what we cannot have." Reynald gripped Liam's waist a little more tightly.

He touched Reynald's fingers with his own. Neither of them wore Liam's gloves because they were far enough south not to need them. Although, Liam would plunge naked into another blizzard if it meant he could spend the winter in a cabin with Reynald instead of being a week out from the capital.

St. George was almost as sprawling and populated as the Citadel. The line into the gates was longer than expected. Liam and Reynald dismounted to stretch their legs while they stood in a growing line of people and merchants trying to get into the city. The longer they waited, the more agitated Reynald became. He tapped his toes, began hopping from one foot to the other like a child, and finally plopped down into the grass to pluck the blades and let them rain from his fingers.

"Stand up. You're embarrassing to wait in line with," Liam hissed.

"This is dull. Why do you think it's taking so long?" Reynald whispered. "Traffic into the city is never this jammed."

Liam shook his head. The people ahead and behind them also complained about the long wait, but nobody explained what was going on. As they drew close to the entrance, they realized a team of city patrol were doing full searches of every single wagon and bag before they allowed people through the gates.

"I'm going to lose my mind if I stand in this line any longer." Reynald dropped his hands to his sides. "Let's just go. No bath is worth this."

"We're close. Why don't you pull some more grass," Liam teased.

"Why don't you go fuck yourself," Reynald muttered as he pulled three small balls from his pockets and juggled.

"Are you serious?" Liam repressed a laugh.

"What?" Reynald added a fourth ball from his sleeve mid-juggle.

"Sir Bord."

One of the guards noticed Liam and bowed. He rushed toward them. Since St. George was a proper metropolis instead of a hamlet or trading town, it made sense that the guards recognized the sigil on his surcoat and the notorious shield strapped to his back. It made Liam miss traveling the countryside. The last thing he wanted was to be *recognized*. He was already stretching the rules with how much he stalled, and if reports reached the king…

"Sir, I didn't know you were in line. We'll have to check your saddle bags, but come, and we'll bring you to the front."

"Thank you, but no need." Liam raised a hand to stop the guard from taking Creed's reins. "I'll wait for my turn."

"Sir, are you sure?" he asked.

"Yes. There's no need for special treatment."

Reynald kicked Liam in the shin. The action was subtle, hidden below his flowing robe as he pretended to lose a ball from his juggling game. Liam confiscated the ball as punishment before turning back to the guard.

"May I ask why you're searching everyone?" Liam asked.

"Goblins have been attacking from the southwest. We've also had a pixie problem, and messuri are starting to infest the slums."

"I see." A lump formed in Liam's throat. He swallowed. "Thank you. I won't keep you any longer"

"Sir." The guard bowed. Liam nodded and allowed the guard to go back to searching the wagon three spots ahead of them.

"Who hates pixies? They're adorable. What's wrong with these people?" Reynald rested a hand on his hip. "Also, what's wrong with you? We could have gone in right away, and you're standing out here like a fool."

"A few pixies, sure, but I imagine a swarm would be a little terrifying. Also, it's not right to use my status when all these people need to sell their wares for their livelihood, and we're here for a hot bath. Waiting a few minutes won't kill you."

"Still…" Reynald paused. "Before we rent a room, I better swing by a physician's office and share my remedy for the blister fever we treated in Birchshire."

Liam nodded, agreeing with the idea. As soon as they passed through the gates, their first stop in the city was the nearest physician's where travelers would most likely go. There was already a small girl at the physician's office unconscious with fever. Reynald shared his process for brewing his medicine. One benefit of the city was that the doctor already had all the ingredients in storage. After they treated the girl, the doctor sent a pigeon to a few of the other doctors and the local churches. Between the two-hour wait to get into the city, and the time they spent at the physician's, they didn't get to a travel lodge until sunset.

The light struck the buildings at a sharp slant. The travel lodge itself, like many other larger buildings in St. George, was cathedral style. The quarries near the town made quality stone at reasonable prices, and gargoyles watched them as they marched toward the establishment. Liam had loved visiting St. George when he was a squire serving beneath his father. The buildings and sculptures and endless spires always made Liam feel like a character in a fairy tale. The quality of the lodge was worth the wait once they managed to check in. There were live performances on a proper stage instead of a platform in the corner. They watched dancers and jugglers and a play where the hero tricked the fates by promising his soul to the fay, the spirits, and a demon all at once.

"I should take notes," Reynald whispered into Liam's ear at the end of the play.

Liam laughed without worrying about possible literal meanings. Three pints of raspberry lambic had him relaxed and easy going, and he didn't want to spoil the calm in his mind. Their baths were giant outside pools filled from natural hot springs. Reynald pouted at the open setup, but Liam was relieved for an excuse not to be able to touch Reynald's naked skin, despite how badly he craved to drag his fingers over every curve. They had to stop. They absolutely had to stop. If they were caught, Liam would be burned right beside Reynald, and he didn't have a phoenix feather to bring himself back. Holding his breath, Liam dunked himself below the water, drowning his own thoughts.

In their suite, a fire was already lit in the large hearth. Vents carried the heat from the fire to all corners of the room. The floor was carpeted instead of wood, and a writing desk rested in one corner with a card table in the other. The beds were simple, but clean, and smelled of dried mint, and outside was filled with the bustle of happy travelers enjoying themselves. Liam stared at the people walking from one shop to the next. He envied their simple lives.

"I can't believe you really rented a room with two beds." Reynald shook his head as he tossed his travel bag onto the first of the two beds.

"If we sleep in one bed, I will kiss you," Liam closed his eyes while he confessed.

"Perish the thought." Reynald stretched on top of the quilt, but kept his mask on.

"If I kiss you even once more, I will not let you step foot into Citadel. I already have half a mind to tie you in a knot with the unicorn rope, drag you back to Doctor Euphrosina, and force you to take the Salt Path."

"Only half a mind, eh?" Reynald's voice was jovial, but there was something restrained to it.

"You're horrible. Do you know that?" Liam dropped to his own bed, removing his gear one item at a time. "I'm aware if I dragged you away, you'd never forgive me."

"I have to do this." Reynald stared at the ceiling.

"Are you going to sleep in the dreadful thing?" Liam asked, referring to the mask.

"Come rip it from my face, if you can," Reynald challenged him.

Teasing, always teasing, that's all the fox knew how to do. But his flirting would never have any true substance behind it—any love—he only wanted Liam as a distraction. Liam shouldn't care; Liam shouldn't want to so desperately save Reynald.

But he did.

"Good night." Liam threw the quilt over his head.

Reynald was goading him into his bed, and nothing would have made Liam happier than playing the knave and "falling" for Reynald's trap, but he was already too in love. If Reynald asked, Liam *would* throw away title and shield and privilege and leave with him. Despite the difficulty of the journey, Liam had lived better—happier—for the last month than for his entire life previously. He wanted to wake up with Reynald heaped on top of his chest each morning for the rest of his life, but Reynald refused to forsake his vengeance. There wasn't much Liam could do, except pray to the saints that afterward, they were both alive and perhaps could try again.

Chapter Thirteen

A scream woke Liam. The red glow from the coals in the hearth transformed their high-priced room into an infernal hellscape. Liam started when he glanced at Reynald's bed. The shadows played on the ivory and made Liam swear it was alive, stealing Reynald's body as its own. Liam shook his head and fisted his eyes to wake himself and dispel the trick of the light.

With a sharp inhale of breath, Reynald woke and jerked to a crouch on top of his bed. His back pressed into the corner of the wall, and his eyes behind the mask were rounded with panic. Liam exhaled and moved in controlled, deliberate inches. Reynald held his carving knife in his hand. His knuckles were white as old skulls on a forgotten battlefield. Grabbing Reynald's flute, Liam eased closer, displayed the instrument like a gift, and knelt near the bed.

"Reynald," Liam said in a calm, reassuring voice.

"I heard dogs," Reynald snapped.

"It's a large city with a pixie infestation. It was somebody's pet waking half the neighborhood. Here." Liam offered the flute to Reynald.

Reynald frowned at the instrument. Liam rose and sat on the edge of the bed, still holding the flute with one hand while sliding his other across the rumpled sheets, but Reynald caught on when he saw Liam reaching for his carving knife.

"Don't." Reynald pressed the point of the blade beneath Liam's chin.

"Nothing's going to hurt you in here," Liam promised.

"I *heard* dogs," Reynald snarled, and Liam imagined the mask curling back its lip and baring its teeth.

"You did." Liam reached out and pushed the mask over Reynald's head.

"What are you doing?" Reynald's hands shook.

"Looking at your face."

"I'll kill you." Reynald readjusted the blade below Liam's jaw in order to steady his grip.

"No. You won't." Liam set the flute near Reynald and kept both his hands in view.

"Why won't I?"

"Because we're friends."

"Friends." Reynald lowered the knife, but his tone was bitter. "They might hang you for saying that."

"We're friends," Liam repeated.

And I've fallen in love with you.

He cupped Reynald's face with both palms and reassured him with tender brushes of his hands. Reynald's chest heaved as he fought for breath, but Liam continued to whisper soothing phrases, comb his hair, and dab the sweat from Reynald's brow with his linen undershirt. The knife finally fell from Reynald's hand, and he clutched the flute to his chest instead. Liam set the knife on the nightstand away from them.

"Good…you did good," Liam whispered and caressed Reynald's face.

"My sister taught me to play." Reynald stroked the flute like it was a doll.

"She must have been wonderful," Liam said.

"She was the only family I'd ever known. I was a toddler when they burned our parents and kidnapped us." Reynald shook his head. "I don't remember my mother's face, just Joan's."

"Would she want you to waste your life on vengeance?" Liam murmured.

"Honestly?" Reynald laughed. "She'd encourage me. She was venomous against the monarchy. She wanted rebellion."

"Oh." Liam hid his grin behind his hand. "So much for that argument, then. I'm not especially surprised. Any sister of yours would be fiery, wouldn't she?"

"Yeah." Reynald chuckled, his breathing returning to normal.

"Are you cold? I could add wood to—"

"Don't leave." Reynald clutched Liam's arms and tugged their bodies together.

"Okay," Liam sighed.

Pulling the covers over their legs, Liam lay in the bed. Reynald clung to him, trembling. Liam rubbed small circles into Reynald's back to soothe him. He kissed Reynald's temple, sucked in the scent of the oils he'd bathed with, and relaxed despite all his anxiety about the upcoming days. Reynald's fingers curled into Liam's shirt.

"I'm sorry." He hid his face against Liam's body.

"There's nothing to be sorry for." Liam shook his head.

"I'm making this more difficult than it has to be."

"I'm not afraid of a challenge." Liam smoothed his fingertips across Reynald's forehead, as if his touch could erase the worry causing the wrinkles in his skin.

"You must relish a challenge indeed, to befriend someone as difficult as me."

"Happily, for you." Liam couldn't form the words he wanted to say. The real reason he'd *happily* endure Reynald's fickleness.

"We should rest." Reynald blew the air from his lungs, sinking closer against Liam.

They allowed silence to wash over them, but it was the comfortable, familiar sort of silence true friends shared. Liam buried his face in Reynald's hair, dozing, but he couldn't fully sleep because he was enjoying the comfort of the moment too much to let his mind slip into unconsciousness. However, long before dawn broke, the echo of dogs barking in the distance drifted to their hotel room close enough for Liam to hear them as well.

"Bastards." Reynald clenched his teeth. "I knew I heard dogs.

Their barking must have filtered into my dreams and given me night-mares."

"That's…a lot of dogs." Liam peeled away from Reynald and opened the window shutters to investigate.

Leaning into the night air, Liam scanned the cityscape. More dogs were joining into the cacophony. Several low horns called out in warning, and Liam tensed. He stared in the direction of the noise and saw a red glow simmering near the gate a moment before the haunting, piercing sound of the church bells rang into the night sky.

"What's going on?" Reynald grabbed his boots. "Who's attacking the city?"

"I can't tell, but there's fire at the northwestern end of town." Liam rushed into his full gear. "Dammit. We have to try and help."

"Come on." Reynald held the door open.

They bolted to the stables and mounted Creed without bothering to saddle him. Creed's hooves clapped against the road as they rode north. At first the streets were empty, easy to navigate, but as the flames rose in the sky and smoke filled the air, they passed citizens evacuating toward the church. Liam slowed Creed down to a safe trot. He tied him to a post far enough away from the flames to keep him safe. Reynald sprinted ahead, and Liam chased him. The noises tore at his skull: the dogs, screams, bells, whip-cracking flames, shouting guards, and roars. They reached a tower where the city patrol divided into groups of men grabbing pails to fight the fire, and men with arrows nocked on their strings. The wall was as chaotic as the rest of the city.

"We're here to assist!" Liam shouted.

"Sir Bord? Thank the Holy Helpers, a knight."

Liam recognized the man. Shamus McCreedy, a captain who'd received medals during the last war. They'd never fought together, but they had shared beer and bread at the palace once or twice.

"McCreedy." Liam nodded. "What's attacking?"

"Blasted wyverns. Ever since His Majesty opened the mills to the south and the mines in the north, we've had all sorts of beasties at our walls. I heard you were able to stop similar attacks in Citadel."

"Let us through. We'll fight them." Liam strapped his shield to his arm.

"Both of you?" McCreedy paused. Despite the flames licking around the edge of the city, it was the sight of Reynald that drained the color from his face.

"Yes," Liam said without hesitation.

"Sir Bord, that is a witch with you."

"He's a poacher being brought to trial. Let him get a good deed in before he burns." Liam waved off Reynald's spell craft as if he'd been caught stealing a flower from a noble lady's garden instead of killing the king's unicorns. As if his crimes could somehow be overlooked, regardless of knowing better.

"Sir Bord, if the king discovered a witch guarded St. George, my entire regimen would be disbanded and I'd be hanged. My men will escort the witch to a holding cell while you fight, and—"

"Of course." Reynald tossed his head up, laughing bitterly. "Wyverns are killing your men out there, but I'm the fucking dangerous one."

"Sir Bord. You know the law." McCreedy's jaw tightened.

"I take full responsibility for him. You can write an official report stating your objections." Liam clapped a hand on McCreedy's shoulder as if they were true war chums. "Say I pulled rank and didn't give you a choice."

"Seigfried would stick your head on a pike." Reynald crossed his arms over his chest and leaned against the nearest pillar. "Go. I'll stay here."

"These are *wyverns*." Liam gritted his teeth. "I can't kill an entire clutch by myself, Reynald—I need you."

Reynald stared at Liam. Even with the mask, he looked shocked. Liam locked his gaze with Reynald's. Stryx had a weak point. Ogres could be decapitated the same as any man. Dire wolves and giant spiders were meat and blood. Wyverns were scale and fire. Liam had his shield; however, taking down one or two would take all his strength, but he knew…he knew Reynald was stronger than him…stronger than all the knights. He knew Reynald could be the savior of St. George if they gave him the chance.

Would Seigfried execute him for that? The king used witches all the time for his personal entertainment. Liam thought it worth the gamble. Who cared as long as the city was saved? Liam would almost certainly die fighting alone anyway, so he might as well help Reynald stop the attack.

Fire exploded from the top of the city wall parapets. Two bodies were flung to the ground, bones broken on impact, but they screamed as flames crackled their skin. Several of the bucket holders doused them, and a field nurse rushed to check their vitals, but their screams died as they did. McCreedy shoved Liam toward the guard's passage near the city gate.

"Go! Go! Damn the paperwork! We'll sort it later, yeah?"

"Thank you." Liam gave McCreedy a final nod before he grabbed Reynald's hand and rushed forward.

Liam and Reynald raced shoulder to shoulder across the boardwalk and out of the city. All the Johnson grass and yarrow growing around the walls smoldered. Three wyverns were on the ground, tearing into charred corpses. Almost a dozen more circled in the sky, swooping to snap at the archers trying, and failing, to plunge arrows through the wyvern's breasts.

"Liam, stand back." Reynald stepped between Liam and the closest two wyverns.

"But—"

"You wanted my help." Reynald gave Liam a quick glance. "So trust me."

"I do." Liam shuffled backward, shield and sword ready if Reynald needed assistance.

White plasma crackled around Reynald's hands. The taste of ozone filled Liam's mouth and the fine hairs on the nape of his neck bristled. The lightning spread from Reynald's fingers like webs, clinging tendrils searching for the ground, but the main bolt accelerated forward and pierced the first wyvern through the heart before angling toward the second, skewering him as well. Only a small, singed entry wound marred the beautiful, iridescent scales before both creatures dropped to the earth. Reynald muttered a quick prayer before dashing to the next wyvern and shooting another arc of lighting. Liam stood and gaped. Reynald had sent gorgeous, magenta fire at him during their first battle, but it'd been almost laughable to block with his shield, but the scales armoring the wyverns did nothing against the plasma Reynald shot into their hearts.

Liam had known Reynald was more powerful than all of them, and yet, he'd grossly underestimated the sorcerer's power.

Reynald's hair whipped behind him like more flame. His robes flashed with pearlescent color as the wyvern-fire played with the magical cloth. A stabbing truth cut into Liam's mind—Reynald could have killed the dragon when Liam first captured him, and Reynald could have slaughtered everyone in the palace. He had *chosen* not to. Whatever spell he was arranging for his vengeance, the unicorns had been the sacrificial lambs to spare the knights, guards, and servants.

One of the airborne wyverns landed in front of Liam and separated him from Reynald. The firelight rippled across the wyvern's sleek emerald hide, and he stepped forward, snapping his jaws. A burst of red and orange exploded in Liam's vision. He raised his shield to deflect the fire, but the force propelled him back several inches. Liam shifted his gaze, searching for Reynald, but the wyvern lunged forward. Rolling to the side, Liam flipped to his feet and drove his sword down. Liam aimed for the wyvern's neck, but the creature swerved, and Liam's blade sunk into the grass.

Arrows scattered around them as archers attempted to provide cover. Liam freed his blade and dodged a stray shot. A dozen arrowheads managed to plunge into the wyvern, but they might as well have been porcupine quills in the muzzle of a dog. The pain infuriated the creature, and he cracked his tail like a whip. Liam jumped, tumbling farther away from where he'd last seen Reynald stand. Liam didn't have a chance to look anywhere but directly in front of him so he couldn't tell if Reynald was all right or not. Liam blocked another blast of fire before retreating away from the scorched grass around him and regaining his footing. Sweat dripped from Liam's chin. The shield against his arm was warm. He circled around the beast and thrust. The wyvern deflected with his tail and faced Liam, jaws snapping. Liam danced backward. The wyvern reached for Liam's leg, and he plunged the sword down, this time piercing the wyvern's neck. The creature jerked. Screaming, Liam hacked through the neck over and over, until the beast was dead in the grass and steam rose off Liam's sleeves from the wyvern's blood.

Liam gasped, exhausted from slaying a single wyvern. Sweat drenched his undershirt and rolled down his neck. The steaming blood on his clothes wasn't cooling, and the extra heat made it hard to control his breathing. Another beast dove from the sky. Liam's cloak and shield saved him from the flames, but the horned male was clever and stayed in the air, so Liam couldn't counter his attacks. The wyvern swept past again, but before he could spit flames, a bolt of white ripped through his chest, and he dropped—deadweight.

Half a thanks left Liam's mouth, but another horned male was charging from behind. Liam spun, blocked, parried. His sword glanced off the hard scales. He ignored his worry about chipping the blade and caught the wyvern beneath the throat where the scales were less tightly packed so they could expand when the creatures inhaled to prepare a blast. Blood fanned outward from the wound. Liam hissed as the scalding blood splattered across his face. After smearing the heat off his face, he advanced, cutting the creature again, refusing to stop his assault until the wyvern lay collapsed at his feet.

Liam scanned the battlefield for his next target. One more, he needed to kill at least one more while he was still standing. Three glided in his direction, but he could barely raise his sword before they dropped like birds as lighting skewered them. Liam startled, distracted by how Reynald controlled the battlefield. With a skyward scream, Reynald forked lighting from his fingers and then, clenching his hand into a fist, managed to curve the arcs to hone in on their moving targets.

All the while, Liam could only stand there and gasp for breath because killing two had worn him down.

"Liam!" Reynald screamed and sprinted toward him with an outstretched hand.

There was something slow and final about the way time flowed around the fight. Liam's head swam, the noises around him were too much, the blood on his skin still burned. Liam wanted to drop his sword—open his arms and embrace Reynald. He wanted to whisper that Reynald was the strongest person he'd ever seen, but horror contorted Reynald's face as he ran. Liam turned to look behind him to see what was wrong and two sets of jaws snapped at him. One clamped onto his calf, puncturing the boot leather like paper. The other caught his throat. Bright red and then deep black overwhelmed Liam's vision. He was choking, drowning in hot liquid that flowed from his lips even as it filled his lungs. Before he could comprehend what had happened, the two wyverns collapsed dead on the ground. Liam started to fall, but Reynald caught him and cradled Liam in his arms.

Reynald's screams were too far away, so was his touch when he slammed Liam on the ground. Reynald pulled a hollow, narrow tube from one of his endless pockets and stabbed Liam with the end. Liam struggled as the cylinder burned his throat, but afterward, he could somewhat breathe through the tube. His vision continued to fade, however, even as Reynald screamed again and stitched the gashes puncturing Liam's neck.

"I should let you die, fool. I should let you die." Tears ran down Reynald's face.

The worst part before Liam blacked out, the most chilling part, was how at peace he was. The night sky above them was salted with endless stars, the dew on the grass chilled his scorched skin, and the burning city beside them washed warm colors over the rest of the landscape. Liam moved his mouth, shaping *I love yous* with his dying breath, but for all the noise assaulting them, Liam couldn't make a sound, though he tried until unconsciousness dragged him away.

He awoke in their room. A dozen needles pierced his throat and leg. He tried to groan, but only a squeak left his mouth.

"Shh." Reynald pressed a finger to his lips. "You absolutely cannot speak. I had to use all my tricks to keep you alive, but even magic has limits. You need some time to heal."

Liam opened his mouth, but Reynald clamped his entire hand over his lips.

"What did I just tell you? Do you want to tear your stitches?"

Shaking, Liam reached his hand high and held Reynald's face.

Reynald was ghastly pale, with deep-purple bruises beneath his eyes, and the white surrounding his blue iris was red from all the blood vessels rupturing.

"Yeah, I look half dead." Reynald dug the heel of his palm into his unbloody eye. "I'm actually shit at controlling the elements. The lightning spell is for emergencies…and healing you took more than some herbs and incantations."

Reynald gave a half-crazed laugh but whimpered and held his side. He moved stiffly as he dug through the nightstand drawer between their beds and displayed his fox mask. A hairline fracture zigzagged across the mask's nose.

"You righteous bastard. Look at what you made me do. Five perfect lives sacrificed for this magical relic and I cracked it like a porcelain cup because I couldn't watch you bleed out in the mud."

Liam cupped Reynald's face again and frowned.

"Oh, don't look sad. I didn't say I regretted my decision." Reynald moved Liam's hands so he could store the mask and fetch a mug of fairly warm broth. "You're probably happy it's damaged. You never really liked it, right? Here, drink this. The salt will help you heal."

Reynald propped Liam up with three pillows and kept the drink steady as Liam sipped from the cup. Liam wanted to thank him, but he couldn't say anything. Bandages hugged his neck, but at least the tube Reynald had wedged into his throat so he could breathe no longer stuck out from him. He pulled air in and out from his nose, savoring the feeling of his lungs expanding and contracting, although a metallic taste clung to his mouth no matter how much chicken stock he swallowed. The salt stung him from the inside out, but in a satisfying way, like scratching an itch.

"We're stuck here for a few days while we recover." Reynald set the cup aside. "The captain of the city watch decided not to mention that I helped in the battle, and the innkeep isn't going to charge us for the room or services. We're both local heroes."

Liam tapped Reynald's sternum. *He. He was a hero.*

"Listen, an entire armed guard couldn't even take out one wyvern, but you managed two on your own. And I cheated. Believe me, I cheated, and I'm paying for it." Reynald held his side again.

Liam touched Reynald's hand and raised an eyebrow to question him.

"I broke my ribs playing battle wizard. I told you, lightning spells are for emergencies. I'm lucky I only ruptured the vessels in my eye, had I torn the veins in my heart I wouldn't be here—don't you dare move!"

Reynald held Liam in place when he tried to jerk upright.

"I know I was reckless, but they were setting the city on fire, and you know I take personal offense to people burning alive." Reynald tried to scoff, but it made him wince again. "Anyway, between stopping the 'monsters' and curing the fever starting to creep into the slums, the people of St. George are head over heels for us."

Liam flushed as a vague memory of him trying to confess his love with his last breath returned to him. He was grateful the wyvern had bitten his throat to keep him from dying as a fool.

"I had no idea Seigfried is mining the mountains as well as gathering the lumber from the Balbraid Thicket." Reynald fidgeted with the empty cup beside them. "I wonder how many attacks and outbreaks it will take before the people are ready to revolt?"

The greater question was why Seigfried suddenly needed to expand his treasury. Like many royals, he had expensive tastes, loved balls, and exported luxuries, and his forbidden books and magical artifacts must have cost their own fortunes, but the sort of money he was gathering now could cobble every road in Phrophis while funding parties every hour with plenty left over. It left a rock in the pit of Liam's stomach, but he was in too much pain to dwell on the problem.

"At least me nursing you evens us for you nursing me after my fever, right?" Reynald grinned.

Liam smiled and nodded.

"You better rest." Reynald kissed the corner of Liam's mouth.

Liam's eyes widened in surprise at the affectionate gesture. His expression screamed for more, but Reynald eased himself to standing and walked toward his own bed. Liam patted the mattress beside him, gesturing for Reynald to lie in his bed instead.

"Should we? Beat up as we are?"

Liam shrugged and splayed out his hands. Reynald did have a bad habit of climbing all over Liam when he slept, but it was worth the risk to be close together. Almost dying had banished all of Liam's worries about the near future. He was alive at the moment and wanted Reynald next to him. Because what was life for if not holding Reynald close?

Chapter Fourteen

Even with doctors visiting and offering their expertise and the best healing herbs available, Reynald and Liam couldn't do much the first week except sleep. When Liam was finally able to try his voice, the cords inside his throat felt as if the wyvern were breathing fire down his gullet. Reynald coached him through retraining his voice with several daily conversations, and the occasional argument. Each day, Liam could speak a little longer before tiring. The scars remained, angry and pink on his flesh, even after Reynald removed the bandages. Liam admired the bite around his neck. He never minded scars—they were an honor to a knight. Although, he and Reynald were quickly becoming a matching set, the way the scars scattered over their bodies.

A knock reverberated in the room. Since the wyvern attack, they kept finding little gifts at their door, pouches of pink or lavender salts, interesting rocks, little dolls twisted from twigs. There was never any sign of *who* left the gifts because the city patrols were supposed to report such things, but that didn't stop people from sneaking to their door in the middle of the night and thanking Reynald in the only small way they knew how. Reynald kept everything, storing them in his infinite pockets. A sheepish grin spread across his face when he heard the knock.

"You're not used to this, are you? The gifts." Liam pushed through the pain in his throat to ask the question.

"Well, I didn't get many excuses to leave my tower. I was afraid of being captured and dragged back to the palace, especially when I was younger."

"Well, let's see what's waiting for you this time." Liam expected another such gift when he opened the door, but one of the physicians stood at the door, surprising Liam.

The doctor, Albert, had streaks of gray in the hair above his ears and a trimmed mustache. He looked cantankerous no matter what he did or said but was a pleasant person whenever Liam spoke with him. Albert had examined Liam's throat and leg after the battle to see how he'd been healing and bragged at how well Reynald had done the field operation. Reynald downplayed his own part by claiming the magic did the majority of the work, but from what Liam could gather, most of what the magic did was cross the line between impossible to possible. It allowed Reynald to reconnect torn tissue, slow Liam's heart enough to keep him from bleeding out and prevent infection from festering in any of the wounds, but all the delicate reconstruction work had been Reynald's skill.

"Doctor Albert." Liam nodded in greeting. "How can we help?"

"You need to leave St. George. Immediately." The doctor glanced down the hallway in each direction before leaning closer to whisper. "Sir Hall arrived an hour ago. The mayor wrote for help after the attacks, and he came with a platoon of soldiers to assess the situation."

"Thank you, but Sir Lennard knows I've been hunting a witch to bring to Citadel. I doubt there'd be a problem if he saw us."

"Sir Bord…you're a knight. Surely you understand the law. You allowed a witch under your charge to use magic freely. The healing might be excused, but the destructive magic?"

"We were under exceptional circumstances." Liam looked away, but his gaze turned to Reynald sitting on the bed and staring at them. Liam's fists clenched around the doorknob. "Surely the king would see the wisdom in using all resources to save a city, *his city*. He keeps magicians in the palace who use magic frequently."

"He keeps a wood full of game for his own hunting pleasure as well," Reynald muttered. "But if anyone else hunts there, they're poachers and are executed. Aren't they?"

"He's right." Albert nodded.

"Thank you, Doctor Albert." Reynald struggled to his feet. "We appreciate the warning, but being here puts your license at risk. Go before anyone sees you. We'll be gone shortly."

"Here." He passed a tattered journal to Reynald. "Payment for the medicine. They're my notes from college. I think you'll find them interesting."

"I'm honored you trust me with these." Reynald bowed and hid the journal in his robes.

The doctor rushed down the hall, and Liam shut the door. Reynald still moved stiffly from his injured ribs, although the white of his injured eye was back to normal. Liam stopped him from stooping to pick up his boots and slipped them on his feet instead while he sat on the edge of the bed.

"Lennard Hall is a good kid. He admires the other knights; he wouldn't report—"

"Do you want to gamble your life on that?" Reynald interrupted before Liam could finish. Reynald didn't blink. His expression silently dared Liam to argue, but Liam couldn't, so he dipped his head and stared at Reynald's boot laces.

"You don't look well enough to travel," Liam said.

"I'm technically being delivered to the king as a fire pit offering. My ribs will burn broken as well as mended."

"Don't speak so casually about your execution." Liam furrowed his brow.

"You know I'm scheming—" Reynald paused for dramatic effect, winking. "—something. I promise you, I'm doing my best not to die, despite my current condition."

"Which is why I want to rest longer. I can find Lennard and talk to him if you're worried he might get the wrong idea. I'll claim it's my injuries I'm waiting to recover from."

"At best, he believes you and offers to escort me to Citadel himself in your absence. At worst, he sees through your candid little lies and sends a pigeon to the king informing him that you're a witch sympathizer."

Liam's arms dropped to his sides. He wandered to the windows and glanced out at the city. The morning light reflected off the buildings, windows, and streets, making everything gleam. It was a beautiful city, and he was glad they were able to help protect both the architecture and the people. His gut told him Lennard *wouldn't* betray him if he told the younger knight the truth, but Liam had to admit the law didn't work how Liam always assumed, and he had no guarantee Sir Hall wouldn't scream *duty* and arrest them both to impress the king. Liam himself might have done the same, once. They needed to flee.

"Put your mask on. I'll bind your hands again and make a show of leaving the city. When Sir Hall investigates, the city patrol can honestly report we're on our way as guard and captive."

"That's the most practical idea you've had since I've met you." Reynald snorted.

"I loathe this with every fiber of my being." Liam found the unicorn-hair rope and twisted the strand around Reynald's wrists in a double bind.

"If you were enjoying yourself, I'd have some questions about your bedroom preferences." Reynald laughed.

Liam grunted but refused to let his thoughts drift to erotic fantasies. Miserable, but feigning grim stoicism, Liam grabbed their gear and marched Reynald downstairs. He noticed the angry looks of the innkeeper and staff as he escorted Reynald from their room to the stable. No one said anything. Everyone bowed and spoke politely when spoken to, but their faces betrayed their fear and sadness…and rage. This was the hero who saved the city. The one they'd risked their own freedoms for to leave tiny *thank-yous* at Reynald's doorstep, but Liam's procession reminded them what happened when witches were brought to trial. Leaving the city was quicker than entering, and Liam made sure he found McCreedy and had a chat before leaving so he and all his men could see Reynald bound. Fortunately, they didn't run into Lennard before escaping. The knight probably went to the mayor's manor to have a feast and chat about the attacks before deciding what to do. Liam's face twisted into a bitter frown. Dinners and plans and laws were all fine and well when men weren't dropping to the ground in smoldering mangled knots of burnt flesh, but actual battles were hellscapes. Why shouldn't Reynald have fought? Personal feelings aside, Liam would have made the same decision all over again. Facts were facts, and Liam killed two wyverns, yes, but Reynald had killed almost two dozen.

About three miles away from St. George, Liam stopped and untied Reynald. Once the rope dropped, Liam ignored the cord and brought both of Reynald's hands to his lips. Without speaking, Liam rubbed above where the rope had sat. He hadn't bound Reynald tightly, and there were no marks, but Liam continued to knead his wrists. Reynald stood still, keeping his gaze locked on Liam's circling thumbs instead of on Liam's face. After massaging the muscles and tendons, Liam held Reynald's right hand and brushed his lips against the blue veins hidden beneath Reynald's skin. He kissed one side and then the other. His mouth moved to Reynald's knuckles, and he kissed each little hill rising from Reynald's hands.

"Why?" Reynald whispered.

Because I love you.

"Because I need to," Liam said.

"Dammit." Reynald knocked his mask away, tugged Liam closer, and smashed their lips together.

They stood on the side of the road, dangerously exposed to other travelers, clearly a knight and a witch locked together like teenage peasants during their first Beltane festival. Liam wiped his mouth after they parted and scanned the road and countryside to make sure they were alone. A flock of geese flew overhead, relocating as the seasons changed, but otherwise the world was theirs.

"I think we need to make camp."

"We're barely out of the city." Reynald rubbed his face.

"If we never reached Citadel, I wouldn't complain."

"We are still *too close* to St. George."

"You're right." Liam groaned. "The problem with you making me forget about all the rules and laws I've followed all my life is that I forget about the consequences as well. We'll ride farther."

"We could walk for a bit." Reynald smiled but held his side. "The jostling was hell on my ribs, even with Creed being gentle."

"All right. Let's walk." Liam held Reynald's hand for a few steps, then released their fingers in case anyone rode down the road and spotted them.

They walked, picked berries to go with their lunch, and hunted rabbits in the brush. Reynald spent half the day as a fox, stalking Liam from bush to bush. Liam laughed each time he saw a pop of orange pushing out from the foliage. When he wasn't frolicking as a fox, he tried to play his flute but couldn't hold a note without gasping in pain. Reynald insisted the problem was the flute and not him, and he'd fix it later. Liam shook his head but let the excuse slide.

At night, Liam tried to make the tent as comfortable as possible. He was mostly recovered, but tender, and Reynald held his side absent-mindedly even as he insisted he was fine. As they lay down, Liam licked his lips, replaying their kissing a thousand times in his mind. His body ached in a way that had nothing to do with his healing injuries, and sleep would not come even after the fire burned down from tall flames to little crackling licks of fire. He decided to add a little more wood to the dying flames. Their tent was warm enough that they didn't need the heat, but it would keep animals distant.

"Are you okay?" Reynald rubbed sleep out of his eyes as Liam slipped back into the tent.

"Restless."

"Don't lose sleep worrying over me." Reynald snorted.

"I can't help but lose sleep over you." Liam lay on his side and stared at Reynald.

"Ah…*that* sort of restless. I could alleviate some of your suffering, if you'd like." Reynald smirked.

"You already hurt yourself taking care of me." Liam crawled closer, hovering above Reynald. "This time, I will take care of you."

He plucked a single kiss from Reynald's mouth and studied his face for his reaction. Reynald's lips were plump, and he stared at Liam with a blown-out gaze. They made another sweep for each other, licking and tasting as they kissed. Liam trailed down Reynald's throat, spending a full minute sucking at Reynald's pulse. Reynald lay still and controlled his breathing to keep from hurting his side, but his fingers grabbed and clutched at Liam.

"I want you," Reynald moaned.

Liam guided his hand along Reynald's leg. His thighs were warm as Liam rubbed circles into his skin. Dipping his head below the robes, Liam kissed his way upward until he was between Reynald's legs. He flung the robe over his head to give himself space to breathe and sucked Reynalds balls.

"Ah…ahh…yes, Liam."

"Tell me if anything hurts." Liam pushed the skirt of Reynald's robe higher so he had more room to maneuver.

"I don't care. I want this." Reynald began to buck but grunted and settled against the blankets instead.

"Tell me—"

"Fine! I'll take it easy, just don't stop."

Liam kissed along Reynald's shaft and fluttered his tongue against the tip. He caught Reynald's gaze with his own and locked their stares together, watching Reynald's expression unravel as Liam wrapped his lips around Reynald's cockhead and sucked.

"Oh fuck. Fuck, so amazing." Reynald's eyes shut as he leaned against the pillow behind him.

Liam began slowly, sliding up and down at his own pace. Reynald whimpered, clawed at the blanket, and curled his toes. His cock swelled in Liam's mouth, hot and throbbing. Liam flourished his tongue along Reynald's tip before swallowing to his base, then repeated the sequence.

"Liam, this is driving me crazy. Please, faster." Reynald rolled his head from side to side, tangling his hair around his face.

Liam obeyed, rising up and dropping low at double his previous speed. Reynald's breathing remained shallow; he trembled as he grew close. Liam went deeper, allowing the tip of Reynald's cock to hit the back of his throat. Reynald muttered half a curse as he allowed his hips a single, controlled thrust. He fisted the blankets, anchoring himself to the ground, and held his breath as he released.

Liam remembered Reynald mentioning the heat when he'd swallowed, but he wasn't prepared for the exact warmth and texture. Still, he managed to drink everything before pulling his lips away from Reynald's dick with a loud pop. Liam giggled, almost dizzy with excitement, especially when he saw how wrecked Reynald looked as he lay on his back and recovered.

"You make me forget what I'm supposed to actually be doing with my life." Reynald closed his eyes, his breathing labored, though he kept the motion of his chest as slow and shallow as possible.

"You do the same to me." Liam brushed the pad of his thumb against his own friction-burned lips, relishing the sting.

"Let me…adjust…" Reynald struggled to push himself upright.

"Stay there." Liam touched Reynald's sternum with his fingertips to keep him still without applying any pressure.

He stripped away his pants and woolen underclothes before straddling over Reynald's hips. Licking his lips, Liam pulled off his shirt and rolled his fingers across his broad chest. Reynald's irises followed his movement, dipping only to glance at his thick shaft before raising higher to admire Liam's face. Liam flushed at the attention. Taking hold of

Reynald's left wrist, Liam pressed Reynald's hand against his sternum so Reynald could feel his heart race. Next he dragged Reynald's hand over to his nipple. Reynald brushed against the darker brown bud, and Liam hummed as his eyelids fluttered shut. Eager, Liam curled his fingers around his cock and stroked with lazy flicks of his wrist. Reynald rested both of his hands on Liam's thighs, a beautiful contrast to his own warm brown skin.

Liam rocked into his movements. His muscles rippled as shivers of pleasure spread through his body. Despite the need to shut his eyes and lose himself in the sensation, Liam kept his stare trained on Reynald, refusing to miss a single reaction from his face without his mask hiding him. Reynald's thumbs traced up Liam's pelvis, the light touch making him gasp. He bucked a little harder, fully into the action of pleasuring himself. Being watched added an extra thrill to the moment.

"Reynald," Liam moaned for Reynald's benefit, enjoying the way it made Reynald's eyes lose focus.

With his free hand, Liam swooped his locs up and over one shoulder. He dragged his fingers down his lips, neck, and chest and pinched his own nipple.

"Damn, you look good." Reynald spoke in a breathless voice.

"Do you want me to come?"

"Yes." Reynald's jaw slacked as he stared. His hands brushed up and down Liam's thighs.

Liam arched, stroking faster, clenching his thighs and ass to tighten all his muscles and help his pleasure climb. His labored breaths filled the tent. The urge to come overwhelmed him, consuming his mind. Moving as fast as he could, he jerked, and bucked, and rounded his spine as he poured out, splashing onto Reynald's stomach.

Before collapsing, he made sure to wipe Reynald and himself clean. Then he crashed onto the blankets, too hot to get beneath them. He stared at Reynald's face, memorizing it.

"Don't put on your mask in the morning," Liam pleaded. "Once we travel, if you must, but not before we ride out."

"You already made me crack the damn thing." Reynald's features crumpled a little. "The metaphorical irony has not gone unnoticed, by the way."

"I literally put a shield between us as we traveled." Liam laughed.

"You did. I wanted to mock you so hard." Reynald grinned.

"I knew it was childish, but I was hurting too badly to stop myself."

"I'm sorry, I never wanted you to hurt." Reynald pressed his palm to Liam's heart. "I really did admire you when I lived in the castle. The knights and squires looked so valiant in their battle gear or formal dress. I should have kissed you the night we played chase. We could have fumbled our way through sex as actual teenagers instead of grown-ass men."

"It would have killed me when you disappeared. I get attached too easily." Liam covered his face with his arm. "I released the fox from the royal trap because his blue and brown eyes reminded me of you."

"Well, yes, because it was me." Reynald poked Liam's side.

"I figured that out afterward, but at first, I only thought it was a coincidence."

"Maybe we'll be like the lion and the mouse in the fable." Reynald shrugged a single shoulder. "Except, instead of a lion, it'll be a stallion, and instead of a mouse, it's an incredibly clever and sexy fox."

"You are incredibly clever…and sexy." Liam curled his fingers in Reynald's hair.

"Keep praising me. It's almost as sexy as when your mouth sucks my cock."

Liam flushed and whispered several more compliments into Reynald's ear before they went to sleep.

Chapter Fifteen

"**I** want to stop at my manor, then pass through the Balbraid Thicket on our way to Citadel." Liam no longer needed his map. They rode through his own lands and the sense of homecoming twisted in his chest with dread because he and Reynald *weren't* going home—they were going to the palace.

"We could be at Citadel by midnight if we keep to the main roads," Reynald said.

"So?" Liam snapped.

"Surely Sir Hall mentioned our departure from St. George. We've dallied at every opportunity, and each day we add is a gamble, Liam. The time for stalling is over."

"Frankly, I no longer care if Seigfried is pissed when we waltz into his castle three weeks late. I need to know what's actually happening in the Balbraid Thicket, Reynald. My *home* is on the edge of the forest. I can forsake the king, but not the people who depend on me for protection—what if they're suffering from plague? What if the Shadows of the deeper woods have leaked to the farms? Do you even know how to fight Shadows? I don't."

"I'm not sure there's any fighting those, but fire usually makes them retreat." Reynald hung his head. "You have to promise me this will be our last detour."

"It's your execution. We can rush to your end as soon as I make sure my house is in order." Liam clenched his jaw.

"If we're going to be seen by everyone in your demesne, you better tie me again." Reynald slipped his mask over his face.

"No," Liam muttered.

"This isn't the time for obstinance, Liam."

"The people of St. George stared at me as if I were Malphas sending one of the saints to my infernal domain."

"That was, more or less, how we wanted them to stare at you. Did you forget you're a knight sworn to the king?"

"I did that so McCreedy didn't get punished for my decisions. This is my home, and I'm not going to bind my guest in my own home."

"Your guest?" Reynald's laughter was slightly muffled because of the mask, but it was no less sardonic.

"Honored guest? Most esteemed guest? Which title would you prefer?" Liam teased as they passed by familiar orchards and pastures, nearing Liam's manor.

"Liam." Reynald gripped Liam's cloak from behind, tugging

slightly. "Don't get yourself killed. You throwing your life away saves *no one.*"

"We'll be all right. You'll see," Liam insisted. "I dare say everyone will struggle to hold in their excitement when they see a steward in our very home. But take off the mask. You'll scare them."

"If you believed all that nonsense about evil witches, why wouldn't you better vet your servants?" Reynald protested but hid his mask in his robe.

"I never had a problem with mages, just criminals."

Creed knew they were going home and rushed onward without any prompting. Liam's manor sat tucked in a mess of fiery-red maple trees. His grandmother Lottie had planted them as a new bride because she wanted the hillside to burn every fall. The sight was breathtaking generations later as they rode up the path to the gate.

Ruth offered to draw his bath while Edward said he'd tell Charity to cook something proper. He had to stop his servants and explain he was only staying for an hour and asked Daniel to send Sam to his study. They'd hardly stepped into the study themselves before Ruth knocked, holding a tray of sliced apples and smoked sausage with bread, apple butter, and three different salt cellars, including his grandmother's holiday stained-glass container full of *fleur de sel*. She placed the tray in front of Reynald, curtsied, and left. Reynald raised an eyebrow, questioning Liam.

"What did I say?" Liam poured them each a whiskey, one for Sam as well, and crashed behind his desk.

"Nice place." Reynald sat and tried the salt on top of a slice of bread and apple butter.

"Thank you."

I wish I were carrying you across the threshold and giving you a proper tour.

"Fuck, this is good," Reynald swore under his breath as he grabbed more of the food from the tray.

Liam smiled as he watched Reynald enjoy his meal. Sam knocked before entering the room. His gaze shifted from Reynald to Liam. He didn't comment but bowed.

"You summoned me?" Sam was tall and too lean, no matter how much he ate. He kept his long hair pulled back in a ponytail.

"Sit down. Have a drink. I can't stay long. I'm overdue in Citadel, but I needed to check on things here before I went to the city."

Liam offered Sam a glass. It wasn't uncommon for them to share a drink while Sam debriefed him.

"I had Daniel personally escort the supplies you requested to Birchshire."

"Was he attacked on the road?"

"They heard dire wolves howling at night, but they kept a bonfire to ward them away. As for musseri, the people here know to guard against them since we've always lived closer to the forest. Still, Master Gau set traps along our borders. There have been more attacks on the outskirts, but the additional training has kept the casualties low, nothing like the first dire wolf attack. I have full reports in my journals if you'd like to see them."

"When I return in a few days." Liam emptied his glass and stood.

"Thank you, Sam. What I've seen on my journey is…concerning, but I can finish my task now that I know things here are holding."

"Sir, do you need my help? With…" Sam swallowed, gaze flicking toward Reynald before returning to Liam. "Travel arrangements?"

"Reynald, I think Sam is asking you a question." Liam spoke in a low voice. "This might be your last chance."

"I assure you, the Bord estate has some experience with these matters." Sam nodded his head at Reynald.

"You do?" Reynald looked at Liam.

"I wasn't aware, but I can't help but notice that Ruth gave you three flavors of salt for your meal." Liam gestured, pacing in front of his desk. "So apparently some of my staff love to frequent the salt merchant, and I paid them as much mind as I would anyone talking about dill or marjoram."

"Just this once, I'll admit that *you* were right, Liam. The hospitality of your home was absolutely not what I expected." Reynald laughed. "Unfortunately, I will have to decline the gracious offer for travel arrangements since I'm already on my way to Citadel."

"Stubborn ass," Liam swore under his breath.

"Are we ready to go?" Reynald stood after finishing the last apple slice.

"Sam…" Liam clenched his jaw, wondering how he should word what he wanted to say. "Have everyone prepare for a hard winter. Help whenever, whomever, we can during the long nights."

"I think I understand." Sam bowed, finished his whiskey, and stepped out of the room.

"There's a spell on the mantel," Reynald whispered after Sam left.

"What do you mean?"

"There are tiny sigils written with what looks like…" Reynald squinted, touching the marble framing the hearth. "A sewing needle and melted candle wax?"

"Is it good? Bad?" Liam shook his head.

"It's a protection spell."

"Well then? What's the problem?"

"Aren't you curious to know who wrote the sigils?"

"Naturally, but sewing needle and candle wax limits our suspects to everyone in the manor. Even I darn my own socks. Didn't you want to go?"

"Yes, in fact. I thought maybe you were going to hire an artist to paint a portrait of us before we left."

"We're leaving. We're leaving." Liam pressed his hand against Reynald's back and walked him to the courtyard where Creed was enjoying a snack and being looked over by his usual stable hands.

They kept quiet as they rode away, but after the view of Liam's home began to shrink behind them, Reynald hummed in thought.

"I feel like you have some explaining to do?"

"I rather think *Sam* has some explaining to do, but we'll have that talk next time I'm home."

"Your people were trying not to look, but I noticed a few girls peeking out of the kitchen, and a lad behind a display case, and several turned heads."

"They ween us off milk long before wet-nurse tales of the Thicket.

I don't feel like they're much different than any of the citizens or villagers I've met while we traveled. Alone as a knight, people were content to hide their superstitions, but when you're with me, they can't help but get a little excited."

"You're flattering me."

"Can you not see it?"

"These have been strange circumstances. I normally don't go walking around and healing plagues like some sort of hermit saint."

"Maybe you should. The life suits you. Better, I think, than assassinating the king."

"Maybe afterward." Reynald snorted.

"I'm still not sure why you need the stupid mask or a demon's help. You're strong enough without those. Surely you could bide your time as a fox in the Royal Woods and ambush him during his next hunt."

"Do you mean the royal hunts, which are essentially Seigfried showing off, so they often have noblewomen and children in the hunting parties?"

"Fair, but what about sneaking into the castle somehow and attacking him in his sleep? You got in easily to steal the phoenix feather." Liam continued to talk as they rode away from the orchards and into the Balbraid Thicket.

"Because he's paranoid and keeps various magical artifacts in his room at all times, and he rotates them out depending on which paranoias are concerning him the most that day. Too risky."

"Maybe I could stab him."

"Also too risky," Reynald said. "You wouldn't, anyway. He'd give you puppy eyes, and you'd forgive him of any atrocities."

"Let's wait and see exactly what he's doing in the forest first. Anything horrible enough to terrify an ogre might be horrible enough to inoculate me to the enchantment of 'puppy eyes.'"

"Liam, do you trust me?"

"Yes," Liam said.

"Stop."

Liam dismounted and waited to see what Reynald would do. Reynald pulled a satin sash from one of his pockets. He brushed the soft material along Liam's neck.

"I thought this time, I'd use a proper blindfold instead of a spell."

"You teased me about the rope, but that is a *satin* blindfold." Liam closed his eyes. "An almost romantic choice."

"But unlike you"—Reynald stepped behind Liam to blindfold him. He arranged Liam's hair around the cloth—"I have no problem admitting that I'd love to blindfold you in bed."

Liam bit his bottom lip. Reynald traced the shape of Liam's mouth to prove his point, and Liam parted his lips.

"The things I could do to you if we had more time." Reynald's breath tickled Liam's ear. He kissed Liam's jaw before tucking Creed's reins into Liam's hand. "Hold onto this, and keep your other arm locked with mine. I won't let you stumble."

"All right."

The ground beneath their feet became less even. Reynald had to hold Liam's waist and guide him over tree roots multiple times. The familiar crunch of armadillos rummaging the forest floor cut through the last of the autumn birdsong. Liam's pulse quickened as he stepped deeper into the woods.

"You're taking me to your meadow."

"Yes. The blindfold isn't because I don't trust you, but my tower wanders. It's easiest to find when I close my eyes."

"Please tell me your eyes aren't closed right now."

"Not yet. Not until the last moment."

"So, you *do* live close to me?" Liam smiled.

"Guess I do." Reynald chuckled. "My Place hangs around this edge of the woods the most."

"I would have snuck blindfolded into the Thicket every night if I had known."

"And probably been eaten by a goblin." Reynald snorted.

"I'd die every night if that's what it took to find you."

"You have to stop, or I *will* kiss you, and I can't promise I'll stop once I start."

"I dare you."

"Sorry. We're here." Reynald tugged the satin away.

Liam blinked as light streamed around them. He gasped—everything was gold. The rays slanting over the gold-green aspens, the fields of yellow and orange yarrow, the goldenrods and the chamomile—everything encircling the crumbling stone tower glowed with bright color.

"I can hardly imagine you living somewhere so…cheerful."

Reynald pressed a finger against his lips, telling Liam to keep the secret to himself.

"What's in the tower?"

"My home. Come on. I saw yours, so now it's time to show you mine." Reynald led him through the arched doorway and into a small foyer.

Dried herbs hung in bundles, all tied with different-colored strings. A chaise sat tucked in the corner surrounded by pots of ivy. They wound their way up the spiral staircase. Every few feet, the wall had a recess filled with potion bottles, clay jars, candles, or figurines. Reynald reached into his pockets, pulling out his corn dollies, ribbons, marbles, rocks, and various other gifts from the people they'd met in their journey. He scattered the mementos along their path as they climbed.

In the highest chamber, musical instruments hung on the wall between more herbs. All the throw pillows were embroidered with bright threads, magenta, violet, cobalt, orange, crimson, deep green. The rug looked like stained glass. Ivy grew up the walls. Large stone pots lined up against the walls held fresh herbs and flowers anywhere enough light spilled in through to hit the leaves. Reynald's desk was cluttered with little mismatched containers of clay or glass full of dirt and various sprouts.

"How many instruments do you play?"

"A dozen or so." Reynald shrugged. "One of the few things I liked about being a royal magician was that we were allowed to learn whatever instruments we wanted."

"So, you learned music when Seigfried watched, and magic when he was distracted?"

"Here are all the pages I stole from his library." Reynald picked up a grimoire that filled both his arms. The stacked pages were varying sizes and colors. It made for ugly binding, but it was amazing how much he'd snuck out of the palace.

"How did you carry so much paper?"

"This robe began with a single pocket, but I wove magic into the material, and the more I added, the more pockets I found."

"Sounds like a fairy tale."

"Fairy tales probably came from real stories about sorcerers."

"How do you sleep with thirty pillows on your bed?" Liam laughed as he dropped face-first into the pile.

"I throw them on the floor." Reynald strolled to the window.

Liam sat on the bed, hiding his face in a pile of cushions. "Mmm. They smell like you."

"Come here. I brought us here for a reason."

A brass cone tube rested on a tripod. A glass lens made the end of the tube look like a giant, blind eye. Curious, Liam crawled off the bed and stood next to Reynald.

"From this high, we'll be able to see everything lost." Reynald caressed the brass.

Liam swallowed, wanting to know, but not wanting to see. Stealing himself, he bent over the thinner end of the tube and peeked through the viewing hole. At first, the Balbraid Thicket stretched across the horizon in her full glory. Creeks and streams flashed like silver ribbons. The fall leaves were as colorful as the pillows and the rug in Reynald's room. The spyglass allowed him to watch a white stag drink from a brook, and hidden glens cut into the woods in sections while hills led up to rocky outcrops. But as he scanned farther out, a flat, gray scab showed where they'd been burning sections after cutting all the trees. The mills were simple enough, square and wooden with enormous wheels at their sides, but there were dozens, and they poured pulp and debris into the streams, leaving them grimy and sick-looking. The Serpent Tail was dry, the trees around the once wide and twisting river were stumps that hadn't yet been burned. The dam upstream stood as a barrier, keeping the forest out of its own land.

And all around, where a rich tapestry had spread, there was nothing but mud and sawdust.

"But *how*? How have they destroyed so much, so fast? It's only been three months."

Liam searched for the men clearing the forest, but there were no camps, no fire smoke or lean-to towns for the workers to rest, drink, and talk after hours.

What he found instead made the hairs on his neck prickle. Huge, eyeless, noseless, mouthless man-shaped creatures of twisted metal wire and stone felled trees with solitary swings from axes as long as men were tall.

"What *are* those?" Liam jerked his head high, as if he could see them with his bare eyes.

"What do you see?" Reynald peeked in the glass.

"They're faceless metal people. No wonder the wolves and imps are fleeing. Men build camps and make noise and are easy to avoid. Those things don't look like they even sleep."

"I've read about these. They're called golems. Servants animated with magic."

"How did Seigfried get *golems*?" Liam tugged at his locs.

"He has a castle full of mages. He could have forced any of them—all of them." Reynald shook his head, hugging himself.

"He's using magic to clear the forest faster than human woodcutters could." Liam dropped into a nearby stool, his hands shaking. "All the while burning actual people in the name of his hypocritical justice. I can't… I can't allow this. Reynald, let me help you."

"What? Absolutely not. I don't need some knight stepping on my toes. I can handle this by myself." Reynald's fists clenched, and his jaw tightened.

"Some knight? Am I only some knight to you? After everything we've been through?" Liam turned away, but staring at the bed didn't help, so he stood and marched toward the door.

Liam continued through the doorway, down the stairs, passing all the little gifts the citizens of Elktrail and Birchshire and St. George had bestowed to Reynald for saving them. Liam stopped at the bottom of the stairs, touching a river pebble that the water had worn to the shape of a heart. Brushing the smooth stone with his fingertips, Liam wondered if perhaps he *would* only get in the way. He had barely helped in the wyvern fight, almost got himself killed, and had never been in control during their entire quest, despite being the supposed "captor."

Reynald's voice echoed, calling Liam's name. Liam flinched and escaped into the meadow. There he stood with his arms crossed over his chest.

"There you are." Reynald appeared a few minutes later, clutching his side.

"I didn't see the way we came, so I don't know where I am," Liam said, and the words hurt because he had trusted Reynald enough to get here, but Reynald didn't trust *him* to help him fight.

"Walk in any direction, and you'd find your way." Reynald tried to bump Liam playfully with his shoulder to ease the tension, but Liam didn't budge.

"You said no more stalling. Let's go."

"Please don't let us part this way." Reynald dug his fingers into Liam's bicep. "Even with an oracle's blessing, I don't know what's going to happen, and if I never see you again"—his voice cracked—"I don't want my last memory of you to be your back walking away."

Liam spun one hundred eighty degrees and encircled his arms around Reynald, careful of his ribs. The momentum caused his cape to twist around them in a spiral, a swirl of metallic blue in the center of a golden field. Reynald's breath hiccupped in his chest. He grew heavy in Liam's embrace.

Liam traced the shell of Reynald's ear with the tip of his nose before whispering, "Then remember me like this, holding you in your meadow."

"Dammit, Liam." Reynald shoved his head into Liam's chest, more of a headbutt than an affectionate gesture.

"You were forced to spend most of your life alone, but you're not alone now. I'm with you." Liam cupped Reynald's face and kissed his forehead, grateful Reynald wasn't wearing the mask.

"It's *dangerous*." Reynald's brow furrowed as he frowned. "Even with Edeline giving me a plan, what I'm doing is dangerous."

"That's not stopping you."

"I don't have any responsibilities. *You do.*"

"I hate this." Liam unwound his arms and turned in the direction they came from, using the tower as a reference point. "I refuse to smile and leave you to deal with this on your own. And why? So I can go home to drink whiskey by the fire like it's another day while monsters destroy everything around me? I can't."

"Don't do anything reckless—"

"You of all people shouldn't lecture others on recklessness."

"Edeline didn't say anything about you joining me. What if your interference changes the future, and we all die, but Seigfried destroys everything anyway?"

Liam clenched his teeth. He didn't have an answer.

"You said you trusted me, so *trust me*, Liam."

"I can't promise what I'll do once we're there." Liam exhaled. "But I did promise I wouldn't make you travel to Citadel alone. We can go. I won't stall anymore. I know I've made that claim several times, but…I don't know what else I could do *to* stall even if I had a mind to."

Chapter Sixteen

"This is it. We'll finally see Citadel again," Reynald said.

"The ride will be a few hours, give or take where we intersect with the road, but not much longer."

"Yeah…and there's no real reason why we shouldn't keep riding. We can reach the palace by nightfall." Reynald toyed with the sleeve of his robe.

"And I said no more stalling. And you said no more stalling. We said no more stalling."

"You did. I did. We did." Reynald nodded.

They turned and faced each other at the same time. Reynald was first to break eye contact.

"Would you like to spend one last night together?"

"Yes." Liam's voice cracked, but he didn't care if Reynald heard the emotion in his tone. "But only if you want to as much as I do."

"I do." Reynald twined his fingers with Liam's and led him back to the tower.

"Don't blame me for stalling this time." As Liam climbed the steps, he swiped the heart-shaped stone he'd seen because he wanted a memento, just in case.

"This one's absolutely my fault."

If Reynald saw Liam's petty theft, he didn't comment on it. Instead, he guided Liam to his bed and made a show of flinging the excess pillows to the ground.

"See? Plenty of room for sleeping."

"How do you not trip in the middle of the night if you have to piss?"

"How do you not break your ankle in the woods?" Reynald snorted. "Kick the pillows aside if you must. You've fought dire wolves, ogres, and a nefarious witch. I'm sure you'll survive the battle of the pillows."

"A not-so-nefarious witch. You could have beaten me. Your bolt punctured the wyvern scales easily, which means you could have destroyed my shield at your merest whim."

"I was never trying to hurt you, only goad you." Reynald loosened the front of his robe.

As Reynald undressed, a familiar iridescent flash caught Liam's eyes. He held Reynald's wrist to stop his movement and checked the inner robe to reveal deep-green wyvern skin lining the underside.

"This is new," Liam ran a finger along the scales.

"Yes. I modified my robes while you were unconscious in St. George."

"You were seeking dragon skin when I caught you."

"Was I?" Reynald asked. "Or was I goading you because I knew I'd have a better chance later after you captured me?"

"Tell me."

"Tell you what?" Reynald pulled the wrist Liam held closer so he could work his lips against Liam's knuckles. "Tell you I want you? Tell you how I plan on making you call my name until your voice is hoarse?"

"If you won't let me help, at least tell me the plan."

"I can't. You'll try to convince me not to cast the spell."

"Then don't cast it!" Liam released Reynald and threw up his arms.

"Liam." Reynald pulled Liam onto the bed, straddled his lap, and held his face. "You trusted me enough to get here, so trust me for the last leg of our journey."

"I trust you with *me*." Liam mirrored Reynald, reaching out and cupping his face. "I don't think you'd intentionally hurt me, but I'm quite sure you'd tear yourself to threads in the heat of a spell if you had half a chance to avenge your sister."

"That's…fair," Reynald said.

"What about afterward? You said you weren't sure we'd ever see each other again."

"I'm not."

"But I want to." Liam swallowed.

"Dammit, Liam. What did I tell you about being so sincere all the time?" Reynald closed his eyes and curled closer, hiding his face in the crook of Liam's neck.

"You should try sincerity some time. Honesty would suit you."

"I'm not an oracle. I can't promise you what will happen after tomorrow. All I can do is give you tonight, if you still want it."

Reynald tilted Liam's face upward and kissed him. Liam relaxed and allowed Reynald to take control. Each drag of their lips warmed Liam's body. Swept away with emotion, Liam grabbed Reynald's sides, causing him to yelp.

"Sorry." Liam winced when Reynald grabbed his sore ribs.

"I'm fine. Tender, but fine." Reynald rubbed his side.

"Maybe we shouldn't do this." Liam shook his head.

"I will break the ribs on my other side to do this." Reynald chuckled. He pressed Liam's chest and pushed him against the mattress to hover over him. "But I'll do my best to be gentle—on both of us."

Reynald removed the rest of his robe, dropping the garment to the ground. He tugged playfully at Liam's surcoat before ripping the fabric away. Layer by layer, Reynald helped Liam out of his armor, riding leathers, woolens, and then linen. When their bare skin finally touched, Liam groaned. His cock was half hard and growing fast, but Reynald focused on Liam's chest and stomach. He peppered Liam's body with kisses. Liam grabbed Reynald's shoulders. He arched, groaning freely.

Through the window frames, the sunset swirled red and orange. The colors were raw and bloody and made it look like the world around them was coming to an end, but in Reynald's tower, the plants sat content in their pots, and the herbs hung from their colored string, and the pillows were scattered across the floor. They were in a dimension of their own, and the destruction outside couldn't interrupt them.

Reynald eased their cocks together. His moves were deliberate and languid for both the sake of driving Liam wild and to keep from hurting his side. The wind slipping in through the open windows caressed their hot skin and made them shiver. Holding out his hand, Reynald sent a spark of flame to the brazier across the room. The fire burgeoned, filling the room with warm light.

"Neat trick." Liam panted.

"You think that's impressive, wait until I show you my special concoction."

Reynald jumped to a bookshelf filled with bottles instead of books and scanned the selection. He chose a tall bottle of dark purple glass. Popping the cork stopper, he drizzled the lavender tinted oil onto his fingers and slipped one between Liam's legs.

"Ah." Liam choked on a breath as his body hitched at the sudden and smooth intrusion.

"Made this for myself. Beats regular oil any day." Proud of his mixture, Reynald flashed a mischievous look at Liam. "Are you ready for more?"

"Y-yes," Liam stuttered, struggling to breathe.

He felt his skin stretch and his hole widen with the entrance of a second finger. The potion allowed Reynald's fingers to ease in and out without too much friction. Liam hitched his hips, arousal already tightening his muscles and making the blood rush through his entire body—especially his cock.

"Another moment. I want to make sure you're good and relaxed before we try this." Reynald watched Liam squirm from just two of his fingers. "Let's see… Here we go."

Reynald brushed against Liam's prostate. Liam's eyes slammed shut; he opened his mouth and screamed until his voice echoed through the rafters above them. His need and desire possessed him. Liam fisted the blankets and rolled his hips to get the most of each jab of Reynald's fingers. When Reynald pulled his hand away, Liam whimpered.

"Please—"

"Don't worry, I'm not stopping." Reynald oiled his cock and lined his tip with Liam's entrance.

"Oh…o-oh, Reynald." Liam gasped.

Reynald hadn't even slid inside yet, but the heat of his cock pressing against Liam's nerves had him clenching in anticipation, and he had to force his body to relax. Reynald applied pressure. Liam's body yielded, swallowing Reynald's cock and wrapping around his girth. Shouting, Liam clawed at the bed beneath him. Reynald's breath came and went in double hitches.

"You're so warm. Saints, Liam. *Ah—*" Reynald slid most of the way out. "I can hardly take this."

He thrust, Liam cried out, and Reynald's face twisted in euphoria. Reynald lowered himself, leaning against Liam's body. In a haze of heat and pleasure, Liam kissed across the curve of Reynald's shoulder as they rocked. Their bodies pressed so close together that Liam imagined his heartbeat was both of theirs.

"Let me look at you." Reynald held Liam's face as he hitched his hips. "I want to memorize every detail—*ah*. And think. Of you. Forever."

Liam's hands found Reynald's ass. Reynald didn't wince when he squeezed, so Liam grabbed and helped Reynald shove deeper with each thrust. His cock twitched as it rubbed against Reynald's stomach.

"Reynald! Reynald!" Liam cried. His legs raised in the air, calves straining.

"You're mine. Mine." Reynald growled in Liam's ear.

"Then touch me."

"Don't hold back." Reynald wrapped his slick palm around Liam's shaft and stroked.

"R-Reynald…"

"Let go. Come harder than you've ever come before."

"Reynald!"

Liam couldn't hold eye contact anymore. His eyes shut, his body demanding he *experience* instead of look. Tingling pressure built inside him, swelling, condensing. When he reached his peak, he moaned until his voice cracked, and he came so hard he saw streamers of light dancing behind his eyelids. After Liam's voice settled to a few gasping breaths, Reynald let go of Liam's cock and moved faster. His orange hair hung around him, tickling Liam's chest. Their sweat mingled, soaking the sheets beneath them.

"Oh…fuck!" Reynald tossed his head skyward, bowed like a cobra, and trembled in orgasm.

They crumpled into a heap together, clinging to each other, falling asleep before they could mutter good night.

In the morning, they lingered in bed. Liam clutched Reynald as hard as he could without hurting him. Eventually, Liam's rumbling stomach and aching bladder forced them to admit the day was passing, and they couldn't avoid the rest of the world forever. They rose, washed, and prepared themselves to ride.

"Are you worried?" Liam scanned the golden flowers and bright yellow leaves encircling them, wondering if he'd ever see them again.

"No." Reynald shook his head.

"I'm worried."

"I know." Reynald hooked his pinky finger with Liam's before they walked to the edge of the field where Creed feasted on goldenrod.

They flushed butterflies from the tall grasses and flowers: swallowtails and clouded yellows. Stray petals blew around them with the breeze. The sun was almost in the center of the sky but angled as the approaching autumn caused the days to fold in on themselves. When they reached Creed, Reynald stopped, gave Liam a final, lingering look, pressed his lips to the corner of Liam's mouth, and secured the fox mask over his face. Liam traced the crack in the center of the ivory.

"Tie me. The city guard need to see me as a prisoner," Reynald said.

"If you insist." Liam closed his eyes and held his breath, composing himself as best he could before finding the unicorn rope and binding Reynald one last time.

Creed snorted at them in greeting and nudged Liam's back. He patted the horse before helping Reynald mount and sitting in front of him. Creed knew the woods and found the road far sooner than Liam wanted him to. He stared at the rocks littering their path. No matter how hard Liam willed for the world to stop, the pebbles kept slipping past with each clop of Creed's hooves. They kept moving closer to Citadel.

Sometimes in battle, time stretched and slowed. During the war a few years ago, Liam would find himself missing out on the details he *should* see, like the blood or the expressions on the other soldier's faces as they died, and instead saw useless things in polished-brass clarity, like a spider clinging to a blade of grass, or the way the earth smelled when his boot dug into the damp soil. Citadel grew on the horizon, rising higher with each mile, but Liam refused to acknowledge the city. It was as if the road and city gates were too horrible for his mind to focus on, so instead it captured how rich and white the clouds in the sky looked as they slid past, or how a single sycamore near the road boasted such bright colors that it resembled the pillows on Reynald's bed. Because his mind refused to pay attention to the path, Liam didn't notice Chancellor Cole escorted by Sir Hall, Sir Oldsworth, and a platoon of their soldiers until the sounds of their horses broke through the fuzziness of Liam's thoughts and forced him to stare forward.

"Fuck." Liam stopped. His battle instinct flooded his body with adrenaline.

"Don't do anything stupid," Reynald whispered behind him, bound hands pressing into Liam's tailbone. "This entire journey has been for this moment. Be the Stallion of Citadel and hand me over to them."

Liam watched the party approach. The yellow and crimson sur-coats made them look like another cluster of autumn trees, but this was not a welcome party—it was a capture party. Liam had taken too long; he'd known so with each excuse. Between his tardiness and the inevita-ble rumors about a witch saving St. George, there was no "playing knight and captor," not anymore.

"They're not here to welcome me, Reynald. This is a comfort, honestly. This way, I don't have to pretend." Liam exhaled in genuine relief. "I can burn beside you."

"No." Reynald remained still, but his body tensed at Liam's statement.

"It's what I deserve. Even if you survive, there have been innocent people who burned because of me. Let me suffer as they did."

"No. Listen," Reynald hissed. "You have to play your role. Convince Seigfried you're still loyal. You'll be imprisoned, but not executed."

"Why?"

"Who will defeat the golems?"

"You. You're an army, Reynald."

"Then because…because…" Reynald paused, his voice strained. "What if there's even a slight chance we can see each other after this is over? Even for a moment. Isn't that worth surviving?"

Liam clenched his jaw, grunting, furious at his emotions, at how easily Reynald could convince him to do anything he wanted. Even when every ounce of Liam's will begged him to say no. *For once, don't give Reynald what he wants.* But he would. Liam would suffer swallowing his pride and groveling for mercy before a king he no longer wished to serve, because Reynald desired him to.

"What are you going to do?" Reynald's voice cracked, no longer a whisper.

"Surrender." Liam dismounted, assisted Reynald to the ground, and guided him to his knees. "Don't move until they tell you to."

"I'm aware." Reynald's glance sharpened behind the mask.

Liam couldn't repress the smile. He opened his mouth, the "I love you" nearly tumbling from his lips, but the armed escort was on them, riding off the path to encircle them and block their escape. Cole edged forward, glaring at Liam and Reynald with equal disgust. Liam walked half a dozen steps forward and knelt in the road, then bent with his lips all but kissing the road. He positioned his sword and shield on the ground before Cole even announced the formal charge. Breath disturbing the dirt surrounding the pebbles, Liam didn't dare glance upward, even as Chancellor Cole's shadow blocked the light above him. The chancellor stopped once he was within easy speaking distance, his tone thick with his usual disdain.

"Sir Liam Bord, you're under arrest for accessory to witchcraft."

Liam remained folded against the road until Sir Hall came to bind his hands. He stood, offering any extra knives to his fellow knight and holding out his fists the same way he'd forced Reynald to do throughout their travels. The act felt just, for Liam to experience the same humiliation as Reynald; he approved.

"Take care of Creed, please," Liam said.

"Why didn't you send a pigeon, Liam? We would have helped fight the wyverns while you delivered your target. The king is enraged. You endangered St. George by letting a witch fight with you." Lennard's face was twisted in distress. He was a good kid, and Liam was sorry for putting him in this situation.

"Men were crashing around us in flames. I didn't have time to write a letter asking for help."

"What about Birchshire? Sir Pines's report said—"

"Sir Lennard," the chancellor interrupted, "leave the interrogation to Seigfried."

"Sir." Lennard finished tying his knots and bowed to Cole before connecting Creed's lead to his own horse's saddle.

Liam held his breath. He wanted to scream about the golems. He wanted to ask how many towns were infected with plague. He was sure Doctor Euphrosina was sharing the recipe for the cure, but how many would die before news spread? And how many would be killed by creatures fleeing the true, man-made monsters slicing through the forest?

Liam and Reynald marched on foot. Now Citadel swallowed Liam's line of sight. He stared at the outermost gates until they passed beneath, and then he stared at the castle in the center of the city. Liam's neck muscles strained. He ached to turn and check on Reynald, but he'd only make their situation worse, so Liam marched—like a soldier stomping toward death—with his gaze locked straight ahead.

Their party traveled past the cathedral, the slums, the markets, and down the winding cobblestone roads of the business and entertainment districts. They passed the statue of Saint Margaret. The Candlewick Inn swarmed with patrons too drunk to notice them. Liam wondered what happened to the shy brunette he'd helped when Reynald summoned stryx on the city. Grabbing the scale image over his surcoat with both bound hands, Liam hoped she was well, and the lad and his mother. He had tried to be an honorable knight, to serve the people. At his core, he'd wanted to protect people, to be their shield.

But instead, he'd been Seigfried's torch.

Liam wished he could speak with Reynald. He never did enjoy walking in silence, but this was how it was supposed to be. Knights on their horses, prisoners bound and walking behind them with their heads hung low. The citizens gathered in clusters near their shops or homes, watching the procession and whispering. Many held their saint medallions and prayed. It was almost unheard of for a knight to be publicly arrested. Liam could slay a shoe cobbler in the streets as the sun gleamed off the blood on his sword, and his punishment would be to meet with the palace treasurer to negotiate a small penance for the widow, but to help make medicine and stop a wyvern attack? *That* was the true crime because he'd "collaborated with a witch."

The city fell away as they passed through the final three walls guarding the palace. The courtyard was deserted except for a few workers who stayed far away from the circle of armed soldiers. The mounted guards stopped. Lennard, Kent, and Cole dismounted their horses. With only a dozen men, the smaller group guided Liam and Reynald into the castle. Liam repressed a snort. Reynald fought two dozen wyverns, what would twelve foot soldiers do if he wanted to escape?

The palace Liam had often patrolled, both as a squire and a knight, felt foreign to him, a maze. The noise of their boots accented the otherwise eerie silence in each hallway. The servants were too efficient at not looking at either Reynald or Liam. They didn't whisper and shake their heads like the merchants and textile workers watching from their shops. Instead, they scrubbed floors and dusted with blank expressions, almost as empty as the golems clearing the forest. No eyes or mouths, just service to Seigfried in their every action.

In the throne room, the king toyed with a puzzle box. He solved a step, and the box rewarded him with a series of colored, magical lights. Seigfried's face beamed in joy as he watched. The porridge Liam had for breakfast curdled in his stomach as he remembered watching similar moments over the years. Liam never thought it strange—the king owned royal magicians, so of course they'd make him the occasional gift, and Liam never dreamed the king would use magic to harm anyone in any way, so he never saw a problem in the small hypocrisy.

The golems had no eyes, noses, or mouths, but they had ears carved into the side of their heads. If they didn't need to see to fell a tree, did they need ears to listen to commands? Or did Seigfried *want* them to have ears for when he ordered them to work, even if he didn't give them a mouth to scream or eyes to cry. Did they exist? Or were they merely animated? Liam swallowed bile from the back of his throat but didn't ask the questions out loud.

"Took you a long time to bring me a single witch, dear stallion." Siegfried tossed the cube to the ground beside him and rested his chin against his hand as he gazed down from his throne.

"Sire, you've read the reports—"

"Silence." Siegfried lifted a hand to stop Cole's protest. "I want to hear Sir Bord's side of the story before I make a decision."

Lennard was inexperienced. Liam could shove him to the floor, steal his blade, and plunge the sword into Seigfried's chest before anyone could stop him. He was close enough. They'd kill Liam the next instant, but did it matter anymore?

Reynald had asked him to live—to gamble on the slight chance they might see each other afterward. Liam dropped to his knees and pressed his forehead to the polished marble floor.

"There was a blizzard, and plague, and monster attacks, but these are excuses, Your Majesty. I should have done better. I failed you. Please punish me as you see fit."

Falling into his old habits and playing the role of the chivalrous knight dedicated mind and soul to his liege was too easy. Reynald audibly sneered in disgust, and Liam hated himself.

"You bootlicking bast—"

"Heel, dog." Sir Oldsworth shoved Reynald to his knees, gripped his hair, and forced his head low.

Liam twitched as he repressed the urge to lunge at Kent and beat him bloody for daring to touch Reynald, but anything he did might ruin Reynald's plans. Right or wrong: Liam was going to trust Reynald and let him lead in this dance.

"I'm curious, Liam." Seigfried leaned forward on his throne. "Why were you playing hero across all of Phrophis when *I* had already given you a quest? Is the petty inconvenience of a pig farmer in Birchshire more important to you than the will of your own king?"

"My liege, your people are extensions of you, so I thought by serving them, I also served you. I was a fool not to write to you directly for your wisdom and stay on task. If you command it, I will cut off my hand as punishment for acting on my own."

Reynald's head jerked in his direction. In the corner of his vision, Liam saw Reynald's mismatched eyes wide with shock. Good. If his acting could convince Reynald, it would convince Seigfried. Liam stared at Seigfried's shoes as he always did, not because he was afraid of getting lost in Seigfried's beauty as he once would have, but because he was too disgusted to look his king in the face.

"All right. Give him a sword." Seigfried gestured.

"My lord, I cannot advise you to give a prisoner a sword." Cole stood beside the throne, his hands folded in front of him, but otherwise motionless.

"Of course not. I can't be trusted, and the king's life is too precious to risk. Sir Hall…" Liam held out his hands toward Lennard.

Lennard stepped backward. He glanced at the king, his expression all but begging Seigfried to intervene. Seigfried bit his bottom lip, smirking. After a moment, he scoffed.

"I told you he was still loyal to me, chancellor."

"Sir Bord could be lying. Give *me* a sword and I'll make good on his offer," Chancellor Cole said.

"How would a knight without hands serve me and my kingdom? Sir Bord has always had a soft spot for the common folk. I'm sure this witch manipulated Sir Bord's charity."

"Well, he is rather gullible." Reynald's laughter echoed in the spacious throne room. "I supposed that's why *you're* so fond of him, Siegfried."

"I told you to be silent." Sir Oldsworth slammed Reynald's head against the floor. The mask absorbed the brunt of the impact, but Liam held his breath and blanked his mind, forcing himself not to act.

"Where's the phoenix feather, Reynald?" Siegfried asked.

"I lost it."

"It's in his tower. In the Balbraid Thicket," Liam said before Reynald could fully finish his sentence.

"Fuck you," Reynald growled. "If you hadn't tied me with this unicorn rope, I would shove a lightning bolt down your throat."

"A witch in a tower?" Seigfried snickered. "Are you a character in a storybook?"

"Yes, and you're Prince Charming."

"If you speak back to the king one more time, I will rip *your* throat out with my teeth," Liam snarled before Kent could react.

"The dinner bell is ringing—come get some," Reynald snapped in retort.

Sir Oldsworth moved to shove Reynald to the floor again, but Siegfried lifted a hand to stop him. Rising from his throne, Seigfried knelt in front of Reynald. His gorgeous silks were embroidered with water lilies and ponds, and the pale blue complimented the king's lemon-kissed hair. Yet he wasn't as beautiful as Reynald despite Reynald's tangled hair and the mask hiding his face.

"I told you if you ever ran, I'd roast you like a pig," Seigfried whispered.

"I swear, you're going to pay for everything you've done. I will sacrifice my soul to see it come to pass." Reynald stared up at Seigfried from his prostrated position on the floor, his neck still pinned by Sir Oldsworth's grip.

"How fierce." Siegfried reached out and stroked Liam's hair. "You'll protect me, won't you, dear knight?"

"With my life," Liam kissed the tip of Seigfried's slippered foot jutting out from his silk robes.

"Fucking groveling coward. You disgust me more than all the other knights combined," Reynald growled.

"Sir Oldsworth, lock this witch in the Cauldron." Seigfried smiled. "Just like old times, right, Reynald?"

"No! Not there." Reynald twisted to his feet and bolted, but Kent and three of his soldiers restrained him.

Liam shut his eyes and counted to ten as they dragged Reynald away, screaming. He'd never heard of the Cauldron, but he could imagine. Had Reynald called out to him, Liam would be on his feet fighting, bound or not, yet Reynald only shrieked and cursed them all to the infernal realms. Liam blinked his eyes open, mentally tracing the veins swirling in the marble below him. Seigfried continued to stroke Liam's coiled hair.

"Sir Bord, I gave you a task, and while you completed what I asked of you, you still broke several laws."

"I know." Liam's voice shook.

"You can't go wholly unpunished."

Liam held his breath. Instead of giving the order to have Liam dragged away, he held Liam's chin in his hand and raised his face so he could stare at him.

"You're smart on the battlefield, but naive in the world, aren't you?"

"That's why I need you to give me orders, my lord." Liam's voice cracked. The tears in his eyes were real enough, if not for the reasons Seigfried would assume.

"Sir Hall, find a room in the east tower fitting for a prisoner of his social standing."

"Immediately." Lennard bowed, buttermilk curls falling in front of his face. He pulled Liam to his feet and led the way.

Upon entering the eastern tower, Lennard borrowed the key ring from the head guard on duty. The keys clanked as they walked. Neither of them spoke until they reached a door with a secure, iron lock.

"If you need something, there's a bell to call a guard." Lennard cut the ropes away from Liam's hands. "I promise I'll sneak an apple to Creed in the stables when I have a free moment."

"Thanks, Lennard." Liam nodded.

"Liam, did you know if you take off your armor, put on some old clothes, and go to the taverns, no one ever recognizes you as a knight? We're invisible without our surcoats."

"It's that so?"

"And I went to a few taverns in St. George. In every one, they toasted you *and* the witch as heroes."

"Not me." Liam shook his head. "Legends of my grandfather be damned. I only killed two out of the entire clutch."

"I even met a man who told everyone about the steward who saved his daughter from fever."

"Yes."

"They also said the same steward saved your life."

"Wyvern bite." Liam showed off his throat scars. "Reynald performed surgery on me in the mud after killing most of the wyverns by himself."

"Then why are we burning him? *None of this makes sense.*"

"Nothing has to make sense. Just do your duty." Liam gestured to his room. "Or you'll end up in a cell beside me."

"But this isn't right." Lennard's hands balled into fists.

"No. It's not."

"What should I do?"

"Your best, Lennard. All a knight can do is protect the citizens of the land the best he can within the confines of the law."

"That's not good enough."

Lennard's eyes pleaded for a better answer. His jaw was tight set, lips pressed together in a stubborn frown. Liam sighed and pinched the bridge of his nose. He'd wanted to keep Lennard out of this mess, but the knight was too young and too idealistic.

"Then go back to the taverns and listen until you figure out who's a salt merchant. Talk to them and they'll show you how you can help others *beyond* the restrictions of the law."

Lennard stood for another instant, thinking. Eventually, he nodded, shutting and locking Liam's door. Liam's gaze swept across the room. The narrow loophole serving as a window revealed the late afternoon light. The space was furnished with a four-poster bed so much like his own, draped with velvet curtains and piled high with goose down cushions. Liam dropped face-first into the pillows and sobbed. He wasn't sure how long he lay, but his face felt fevered, and his throat ached. Once the tears ebbed, he scrambled to his feet, poured himself a tumbler of water from the ceramic pitcher on the nightstand, and gulped the entire glass before gasping.

Liam checked behind the tapestries, hoping to find a forgotten door or some escape route. He checked under the rugs, the bed, the heavy chest in the corner, full of night robes and extra quilts. He had water and wine and a small shelf with books, but nothing that could be used as a weapon or lockpick. Liam kicked the stone wall. For all the fairy stories and novels about castles full of secret passageways and trapdoors, this was an ordinary room in a tower. Security had probably investigated it thoroughly to make sure there was no escape.

Chapter Seventeen

The sky darkened beyond the narrow view of the loophole, but there was nothing Liam could do while trapped in his room. When Liam heard a key click in the lock, his guts cramped. He sat on the bed, waiting to see if it was a guard with supper or the king come to chide him. When Reynald stood in the doorway instead—mask skewed on top of his head and smirk visible—Liam scooped the sorcerer in his arms and spun him in the air.

"Ribs." Reynald squeaked, trying to stay quiet. "Still a little tender."

In lieu of apology, Liam smashed their mouths together. He didn't bother wiping at the tears welling in the corner of his eyes, needing both hands to hold Reynald's face. Reynald slipped his tongue into Liam's mouth, indulging in the kiss before pulling away.

"Wasn't expecting such a warm welcome after the way we screamed at each other in the throne room."

"You told me to play along." Liam peeked out the doorway. "Where's the guard?"

"Sleep spell." Reynald pulled Liam into the room and shut the door. "Your double agent act was far more realistic than I could have imagined. I had a heart attack when you offered to chop off your own hand."

"Lennard's too green for that sort of brutality. I'm lucky Seigfried stopped Cole, however, because I would have had to improvise." Liam lowered his hands so he could hold both of Reynald's. "What do we do now?"

"I should go back to my prison before they notice I slipped away. I didn't actually think about what I was doing when I snuck out. I heard the execution is at midnight, and I really wanted to see you before then." Reynald stared at their joined hands.

"Missed me?" Liam pressed their foreheads together and kept his eyes closed.

"You've grown on me," Reynald confessed.

"What can I do to help you?"

"Nothing, Liam. This is going to be between me, Seigfried, and Darius. I don't want you getting hurt in the crossfire."

"Fuck the oracle's prophecy, Reynald. Let's think of our own plan. This isn't you alone anymore. How can *we* solve this?"

"Listen to me." Reynald tugged on Liam's locs to force their gazes together. "I'm not risking you. I… I… I'm not."

"What do you expect me to do? Sit in this room and pray to the saints that you come back for me after it's all over?"

"Here." Reynald slipped the key to Liam's room into his palm. "Once you freed me from a cage; let me return the favor. I'll let you choose for yourself what you do, but stay far away from Seigfried, and don't you dare try to rescue me."

Reynald opened the door, dropped to the floor as a fox, and dashed down the hallway. Liam stood in the doorway, half free, half in his prison cell. The orange fox winked out of view as Reynald turned the corner. A guard leaned against the wall, snoring. Liam stepped fully into the hallway, locking the door behind him.

The first thing he was going to do was retrieve his shield.

Liam slipped the key back onto the guard's belt before rushing out of the eastern wing of the castle. The servants didn't look at him when he passed by, and it was easy to avoid patrols by listening for the clunk of their boots against the hard floors. Liam retraced his steps to the gallery where Reynald had revealed the hidden stairs leading to Sigfried's forbidden museum. The signs of his and Reynald's battle had long been cleaned and erased except for the faint scar on Liam's inner thigh. He pressed the trick stone and descended into the lower level before anyone noticed his presence.

At the bottom of the stairs, Liam hesitated. Reynald mentioned some items in the room were dangerous. He scanned the shelves and remaining curios. His iridescent blue shield sat on a stand in the back with two others. Liam swallowed a surge of rage. His family heirloom wasn't meant to sit in a private museum. The shield was made to protect people, and Liam was going to. Next to the shields was a rack of swords. Again, Liam paused. He had no way to know what sort of enchantments were on any of the relics. Cursed or not, they'd confiscated Liam's blade when they arrested him, so he grabbed a saber with a stallion pommel and tested the balance. In his hand, the sword felt like being home.

Liam marched to the staircase, staring up at the rectangle of light from the gallery above.

"What the fuck am I doing?" Liam asked himself.

He had no plan. A soldier, he really had spent his life following one order or another. Liam touched the golden scale on his surcoat. If he couldn't rescue Reynald, then perhaps he *could* free all the other mages in the castle. Without them, Seigfried shouldn't have the power to make any more golems even if he did survive Reynald's assassination attempt. Decision made, Liam dashed up the stairs and listened for bootsteps before sneaking down the hallway. He snaked his way to the magician quarters.

Liam waited for two guards to pass before knocking them both unconscious. Liam pulled the key ring from the older guard, then used the belt to tie him. He also tore a strip of cloth from the man's shirt to gag him. Finished, he repeated the process for the second guard and pulled them both into an empty room. Keys in hand, Liam unlocked the first chamber and flung the door wide. The sorcerer within flinched on his bed, staring at Liam in fear.

"It's all right." Liam held out his hands in a placating gesture. "The king is headed to the town square for an execution. Change into your familiar form and flee."

"No." He shook his head. "He'll hunt us."

"Find a salt merchant and leave Phrophis." Liam stepped away, hoping the mage would take the opening, but the magician refused to escape.

Each time he unlocked a new door, the response was the same. Every single mage pressed against the wall of their cell or curled on top of their bed when they saw their door opened. Some would stay and some would flee after they realized Liam wasn't a guard. He couldn't bear to ask what exactly Seigfried was doing to make them so afraid. Reynald had explained enough and he had witnessed enough for him to know their ordeals were no less traumatic than what the solders went through during war. After explaining he was there to help, some of the sorcerers leapt from their beds, running, flying, slithering in their various animal shapes. A few remained half-hidden in the corners of their small cells and shook their heads *no*, like the first mage, too terrified to move. Liam didn't push them; he simply ran to the next room to free the next slave. Near the end of the hall, Liam opened one of the last remaining doors and jerked backward. Edeline stood in front of him. She pounded both fists against his chest.

"You fool! Do you have any clue what you've done?"

"Edeline? Why are you in the castle?"

"I'm here because you changed my prediction, proved me wrong for the first time in my *life*, and Seigfried locked me away in a fit of paranoia. You weren't supposed to go to St. George. You certainly weren't supposed to fight the wyverns together! You damned fool!" she swore again. "He cracked his mask saving you!"

"I know."

"You know? What do you know? Do you know what this means? Reynald won't be able to contain Darius with a broken mask. He'll be devoured, and Citadel will be obliterated!"

"Why did you give him such a stupid prophecy to begin with?" Liam clenched his fingers around the key ring. "If you were a man, I'd punch you."

"If I were a man, you'd kiss me."

Liam shot her an angry stare, but she only laughed. Stepping out of the room, she stole the keys from his fist and released the next captive.

"Go to the baker on Cherry Street. He'll help you," she said to the prisoner.

The magician nodded before changing into a raccoon and fleeing down the hallway. Edeline glanced over her shoulder.

"Everything I've done has been for the betterment of Phrophis. Seigfried will destroy the entire kingdom if he isn't stopped."

"By sending Reynald on a self-destructive spiral, where he lets himself burn at the stake, then go to hell, grab a demon, use the phoenix feather to rise from his own ashes, and what? Let the demon get venge-ance *for* him?"

"There's a lot of negotiating contracts involved, but more or less, that was the original plan," Edeline said before releasing an eight-year-old from his room.

Liam grimaced as the lad ran past him but didn't let his guilt dis-tract him.

"And what was going to happen when Seigfried was dead? The

demon just goes home after a job well done, leaving Reynald healthy and happy to die of old age afterward?"

Edeline stopped, staring at Liam. With her crown of curls, she almost rivaled his height but had to tilt her head upward to match his gaze.

"Answer me," Liam said.

"The future isn't a line. There are endless branches, some wide and easy like a road, some tentative like a footpath. What happened to Reynald afterward was going to depend on the contract he offered Darius, and the possibilities were many, but it was Reynald's decision to make."

"And I'm sure those wide paths were happy ones." Liam crossed his arms over his chest.

"His decision to make." Edeline refused to break, adding," Even death is arguably better than having one's soul burned to oblivion, which is currently the *only* path I see for him."

"Fuck." Liam dropped his arms. "What do I do? How do I make this right?"

"You can't."

"Then let me die trying!" Liam's voice ricocheted off the walls and down the hallway. "I broke your prophecy once, maybe I can again."

"Then do what a hero is made to do. Go save him."

"How?" Liam smacked his forehead against the wall. "I don't want a map this time, but a little guidance would be appreciated."

"How does one be a hero, Liam? I'm still learning the answer myself." Edeline swung the key ring around her wrist like a charm bracelet. "And seeing possible futures only makes the weight of my actions *heavier*. I don't want anyone to suffer, but someone always does."

"Reynald makes it seem so easy. He just rushes in and does whatever he can." Liam kept his head pressed against the cool surface, closing his eyes.

"Well, we'll both start there, then. One way or another, I'm going to fight Darius. You can join me in the battle, or you can fling yourself into the flames and burn with Reynald. Your choice." Edeline dropped the key ring on the ground, all the doors now opened, and left Liam with his face leaning into the wall.

Liam turned his head to watch her go as he gathered himself. Reynald had told Liam not to dare rescue him, but this wasn't Liam going after Reynald as a knight trying to fulfill his duty—this was *compulsion*. Pushing off from the wall, Liam made his way out of the castle.

Memories of his game with Reynald during the harvest masquerade flashed through Liam's mind as he crouched beneath tables and behind potted plants to avoid the guards. Never would he have imagined his hiding games would have prepared him for escaping the palace as a fugitive. He avoided the main entrance, turning down a side hall and heading toward the servants' quarters. One of the maids walked down the hallway. She started when she saw him, lowered her head, and kept walking. Liam bowed but didn't speak to her. She was making a point that she couldn't see him, and he wasn't going to spoil her efforts with chatter.

Near the servant's exit, there was a small, not so much parlor, but a room with sturdy chairs and a kettle kept in the hearth in order to serve tea or coffee to couriers or workers stopping in for a task but not staying long enough to need room and board. Liam saw a closet with half a dozen wool cloaks inside. He chose the largest one before stuffing his cloak in a messenger bag. Liam left his surcoat and armor near the fire. He fitted the borrowed cloak over his shoulders and shield before using two of his locs to tie the rest of his hair behind his head and tugging the hood in place.

"See Reynald?" Liam spoke to the empty room. "It's not that hard. Like Lennard said, the moment we take off the armor and surcoats, we're just men."

Liam ran toward the stables. Shouts echoed throughout the courtyard. Liam snuck toward the sounds. It was one of the magicians who'd originally refused to leave her room. She crouched behind a barrel with her arms over her head as four royal guards surrounded her in their green-dyed leather breastplates embellished with real gold in the shape of a crown. Roaring, Liam charged into them, slamming them to the ground.

"Go! Now's your chance!" Liam pulled the girl upright and shoved her toward the main gate while he ran out as a decoy, waving his arms and screaming.

"Come on, you bastards! Let's have a real chase!"

Several men followed Liam into the castle. Someone screamed to the others to "Stop the witch," which suited Liam. Better they think he was an escaped magician than a knight. He circled them around the first floor before sneaking out through the servant's passage a second time. More screams echoed around the palace, alarm bells blurred together, someone shouted that the dogs were dead. Liam's stomach cramped when he heard the far-off announcement, but it would allow the others to get away…help him get away.

Liam kept his gaze set on his goal: the stables. He dashed from tree to tree, crawled on his belly behind a stack of hay bales near the stables, and slipped in around the back of the building. The smell of horse and hay anchored him, something good and familiar in the center of the chaos. When he saw Creed in one of the stalls, he flung his arm around the horse's neck and nuzzled against his coat.

A stab of guilt struck Liam when he realized he was going to have to leave Creed behind. Even if he somehow managed to use the chaos to get out of the courtyard without getting his horse maimed, riding Creed—with his mane and tail oiled and plaited—would be too obvious. He stroked Creed's neck, found where the stable master kept the sugar cubes, gave Creed several, and kissed Creed's nose before leaving the stables. Instead of riding out of the palace like a valiant hero as Liam had planned, he stole a rope from a gardener's shack, snuck up one of the watchtowers, knocked yet another guard unconscious, and climbed out like a thief.

Disguised and on the streets, Liam slipped through the back alleys of Citadel to make his way to the city square. The outer shell of the city was planned with streets expanding out and connecting like a spiderweb, but the heart of Citadel was a labyrinth, fragmented from the days of being a town instead of the capitol hundreds of years ago. The original roads and architecture had been remade, built upon, destroyed, and re-modeled dozens of times over. Occasionally, people would discover sealed off basements or a stretch of forgotten alley wedged between two buildings and later walled away. Some of these lost spaces became a se-cret realm for each generation of children to explore as they played, but

Liam only knew the main streets: turn on Seller's Place, find Huckleberry, travel past Old Way until the city made sense again. Liam did not know these winding side roads, however, and he swore every time a dead end forced him to turn around and backtrack. Then the church bells rang for midnight, and Liam started running.

"Shit!"

A few areas looked familiar, but he couldn't figure out how to get from the slum he was trapped in to the main shopping district. Liam searched for someone to ask for directions, but everyone was locked in their homes or gathered in the center of the city to watch the execution. The street sign at the corner said Poplar and Maple. Did Poplar connect to Huckleberry? Liam dashed right and cursed all fourteen Holy Helpers even while secretly begging them for help.

The church bells faded, and Liam picked up his pace. He made some progress but still couldn't find Huckleberry or another through street to exactly where he wanted to be. A horn called out in a forlorn tone, and Liam grabbed the handle of his sword on instinct. A second blow echoed the first. They were the horns of the city patrols, a signal for the church to begin ringing the bells for everyone to take shelter. As the church bells clanged in warning, a column of fire lifted into the air. Reynald's stolen phoenix feather.

"No. No. No. No. No!" Liam's chest burned from sprinting. The impact of his boots smacking against the cobblestone shot up his ankles and calves.

The burning column thinned and dissipated. Was the spell over? Was Reynald alive? Liam ran, panicked.

Another light flashed. Red, as before, but dark like clotting blood. The clouds began to spiral, flicking with rust-colored lightning. A dim maroon glow remained in the center, throbbing and stretching tendrils through the clouds between the flashes of lightning.

The red pulsing in the sky continued to spread like the dark markings of blood poisoning. Liam turned a corner to find another dead end, forcing him to turn around once again. With a roar, he leapt over the privacy fence of a rich merchant's manor in order to cut through the maze and get to Cherry Street. As he raced toward the square beneath the red-infected sky, Liam heard people shriek. Smoke thickened the air, and all reason fled Liam's mind. He screamed, pumped his arms, and ran, ran, ran, ready to jump into the fire himself to pull Reynald free if that's what it took.

People fled toward the cathedral, pushing their way past Liam. As the crowds thinned, Liam burst into the square, crashing to his knees and gaping in horror. Above, the sky ripped, and brimstone hurtled into roofs and through windows. The debris exploded in blue-violet sparks and dozens of fires sprang up like a swarm of fireflies invading the city.

Reynald stood in the center of a burning pile, laughing. But it wasn't Reynald. The laughter was dark and gleeful, not haughty. His orange hair was an inferno rising above him—actual flames, burning and smoking. The mask was flesh with two glowing orange eyes and a scintillating red wound where the mask had been cracked. The king was gone; the throne erected for him to view the execution sat empty. Reaching out his hand, Reynald pointed at the throne and a chunk of flaming sulfur hurled from the sky and crashed into the wood—good walnut stripped from the Balbraid Thicket now a wreckage of flames and ash.

Chancellor Cole held a crosier in both hands and attempted to strike the mask with the blunt tip. His movements were slow and clumsy. Reynald gripped the crosier and snapped the metal in half like a match. Then, his other hand shot out, clutching Cole's throat and lifting him in the air.

"No." Liam pushed himself to his feet and stumbled forward. "Reynald, no!"

With a flick of his wrist, Reynald snapped the chancellor's neck and dropped him in front of the burning, shattered throne. The chancellor landed in a heap, mouth ajar, eyes blank and wide. With the chancellor dead, the demon spun around and narrowed his bright gaze at Liam. He raised his hand, but paused…conflicted. Instead of attacking, the demon dashed down Market Place, spreading flames around him as he walked.

"Reynald! Come back!" Liam chased him.

Liam had chased him during a harvest masquerade, he'd chased him through the palace in the heat of battle, he'd chased him from Citadel to the Northern Wilds, and he'd chase Reynald into hell itself if he needed to, and so he'd chase him now down the street. Liam didn't draw his sword, nor did he pull his shield from the strap keeping the heirloom hidden below his worn-out cloak. Instead, Liam darted through an alley, behind the fletchers, and cut off Reynald's progression through town. He held his arms spread wide.

"Reynald! Stop! Your vengeance is with Seigfried, not the entire city!"

Reynald growled, teeth dripping spittle that hissed and boiled on the cobblestones near his feet. His fingers were now black claws. He was gradually becoming more demon and less human the longer Darius inhabited his body.

"I can't let you hurt people! I know you don't want this!" Liam stretched his arms wider, as if inviting Reynald to embrace him.

Reynald shoved him aside. Liam crashed into a stall where a girl named Margaret sold flowers during the day. Liam's weight smashed the wood, splintering it. The hood fell away and wood chips fell into his hair from the wreckage. The strands came untied, falling to his shoulders. Reynald froze, eyes narrow slits. They were pure orange now, not white or pupils. Liam brushed the scraps out of his locs.

"Reynald, it's me. Liam. Look. I can wear a wool cloak after all. I don't have to be a knight, but I have to be with *you*. I…"

Liam lost his nerve. It shouldn't be hard to scream out the very phrase that had been tormenting him for weeks, but he wanted to see Reynald's face when he said the words.

"Please take off your mask," Liam begged. "I need to talk to you, not Darius. Really talk to you, and you know I hate when you hide behind that thing."

Reynald summoned a shard of brimstone. Liam dashed out of the way, rolling onto the street. His training allowed him to jump to his feet even after the tumble. He grabbed his shield but kept his sword tucked away.

"Reynald! I have to tell you something! Look at me when I speak to you!"

The demon screeched. Reynald shoved Liam to the cobblestone and fled.

"I'll chase you!" Liam rushed to his feet again and sprinted after Reynald. "You know I'll chase you until I'm out of breath!"

He ripped off the dull gray cloak and allowed it to rise into the air and billow to the ground. Liam pulled his dragon skin from the messenger bag to protect himself from Darius's attacks and dumped the rest—the weight slowing him down. The last stragglers working their way to the church screamed as they fled, while the demon called fire and burned the city just as the city had tried to burn him. It no longer mattered if they saw Sir Bord in his cloak or not. Let them see him. Let them tell the king he fought while the other knights were nowhere to be found. Liam slipped his shield around his arm. Unlike the slums, he knew the Market District, so he was able to take another shortcut to cut ahead of the demon.

"Reynald! I'm sorry! I thought you knew how I felt! You're so clever, and quick with words, and always implying instead of saying things outright! Surely you know how I feel, but I guess knowing isn't enough. You need to hear it, so listen—" Liam screamed enough for his throat to crack. He felt the strain in the vocal cords Reynald had mended with magic. He coughed, doubling over.

Reynald paused, flaming tails now whipping behind him, at least a dozen of them. The fur crept down his neck as Darius continued to overpower him. He cut through an alley. When his foot landed in a puddle, the water boiled and evaporated in a mushroom of steam. Liam kept at his heels. He reached out and grabbed Reynald's hand, but jerked away, palm stinging from the heat. The demon turned and lunged close, slamming Liam against the nearest brick wall. He used his forearm, the wyvern scale-lined magic cloth kept Reynald's touch from burning Liam's chest.

"Please, take off your mask."

The demon's breath reeked of sulfur, and he growled a single word close enough to Liam's lips that he felt them singe with heat.

"Run."

"Your eyes are so beautiful. I want to look at them, not fire." Liam's expression crumbled. "Don't make me say this to Darius, Reynald. I know you can hear me, but…please, this is important."

"Run!"

He slammed Liam to the ground. The air was knocked out of Liam's chest. He struggled to hands and knees before crawling forward.

The children's screaming brought Liam to his feet and running again.

Chapter Eighteen

A beam had crashed to the ground and pinned a woman's ankle. She lay sprawled against the cobblestone. Three children surrounded her and tugged, but their tiny hands weren't enough to pull her free. She shoved and screamed at them to run when the demon noticed them. The youngest stood near the mother's trapped feet, openly wailing while clutching a plush rabbit. The oldest avoided her mother's shoves and grabbed her arm, tugging with all of her meager body weight. The middle child hoisted a splintered chunk of wood in both his hands and charged at the demon to fight it.

Before he could strike, Liam intercepted, crashing to his knees, pulling the child to his chest, and using his cloak to deflect the fire spewing from Darius's hands. As soon as there was a pause in the attack, Liam carried the boy to his family, rolled the beam away from the mother's foot, and faced Darius.

"Run! I'll cover you!" Liam shouted at the mother and children but kept his gaze locked on the demon wearing Reynald's body.

The eldest daughter swung her mother's arm around her shoulder and acted as a crutch. Panicked, the family raced toward the church. Darius moved to follow them, but Liam body blocked him, using his shield to get close without burning himself.

"You're always like this! So stubborn!" Liam screamed, forgetting about Darius and thinking only of Reynald. "Fine! If this is how we have to talk, so be it! Reynald! I—"

Reynald tackled Liam to the ground. The back of Liam's skull smacked the cobblestones, and the red sky above seesawed in a sickening way. The brimstone still raining to the ground winked in beautiful flashes, but the smell of smoke turned Liam's stomach. He felt the pinch of Darius's claws poking into his scarred throat. Fitting as it was—since the demon was only out of control because Reynald cracked his mask using too much magic to heal Liam—he couldn't die in the street. If he died, Darius would consume Reynald's soul and slaughter the entire kingdom.

Ignoring the prickling pain against his skin, Liam grabbed Reynald's masked face. Tears welled in Liam's eyes as his skin blistered beneath the burning touch.

"Listen, Reynald..."

The claws pushed deeper, enough to dimple his skin, but he only needed three seconds.

"I love you."

Darius jerked away, pulling free of Liam's hands. The glowing slits cutting through the mask sparked, becoming blue fire on one side, rich anise-brown flames on the other side. The tower of Reynald's hair fell, cascading around his shoulders, and the fox face itself hardened, more ivory than flesh.

"Reynald, I love you," Liam repeated, relieved that it was easier the second time. "I figured you knew but didn't want to give up your vengeance. But if there was ever any doubt, I love you."

The tears lining Liam's eyes because of the heat now spilled because of the emotions lacerating his chest. Reynald reached out with his flared sleeve in his hand and mopped the tears away from Liam's cheeks. One at a time, the flaming tails began to snuff out like candles, and the fur receded down Reynald's arm, showing skin.

"I'm sorry I didn't say it sooner. I'm sorry I lost focus in battle and forced you to overuse your magic. I was so impressed with how you fought, so enthralled with how brilliant you were while using your magic freely, that I completely lost track of my surroundings. It was a greenling mistake, and I only survived because you were able to operate on my throat while killing the last of the wyverns." Liam shook his head. "Don't leave me, Reynald. I love you."

Reynald shook, hugging himself. The mouth of the mask opened, still mobile even as ivory. Reynald turned to the side, body jerking as he dry heaved. Liam sat, reached for Reynald, but Reynald crawled away several feet. With another gag, fire rushed from Reynald's mouth and sparks showered across the cobblestones. He sucked in a labored breath, and more fire and sparks splashed from between his lips.

Liam gripped the stones, eyes wide and unable to look away as Reynald vomited flames. The fire pooled near Reynald, growing each time another mouthful of sparks hit the ground. As he retched, the long black talons rounded and paled, the last of the fur fell to the ground, and his flaming hair simmered low until only matted, tangled orange strands remained. Then the mask was lifeless, only carved ivory. Reynald dropped to his side, drenched in sweat and gulping for breath. Liam inched closer but was careful because the flames next to them were shifting, forming into a shape.

Liam offered his canteen, but Reynald only pushed it aside. When Liam reached for Reynald's mask, Reynald whimpered and turned away.

"It's fused," Reynald said in a gruff, damaged voice.

"Fused?"

"We'll worry about the mask later. Help me stand."

Liam lifted Reynald to his feet. They backed away from the fire. The flames rose taller than them and were still growing. Reynald pressed his masked face against Liam's chest.

"I'm sorry."

"This is my fault. You were never supposed to crack your mask."

"But I did, and I thought I could control Darius anyway."

"None of that matters right now. How are we going to solve this together, Reynald?"

"I expelled him from my body, but the portal is still open. We have to banish him and mend the tear between our realms." Reynald pointed above, at the swirling red clouds slowly spinning over the city.

"What do you need me to do?"

In a sudden swirl of smoke and fire, the flames leapt taller than the buildings around them. The orange and yellow smears took the shape of clawed limbs and swiped at them. Liam jerked Reynald away from the attack. They stumbled backward until their backs pressed against the seamstress's shop.

"Run." Reynald grabbed Liam's hand and dragged him down a different street.

Liam shot a glance over his shoulder as they ran. The growing fire elongated. Wings rose from the center mass. A long tail whipped behind the forming beast. Neck curving out like a swan's, the flames went from shapeless fire to the recognizable bulk of a dragon.

"Fuck! Fuck! Fuck!" Reynald cursed as they retreated.

The dragon's eyes were as molten and orange as steel in a blacksmith's forge. Darius raised his snout into the air and bellowed a roar that shattered the glass in the shops around him. Out of the portal in the sky, a vast murder of stryx flew from the clouds and circled the city like vultures. Several of them dipped low, and when they then ascended into the sky, they held people in their claws. Those who'd captured prey spiraled higher, disappearing through the portal and into the infernal abyss above.

"Fuck." Reynald pressed his back against the wall, making himself less of a target.

"Can you control the stryx?"

"Not against the commands of their master."

"Darius is fire. What if we lured him beneath a water tower and ruptured the barrel to douse him?" Liam asked.

"No good. Too hot. Too much sulfur." Reynald ducked beneath the eves of the buildings to avoid being spotted by the stryx.

"Okay. I'm out of ideas."

"I'm thinking." Reynald tested the mask on his face, tugging with a ginger pull, but the action made him whimper and he dropped his hands. "A banishing circle. In the square where I summoned him. I should have the herbs and chalk."

Reynald patted his robe, thrusting his hands in various pockets and pulling out bags and tins, checking each, sniffing a few, and setting what he needed aside while shoving the rest away. He also pulled out a nub of pastel pink chalk.

"When did I use pink chalk?" Reynald tilted his head, shook his thoughts away, and refocused. "The spell won't care, but I need time to draw—"

A shriek cut through Reynald's words as one of the stryx dove toward them. Acting on instinct, Liam jumped in front of Reynald, raised his shield, and pulled his sword. He aimed for the eyes, but the beast moved too swiftly, and the blade sliced through her neck instead. The steel should have passed through the shadows, but the creature burst out of existence, raining feathers onto their heads that hissed and dissolved into dark steam before floating into nothingness.

"How did I...?" Liam's jaw dropped as he stared where the creature should be.

"The sword you're holding is Marseilles." Reynald laughed. "You stole from Seigfried's collection."

"Seigfried stole my shield." Liam held the sword between them so he and Reynald could examine the blade. "And my old sword. I made do."

"Well, whether by fate or dumb luck, you grabbed a sword created by a sorcerer who specialized in seals and banishment rituals."

"I liked the stallion pommel."

"Of course you did."

"If I stab Darius with this, will he vanish?"

"No. It will hurt, but he's too powerful to be unmade from an enchanted blade. However, you can wreck the little ones without aiming for the eyes."

"Good enough. How long will it take you to draw the circle?"

"An hour. It's not an easy sigil, and I need the circumference to be as big as Darius."

"I'm going to save who I can from these damn stryx before leading Darius to the square. Can you signal me when you're ready?"

"Watch the sky for fireworks." Reynald nodded.

"Fireworks? Is that a spell, or do you literally have fireworks stashed in one of your pockets?" Liam's jaw dropped at the thought.

"A wizard doesn't have to give away all his secrets. Go do something heroic!" Reynald waved him away before pivoting to dash toward the city square.

"Before you go." Liam grabbed Reynald's wrist, spun him to Liam's chest as if they were dancing, and whispered against his ear, "I love you."

Reynald's breath hitched. With a parting kiss against Reynald's earlobe, Liam ran after the shadow creatures and left his fox standing in shock.

Once out in the open, a stryx swooped to capture him. Liam waited until she was low and sliced into her belly, destroying her. Each creature that dove down to attack him was sent back to their hellish dimension, but it wasn't enough. Liam scanned the streets. He was lost again, but Darius lumbered just ahead, crushing any buildings standing in his path.

"Hey!" Liam screamed to get Darius's attention. "Attack me!"

The dragon's roar expanded across the city, shaking the windows in their frames, and a small flock of stryx swerved in his direction. They circled above him before diving closer.

"Yes! Come for me!" Liam shouted.

Unlike love, battle was simple, battle Liam understood. He zigzagged through the beasts, slicing into them with his blade as he passed. Any deep cut caused the creatures to dissolve, and the sword felt light in Liam's hand. He loved magic! Feathers danced around him as he pivoted at a dead end. Making another pass through the alley, Liam managed to cut down the few stryx he missed the first time.

Liam flattened himself against a wall and checked around the corner to spy on Darius. The demon rammed through a brick wall to reach the next street. Bricks showered down behind him, crashing into the streets and cracking into chunks. Liam stepped out into the open, sword and shield ready, but before he could charge, another set of bells cried out from the cathedral. The sound wasn't the long, mournful dongs of the evacuation bell. These clangs were shrill and short—a signal that the cathedral was under direct attack.

Liam watched the burning dragon smash through buildings and melt iron gates with his flames, his orange eyes locked on the palace.

Whatever contract he'd arranged with Reynald must still be—at least partially—intact. Darius was after Seigfried.

Years of training and conditioning and fealty to his liege urged Liam to catapult forward, block the path, die fighting to protect king and castle. Liam swallowed, taking heavy steps backward. He gave the palace a final glance, before bolting toward the sound of bells and the steeple rising above the rest of the buildings.

He didn't have Creed, but there was an inn nearby with a stable. All the patrons and workers had fled when the evacuation bells rang, but Liam checked the stalls to see if he could find a horse to commandeer. The air was still. This block had little damage from the random falling brimstone destroying sections of Citadel. A quiet snort drew his eye to the back where four horses stood and watched him, leery of his unfamiliar battle sweat. None of the animals looked fit for a fight, but Liam chose a sturdy, black stallion and guided him outside. The horse reared, spooked by the sky, the smoke, the screams as people rose into the air in the claws of the stryx, but Liam managed to stabilize the animal. Hopping onto the horse bareback, Liam trotted through the streets toward the cathedral where the rest of the stryx swirled in a vortex.

The wind cooled Liam's sweat-drenched body, and even the quick rest was enough for him to gain a second wind. At intervals, the stryx crashed against the church. Their bodies shattered the gorgeous windows; a kaleidoscope of glass sprinkled about the ground. The shadow creatures crawled through the broken windows. Screams reverberated from the cathedral, and when they crawled out, each stryx held a screeching victim in their talons as they flew into the pulsing, red portal wounding the sky. Liam tied the horse far enough away to keep him safe and ran the rest of the way. As one of the stryx spread her wings to take flight, Liam pierced Marseilles through her ribs. She vanished, dropping her hostage, and Liam grabbed the boy, a lad of seventeen or so, and helped him through the window back into the building.

"If you strike them in the eye, they die. Tell the others. Find whatever you can to use as weapons and defend yourselves." Liam jumped through the window after him.

"Okay." The lad kept his head down as he ran toward the cellar where the civilians were sheltering.

Liam scanned the inside of the cathedral, searching for movement. All the pews lay shattered or on their sides. The fourteen saint statues were spread in a semicircle at the front of the church, but St. Blaise lay face down beneath a pile of wreckage where a section of the ceiling had caved in. Liam scanned the first floor, ignoring the torn silk tapestries and dented golden candelabras. A shadow dimmed the ruddy light spilling from the window behind Liam. Pivoting, he kept his shield raised as he lunged forward. The stryx screeched, flapping her wings. She burst into a shower of feathers as Liam banished her back to her own realm with a thrust of his sword. He circled toward the stairs; another stryx landed at a nearby windowsill, and he dispatched her before she managed to step into the room. As he fought, he kept glancing out the busted windows for fireworks.

Screams echoed from above. Liam climbed the stairs until he reached the second floor. Nuns and deacons guarded the windows, fighting with spears and piercing the creatures' eyes to banish them, but they were outnumbered. Liam jumped into the fray, covering the other fighters. With Marseilles, he didn't have to aim as carefully, so Liam slashed at every patch of shadow he saw, culling the numbers until they were able to stop and catch their breaths between waves of attacks.

"Ha! Lottie's grandson has saved us, after all." The oldest nun, wrinkled, hair very white, snorted as she rested her spear over her shoulder.

"You knew my grandmother?" Liam blinked in surprise, despite the mayhem around them.

"Long before she was Lady Bord."

"I never knew the clergy were trained to fight."

"You think a nun can't fight against the servant of a demon?"

"Augustine, please. Sir Bord, thank you. My name is Mary. If there's anything we can do to assist you, let us know."

Sweat trails cut paths down the grime smeared across Mary's face. Her habit was shredded at the bottom, and her sleeve had been ripped away. Below the scratch marks and blood, Liam saw most of a tattoo, fine cursive ink stabbed into her skin and reading, "Saint Margaret with the dragon, Saint Barbara with the tower, Saint Catherine with the wheel." Liam's father hadn't been a churchgoing man, but Liam remembered seeing this phrase, honoring the three holy maidens, embroidered on several pillows in their solar and guest rooms.

"Where are the other knights?" a deacon asked. "There's usually a few running guard around the church to keep everyone safe, but I haven't seen anyone but the city patrol, and they're all dead."

"All of them?" Liam's grip tightened on his sword.

"Or worse…" Another deacon used his spear to point at the red swirl in the sky. "They were carried off."

"Did the knights die as well?" another nun asked, eyes wide and glassy despite her tight expression masking her fear.

"I…don't know." Liam couldn't bring himself to lie in a church.

"At least you came when the other knights were nowhere to be seen." Augustine nodded with her arms crossed over her chest.

"Watch out! More stryx!" A deacon with buttermilk pale hair pointed out the window.

"We do not fear demons! We are the followers of the Fourteen Helpers," Mary chanted. "To die protecting others would be an honor."

"Amen." The rest closed her prayer.

"Amen." Liam nodded.

The wooden windowsills creaked beneath the weight of the perched fowl. They snapped their beaks at the deacons and nuns who charged toward them, but the spears kept their maws out of reach. Mary angled her spear tip and managed to pierce two of the birds through their eyes at the same time. Liam caught one beneath her jaw. Feathers sprayed out the window. Liam pivoted, blocked a lunge from a second bird as she whipped toward him, and ducked to avoid a separate attack. Augustine pressed her back against Liam's and pierced the crimson eye of another stryx right as she dipped close for a bite. Once her feathers scattered across the floor and dissolved, the old nun rushed to help two of the deacons retreating from a fresh onslaught of birds spilling through the windows.

Liam joined her. Swinging, his blade glided through a stryx. But as long as the portal pulsed in the sky above them, the stryx would keep hunting. Their shadow-dark bodies swarmed the room. Liam and the clergy had to pool into the center, fighting back-to-back-to-back. So many stryx swarmed the cathedral that the air outside looked like a moonless night. Liam hacked at the beasts, careless, desperate to thin their numbers, but even banishing three or four in a swing, he couldn't compete with the press. A scream pierced through the chaos of battle as one of the nuns was plucked into the air and carried out the window. The rest of them closed the gap to mend their formation. Augustine roared in rage, stabbing so fast, Liam wasn't sure how she managed such dexterity with fingers swollen with arthritis.

Liam screamed, refusing to slow down his strikes despite his burning shoulders. He couldn't be selfish. He couldn't die here and abandon Reynald to fight Darius by himself. Tears singed Liam's eyes as the wave of black feathers pressed closer, but he refused to blink. He would fight until dragged away.

Echoes bounced into the room from the stairwell. Screeching. Shouting. Boots against stone. Three dozen extra men stormed into the room. The instant they filed through the narrow passage, they fanned out, trapping the stryx in a pincer attack. The reinforcements were enough to recover the morale of the clergy. Mary shouted, "Amen," the others repeated the word, and they fought until both groups met. Sir Tobyn Stelis and Lennard Hall appeared. More importantly, a contingent of marksmen circled the perimeter of the second floor, covering each window and preventing more stryx from spilling inside.

"At last. The knights have made an appearance." Augustine wiped sweat from her ruddy face. "Thank Saint George."

"Secure a perimeter. Send a scout party to search for survivors in the area," Tobyn delegated to various soldiers. "You. Get some of the men downstairs to salvage the broken pews for barricades. This is going to be a longer battle than our last stryx attack. We need to be able to hold out."

"Sir." The bowman bowed and ran downstairs.

"We're sorry," Lennard whispered to Liam once he was close enough to speak without the clergy eavesdropping. "Seigfried had all the knights and guards escort him to the castle. When Abacus asked to escort a platoon to the church, Seigfried forbade us to leave."

"Of course he did." Liam sheathed his sword and rubbed his shoulders while he had a minute to catch his breath.

"He's insane," Lennard hardly spoke above a breath. "Our king is mad."

Liam nodded, unsure what to say. Finished giving instructions, Tobyn joined their parley. He gazed around him to make sure no one was listening. His own guards were following his orders while the clergy helped with barricades and tended their own wounded. Tobyn spoke as quietly as Lennard had.

"After His Majesty ordered all the guards and knights on-site to retreat into the castle, we thought he was regrouping before planning a defensive for the city, but Seigfried took the six bodyguards you gave him down into a secret chamber and refused to come out or speak to anyone."

"That chamber is filled with magic relics. I'm sure he's grabbed everything in there he can to protect himself against Darius," Liam said.

"Then the rumors of the king's collection of magical contraband are true." Lennard shook his head. "I wonder if some of the more…disturbing rumors are true as well."

"I don't know what you've heard, but I'm sure it's all true," Liam said.

"I've told you, Lennard, magical metal and stone men destroying the forest is a tale for drunks and children." Tobyn shook his head in refusal.

"They're called golems, and I've seen them." Liam drank from his canteen. "At a distance, but with my own eyes. They have no faces, but never miss a single tree. That's why so many creatures are fleeing the Thicket."

"Just what we need." Tobyn's jaw clenched. "As if demons weren't enough to deal with."

Liam's eyes darted toward the window—no fireworks yet—but plenty of shadows as the stryx circled the church. The fiends hung farther back now that the archers were guarding each window, but they hadn't given up their hunt.

"If Seigfried ordered you to stay in the castle before hiding, how are you here?" Liam asked, eyes still trained on the windows and the sky.

"House Stelis serves the oracle, not the king." Tobyn shook his head, a hint of a smirk at the corners of his mouth as he tapped the crest on his surcoat. "These orchids, after all, are a disgrace to the kingdom. Edeline ordered me to protect the church and keep you alive if possible, so here I am."

"And I joined him, because it was the right thing to do." Lennard shrugged. "And I see you weren't content to stay imprisoned. How did you escape?"

"A fox let me out of my room."

"The one who turned into a demon?" Lennard asked.

"That story would take more than a beer or two to explain." Liam shook his head. "But he's no longer physically connected to Darius and is working on a banishment circle to get the demon back to his home realm."

"I've never seen Edeline impressed before, but I think you two have managed it." Tobyn snorted. "She thinks his plan might work."

"If not, we're all dead," Liam confessed.

The stryx outside squawked as they shifted in the air. Dozens of glittering, golden explosions bloomed in the sky, whistling and crackling as they showered down in golden embers. Liam released an exhausted, relieved breath because the fireworks meant Reynald was all right. He turned to the other two knights.

"I have to go."

"Very well." Tobyn nodded. "But after the battle, the remaining knights need to discuss what we plan to do about the king. Especially if what you said about the golems is true."

"Do you think the other knights will side with us?" Liam asked.

"Most," Tobyn clapped Liam on the back. "Until then, may Saint George watch over you."

"Don't you dare die." Lennard shook his head. "That damn horse doesn't like anyone but you. He nipped me for giving him an apple."

"He likes Reynald." Liam grinned.

"Sir Bord." Mary marched to him as he headed toward the exit. "When this is over, find me. We also need to talk. Your father was a great friend of the church, and I think you might be as well."

"My…father was?" Liam wrinkled his brow, confused. His father never attended mass.

"Yes."

"All right. I'll seek you out as soon as I'm able." Liam nodded before dashing to his borrowed horse and riding out to find Reynald.

Chapter Nineteen

Liam left the view of the cathedral shrinking behind him and trusted the others to survive until he and Reynald were successful. On horseback, he wound through the streets. Unlike his usual rides, Liam had to dart the horse around any burning wreckage until he slipped through the gates surrounding the castle. The final gate guarding the palace lay in a heap of ruined masonry with mangled gate bars twisting up from the stones. Liam's poor untrained horse reared as the wind shifted and the stink of burning—burning hay, burning wood, burning flesh—grew overwhelming.

"Easy, boy, easy." Liam patted his neck and steered him away from the shattered gate.

Dismounting, Liam tied the horse away from any potential danger and ran the final distance on foot. He coughed as smoke blew across his path. No living guards remained near the gate entrance to stop him from heading directly toward the palace. He jumped over half a leg. Memories of the front lines on the Prophis-Valan borders from the war clawed at Liam's thoughts, but he shoved them away, shoved them away, shoved them away. He couldn't help the dead and more would die if he didn't find Darius and lead him to Reynald's banishing seal. Screams echoed through the smoke and rubble, guiding Liam.

From within the chaos, Sir Kent Oldsworth's shout of "the traitor" echoed to the courtyard. Liam flinched when he realized *he* was the traitor and scanned the wreckage for cover. Kent called for his archers to nock, aim, and loose a round of arrows, but Liam sheltered behind the wooden stage where the royal magicians often performed.

"Stop! I'm here to help!" Liam shouted as a dozen arrows sank into the wood and ground around him.

"I'm going to make sure you burn with the rest of them!" Kent screamed.

"Wait until after we deal with the demon!" Liam raised high enough to peek over the edge of the stage, then had to duck to avoid another round of arrows.

Teeth clenched, Liam circled around the stage to examine the castle entrance. Harold and Abacus guarded the main entrance. Blood caked around Abacus's face, and one of Harold's arms was tucked into a green sling made of his torn surcoat. Their infantry stood in formation up the stairs leading to the palace. Most of the soldiers maintained their composure as they dodged brimstone attacks from the flaming dragon trying to force his way through their lines. However, several dozen men on either side of the stairway were obvious reserves. They didn't hold their spears with the same confidence as the clergy had when fighting the stryx in the cathedral. Yet they were swarming Darius, doing everything they could—despite the singe marks on their quilted armor—to keep the dragon away from the castle. Except one man who wept and pressed as far back as he could. He'd be court-martialed if they survived the battle, but everyone was too busy to deal with him in that moment.

"Save the arrows for the demon, Kent!" Harold shouted.

"Seigfried wants Liam dead!"

"Fine!" Liam growled. "After the battle, arrest me again, but let me help first!"

Using his flaming bulk to advance, Darius drove the soldiers backward, and the *cheval de frise* meant to protect them trapped them in a flaming pen.

Another infantry soldier dropped his spear in sheer panic. "We're doomed! We're already dead!"

He crawled under the flaming spikes to flee. Kent ordered his men to shoot him. Before the arrows loosed, a stryx swooped down and plucked the soldier into the air, carrying him to the portal. Liam's gaze lifted, and he saw the birdlike creatures perched all around the castle, but none of the windows were smashed open the way they'd broken into the church. Liam guessed Darius himself must kill Seigfried according to whatever pact he made with Reynald, so he kept his stryx hunters on standby until his agreement had been fulfilled.

"I can wound Darius! Stop shooting, and I'll show you!" Liam called.

"Can you really wound him?" Abacus shouted. "How?"

"I stole a sword from Siegfried's collection!"

"He's confessing to more crimes! Kill him!" Kent screamed, but his voice was drowned by the dying screams of several soldiers as Darius trampled over their bodies.

The dragon snapped at a soldier. The man ignited in Darius's jaw. The stench, the death keens… Liam's heart pounded in his ears, and he knew the others had to be struggling with the horror as much as he was. Harold and Abacus had their backs pressed to the palace door. Kent was near the stables with his archers. They took cover beneath the awning with hay bales stacked around them to prevent the stryx from snatching any more of them. A few sharpshooters hid in the loft itself. When they had a shot, they'd pick off the stryx, but each time one burst into feathers and smoke, another one would eventually replace her. Kent attempted several attacks on Darius himself, aiming for the eyes or snout or where the heart should beat, but his arrows slipped through the fire without piercing.

"Kent!" Abacus shouted as another one of his men was picked off. "We can't stop him!"

"Hold your positions!" Kent ordered.

"How?" Harold flung his sword at the demon to show how useless the fight was.

The blade spun through the fire and landed in the dirt behind the dragon. Flames reflected in Harold's eyes; sweat poured down his face. The front lines crumpled as Darius took another step forward, growing impatient.

"Fuck it! Get out of here, men!" Harold held his shield and charged forward, crawling over the dead to reach the demon in a desperate attempt to cover so they could retreat. The flames heated the metal, and Sir Pines screamed.

"Harold! Stop!" Liam risked the arrows and charged forward.

His boots kicked up clumps of grass as he ran along Darius's side, drawing his blade through the flames of the dragon's flank. The demon roared, feeling the sting of the enchanted steel of Marseilles. Darius quartered away from the castle to face Liam instead. His body blocked the archers from shooting at Liam and created enough of a gap for the remaining soldiers on the steps to regroup and tend to their burns. Liam swiped through Darius's leg, shouting to keep his attention.

"Come for me, demon! Or I will send you to hell piece by piece!"

Sweat drenched Liam's neck and soaked his underclothes. He leapt and thrust Marseilles into Darius's eye. The demon shook his head, blinking as if blinded on one side. Liam didn't give him a chance to recover. He blitzed the dragon with several attacks, making damn well sure he had Darius's full attention.

"You're not killing anyone else until you deal with me!" Liam attacked again, exhausted from the heat but refusing to ease his assault.

Kent ordered more arrows released on Liam, but none of the archers had line of sight with the demon between them and Liam, so the attacks all scattered the ground around him. Liam ignored Kent, slowly drawing Darius away from the others and into the city.

"What are you doing? Stop shooting!" Abacus shouted. "Liam just saved our lives!"

"He's a traitor!" Kent insisted.

"The demon is a bigger priority!"

Liam couldn't process their argument. His entire focus locked onto Darius as he wove around the dragon's feet. He thrust Marseilles repeatedly into the flames, an angry wasp refusing to stop stinging until one or the other was dead. Darius lingered, magically drawn to the palace despite Liam's attacks. Liam continued to stab until, pact or no, Darius lunged away from the castle and closer to Liam, snapping at him and kicking his clawed feet. Once Liam was sure Darius would follow, he marched backward toward the mangled ruins of the gates out of the courtyard.

A shadow caught the corner of his vision, and he blocked the blur with his shield. It wasn't until the mace struck his shield that Liam understood Sir Oldsworth had decided to fight Liam, despite Darius snapping at them both. Kent jumped away from the dragon's bite and stepped in again for another swing at Liam. His mace crashed into Liam's shield three times, and Liam had to dodge both Kent's attacks and Darius's.

"Are you crazy?" Harold's face twisted in disbelief. "Fuck this! Everyone retreat into the castle!"

"Our orders!" Abacus reached out for Sir Pines's good arm to grab and stop him. "Our honor!"

"Our weapons are useless. Our men are pissing themselves as they die. Let a Bord fight a dragon. We're retreating!"

"You're next, Harold!" Kent pointed his mace at his fellow knight. "I won't suffer a traitor to live!"

"Go fuck yourself, Kent." Harold kicked open the castle door and gave the command for a retreat.

Soldiers in both green and coral colors stampeded into the palace. Most of Kent's men, in deep red surcoats, risked the stryx to make a run for the doors as well. With their leadership fighting each other, with Sir Pines's sword lost beneath the burnt remains of bodies and broken pieces of *cheval de frise*, even the war veterans didn't have the discipline to hold their position after Harold called for retreat. They slammed the doors shut once everyone was safe inside, but Liam didn't have time to feel relief on their behalf because Kent consumed his attention. With Liam occupied, Darius turned toward the castle.

"No!" Liam broke away, but his attack was shallow because Kent was on him an instant later.

"Kent! Back off!" Liam warned. "He's going to destroy the palace while hunting Seigfried if I don't get him to the square!"

"Die!" Kent choked his grip higher on his mace to increase the force of his blows.

Liam dodged and closed the gap between them. Marseilles slipped into Kent's ribs. Liam kicked him and shoved him into the open before jumping away. As Kent stumbled backward, one of the stryx plunged her talons into Kent's armored shoulders. The remaining sharpshooters in the loft made three shots at her but couldn't get the creature's eyes. Liam *could*, one prick of Marseilles would banish the beast back to hell, but Liam only glared at Kent, jaw tight. He wasn't bitter about being called a traitor, or even being attacked, but Kent had pulled Reynald's hair and smashed his face against the marble floor in the castle.

"Enjoy hell." Liam turned away from Kent, dipped below Darius, and thrust his sword into the dragon's jaw as Kent was lifted, screaming, into the red sky.

His attack was enough to seize Darius's full attention once again. Liam jabbed the beast's face with his shield for the sake of being a nuisance and lured the demon into the city. Meanwhile, the stryx still guarded the palace, but for the time being, they only waited and watched their master follow Liam past the other gates into the streets.

Liam diverged onto an adjacent road to avoid hurting the horse tied outside the gates before curving back to King's Way. Darius glared at him. Brimstone fell from the scarlet clouds. Liam lifted his shield over his head to protect himself. The searing stones bounced off the dragon hide and crashed onto the cobblestone. Liam checked over his shoulder for craters in the road or wreckage blocking his path, detouring when he couldn't climb over the rubble, but he never stopped driving Darius toward the center of the city.

Liam was running off his soldier's sense of fight or flight and willpower alone. As often happened in battle, the dragon-shaped demon was nothing more than an orange blur for him to dodge as Liam's thoughts scattered, but the way McCarthy's jewelry store stood unharmed between the completely smashed perfume shop and hatmaker imprinted itself in Liam's mind. On his deathbed, Liam would remember the way the red sky reflected off the jagged edges of broken glass windows from the cobbler's store more than the way his muscles were hard as rocks and quivering with fatigue. For now, there was only his task: get Darius to Reynald. Banish him.

Their progress through Citadel was agonizing. Step by step, Liam taunted and jeered the demon, rushing forward to attack, then retreating to inch them closer to the square. Liam's foot caught a crater, and he fell. He managed to roll, avoiding any injuries or attacks, but the trembling in his limbs was noticeable now.

"A little farther." He spoke to himself, convincing himself to move.

"You're taking too long!" Reynald's voice called out behind Liam.

"Reynald?" Liam blinked as Reynald appeared and lifted him to his feet, pulling him away from Darius.

"Come on!"

"Good to hear your voice." Liam released a whoosh of air, sinking a little into Reynald's arms.

"I signaled you forty minutes ago!" Reynald grabbed Liam's arm and dragged him the last half block.

"He was attacking the castle."

"Ha! Glad to see the pact is still holding even with the mask cracked." Reynald barked a single laugh as they moved. "It's a shame we have to send him away before he kills Seigfried."

"Dammit, Reynald, you never change." Liam recovered enough to put full weight on his feet again and run with Reynald beside him. "I saw a leg."

"What?"

"A leg! Just a leg in the street! Hundreds of people are dead!"

"I know! I've seen—Liam, I promise you can scream at me later. Let's get this done first!"

Darius lumbered after them. They passed the Candlewick Inn. A bright pink sigil consumed most of the space between Reynald's burnt pyre and the statue of Saint Margaret. Several circles ringed within one another. Between the layers were so many symbols and designs that the markings resembled lace, or the calligraphy the nuns used in their holy books. But Liam only had a few seconds to admire the circle before Darius barreled into the square. The demon caught sight of the sigil and dug his feet into the cobblestone to prevent touching the lines.

"No, you don't!" Liam rushed behind him, cutting off his escape path.

Darius's nostrils flared, and his slag-glowing eyes widened in panic. He reared on two legs and crashed his front feet down to crush Liam. Rolling out of the way, Liam regained his balance, closed the space between them, and thrust his sword in a series of simple attacks meant to drive Darius backward. Reynald slid next to him.

"Get back!" Liam screamed.

"It's going to take both of us!" Reynald formed an icicle in his hand and threw it like a javelin.

The ice glided into the flames of Darius's body. Darius's fire sputtered in his chest where the water hissed into steam and rose above the flames. The demon lurched and twisted, suffering but not corporeal enough for the injury to last. The dimmed patch in his chest filled in with fresh fire, even as Reynald aimed another ice bolt. The spells, and Marseilles's bite, forced Darius closer to the sigil, but as his feet touched the seal's border, Darius shoved forward in wild desperation. He thrashed the air with his flaming wings. Liam and Reynald scattered to each side to avoid being impaled by the tip of his tail. With a gap opened, Darius leapt forward to escape.

"No!" Reynald flung another icicle at the demon.

Liam pushed himself up, but his arms collapsed from exhaustion, and he had to suck three deep, painful breaths into his lungs before he succeeded in standing. He prepared to run after Darius, stumbling forward, but the demon froze in place before Liam reached him. He roared in pain and stepped backward again. Reynald ran until the demon was in front of him, flinging ice spells to drive Darius deeper into the town square. Through the smoke and red light, Liam saw Edeline beside Reynald. She held two butterfly swords. Each time she swung a sword, a crescent of silver ice whirled through the air, slicing into the fire of Darius's body. With two mages attacking, Darius shrieked but lost ground. A dozen stryx plunged toward them to come to his aid, but Edeline crossed her blades, pointed them at the onslaught of monsters, and branched lightning through each shadow, destroying all of them.

"Oh, now you show up!" Reynald scoffed at her as she attacked the stryx.

"I was saving who I could from *your* mess!" she snapped in return.

"*Our* mess, dear oracle!"

"I told you, specifically, to do nothing to jeopardize the mask's integrity."

"Yeah? Well, you didn't tell me keeping Liam alive would become more important than watching Seigfried die."

"You're right. I seem to have underestimated both of you." Edeline kept attacking as they spoke.

Liam did his best not to be distracted by their conversation despite Reynald's confession about wanting him alive more than Seigfried dead.

There would be time for joy after the battle. He held his sword in his blistered hand, but he couldn't lift it much higher than his waist because he was exhausted. Still, he refused to be as useless as he'd been when they fought the wyverns. He sheathed Marseilles and steadied his shield in both hands. If nothing else, he could jump in front of either of them to protect them from an attack if need be. Edeline nodded when she caught sight of him.

"You managed to save him."

"Have I?" Liam asked. "Because this dragon looks pissed."

"Leave Darius to me. Reynald, finish the ritual."

"On it." Reynald rushed to the circle, touching the outer ridge and chanting.

Edeline advanced, spinning in a dance and imbuing her blades with glittering silver frost. The way Edeline controlled Darius was stunning. Each time the demon feinted or rushed to get away, she'd spin, slice, lunge, her swords flashing in the crimson light. Liam stood and coughed from the thickening smoke spreading through the city. While Seigfried cowered in a room of pretty magical baubles, here was a true sorcerer out in the rubble and flames, fighting beside them, no less glorious than Saint Margaret when she burst from the dragon's belly—alive after being swallowed.

With a final leap into the air and a triple rotation, in which she shot off six consecutive crescents of ice, Edeline pushed Darius into the banishing circle. Darius roared, calling forth a storm of flames from his mouth. Liam wrapped her in his cloak and used his shield to cover their faces. After the blast, they stood. Smoke rose from Liam's cloak, and sweat dripped down his and Edeline's faces. The dragon gasped, his panting as rapid as theirs. The blast took a lot of his power, probably why he hadn't used the attack before. Edeline refused to give him an inch of ground, pressing him backward the last three feet.

"Got him!" Reynald smacked the cobblestone outside the magic circle.

Darius stood in the center of the circle. He roared and rammed his head against an invisible wall, trapped. Fire dribbled from his form as he lost shape.

"Banish him!" Edeline dropped to her knees.

"I'm sorry I got us into this mess." Reynald stared at the sigil on the ground. "But I'm going to make it right."

Reynald tiptoed over the outer line until he nestled between the first and second ring of the sigil. Careful not to scuff the chalk, he pressed his hands against two hand-shaped symbols within the network of images, then chanted in a low voice. The pink lines lit up, locking Darius into place. The light reached skyward, the soft pink a strange juxtaposition to the pulsing red above. As Reynald chanted, charging the spell with power, yellow branches of energy crackled from cloud to cloud. The flock of stryx circling the portal exploded. Their feathers floated down like ash before blowing away in the increasing wind.

"Why are you in the circle?" Liam shouted, afraid to cross the threshold lest he interrupt the magic, but more afraid that Reynald was too close to whatever magic was about to happen.

"Because he wants to atone." Edeline rested a hand on Liam's shoulder. "The portal can only be closed from the inside."

"What?"

"He had no intention of surviving this, Liam. He never did."

"I don't accept this! There has to be another way!" Liam fastened his shield in its sling before stepping closer to the sigil.

"Not that I can see." Edeline held onto Liam's shoulder. "What do you want to do?"

Her swirls of hair swayed in the storm twisting around them. All her jewelry jingled as the wind struck the bangles and bracelets. The sound reminded Liam of the small bells people used during individual saint day festivals. The light from the sigil brightened, pink deepening into a vibrant fuchsia.

"Do you promise to take care of Citadel once I'm gone? And do everything you can to save the Balbraid Thicket?" Liam stared into her gaze, wanting to see her eyes when she answered.

"Yes, Sir Bord." A sad smile struggled on her face. "I will spend my entire life protecting Phrophis as an oracle…and queen is meant to."

"Thank you. I think you'll make a fair queen." He removed her hand from his shoulder, kissed her knuckles, and walked to the edge of the sigil where Reynald knelt.

"I'm sorry, Liam. You can yell at me all you want now. For killing the unicorns. For tricking you. For summoning Darius despite knowing it was a shit idea." Reynald glanced up from the symbols before continuing his chanting, but he swept his gaze back and forth as if trying to read Liam's face.

"I told you not to leave me," Liam said.

Reynald closed his eyes, avoiding Liam's words and finishing the chant. The light was blinding as it reached to meet the portal above.

"I told you I would chase you anywhere!" Liam flung himself through the barrier and into Reynald's arms.

Liam crashed against Reynald, locking their bodies together. He buried his face into Reynald's hair and sucked in a deep breath despite the air being filled with smoke and sweat and battle.

"Liam, no!" Reynald shoved Liam, but Liam kept his arms twisted around Reynald.

"I'm going with you!"

"It's a dimension of fire and brimstone! It's hell, Liam! Jump out or you'll die!"

"Who cares?" Liam laughed to hide the pain in his chest.

He hadn't wanted to die with Reynald—he'd wanted to live with him—but this was better than living without him.

"I do! I care!"

Reynald struggled to knock Liam free before they were taken, but their bodies lifted higher and the pink faded into the deepest red as if they were sinking into a giant, beating heart. The demon dissipated into the sky. His flames stretched out into an endless expanse, becoming one with the swirling brimstone. His essence flashed from red to blue violet. The flames shaped themselves into a face. He opened his enormous maw and swallowed them. The air burned to breathe. Liam coughed; blood splashed from his lips. His cloak wasn't enough to stop the searing wind or the poison filling his lungs.

"You don't deserve to die here!" Reynald shouted as tiny, white blisters bubbled on his exposed hands and neck from the heat.

"For all your sins, neither do you!" Liam screamed in return. He stared at Reynald, demanding eye contact.

Thunder blasted around them. The sound rumbled through the plains. The clouds sucked into themselves, pulling them into the hellish otherworld. With a final crack, the portal sealed itself. Liam slumped in Reynald's arms. Citadel was safe now. Edeline had promised to take care of the people of Phrophis, and Liam was in Reynald's embrace. He could accept this fate.

"No!" Reynald wailed as if reading Liam's thoughts and disagreeing.

The mask on his face shimmered, surrounding them in a sphere of white. Liam sucked in a desperate breath of air. His sore muscles relaxed, the blisters on his hands mended, the pain in his lungs evaporated.

"My face…" Reynald slipped the mask off. He brushed the skin of his cheeks, still clutching the ivory in one hand.

"Finally." Liam held Reynald's cheeks and kissed him. He separated enough to brush his thumbs across Reynald's skin. "I've missed your face. I'm happy to see you one last time before the end."

Reynald's expression crumbled. The mask still glowed in his hand, magic pushing back the burning air and giving them a sanctuary amidst the swirling red fire. A prism of light poured from the fracture running across the mask's nose, growing brighter as the crack widened.

"Why wouldn't you let me save you? Why do you always have to jump in and be a hero?" Reynald's hair was tossed around his head, and his robes fluttered along with Liam's cape.

"There was nothing heroic about going with you—I told you—I

love you." Liam twisted the fingers of their free hands together. "Wherever you are is where I'll be."

"The magic in this mask is finite. Once it runs out…" Reynald lowered his gaze.

"I know. Hold me while we can. That's all I want." Liam curled against him, wanted Reynald wrapped around him until their very last second of existence together.

"Listen…there's one spell I can try. A teleportation spell, but it'll be unstable, because I have no way to draw a circle or properly prepare. We might end up back in Citadel… We might end up in a boiling ocean in a pitch-black void." Reynald stared into Liam's eyes. "Sometimes magic is a recipe, and you mix the right ingredients to get cookies, sometimes it's a dice roll with your life on the line… It's your choice to try it or not."

"I'm not much of a gambler." Liam smiled, bumping their noses together. "But you're a bad influence on me, so I'm feeling reckless in your arms. Roll the dice. I believe we can beat the odds."

"All right." Reynald exhaled, closing his eyes. "Let's try."

The crack in the mask spread out like dew-beaded spiderwebs caught in the morning sunlight. The ivory shattered, the sound of distant wind chimes surrounded them, and glittering dust engulfed their bodies, whisking them away from the flames. For an instant, Liam saw the heavens, stars glistening in emptiness and stretching onward endlessly. The flash was gone before he could soak in half the details: comets, dying stars, their own sun burning bright and yellow. He felt the tug of gravity dragging him downward to some unknown, faster and faster, until everything spun into a whirlwind, and there was nothing but the two of them in a cyclone of prismatic light, the last spark of unicorn magic redeeming them from the clutches of hell.

"Hey, Liam?" Reynald whispered, magic surrounding them as they plummeted.

"Yes?" Liam kept their fingers interlocked but used his other arm to hook around Reynald's waist to keep them close, no matter where the magic sent them.

"I love you too."

About the Author

Sita Bethel is currently seeking a professional, high-quality necromancer for two pet resurrections. All interested applicants can send references and portfolios through their nearest magical mirror. Other than bringing back Odin and Anpu so they can fulfill their plans for world domination, Sita Bethel has been busy fleeing the Bible Belt, working on new stories, drinking coffee, and training for the zombie apocalypse. Had enough of Sita Bethel yet? If not, check out @sita_bethel on Twitter, or sita-bethelfiction on Facebook, or even www.sitabethel.com.

Email
sitabethel@gmail.com

Facebook
www.facebook.com/sitabethelfiction

X
@sita_bethel

BlueSky
@sitabethel.bsky.social

Website
www.sitabethel.com

Other NineStar books by this author

Cold Like Snow
Saved by Grace
Only Love is Deathless
Plague and Ash

CONNECT WITH NINESTAR PRESS

WEBSITE: NINESTARPRESS.COM

FACEBOOK: NINESTARPRESS

X: @NINESTARPRESS

INSTAGRAM: NINESTARPRESS

BLUESKY: NINESTARPRESS

THREADS: @NINESTARPRESS